Praise for Oscar C.

Where We Come From

"A story that transcends politics—a fiction to tell a truer truth. . . . A thought-provoking read from a master storyteller whose unrelenting realism is often heartrending." —*The Brooklyn Rail*

"We need more border stories like this: insightful, compassionate, and not actually about politics or walls or you-know-who, but about humanity, family, and home—also known as the things that really matter." —Literary Hub

"[An] instant classic. . . . Cásares tight-weaves his words together as if he were working a loom on a fabric that is guaranteed to last." —*Litbreak Magazine*

"Well-researched, not sensationalized and related with a dispassionate yet tender voice. . . . Cásares's narrative soars . . . with moments of humane beauty." *AM New York*

"Through this deeply human and intensely powerful story of identity and family, Cásares beautifully explores American immigration and the power of compassion." —*Deep South Magazine*

"Evenly and quickly paced. Finely wrought. . . . Cásares is making a bid for our humanity, but he isn't peddling fairy tales." —Lone Star Literary Life

"[A] deeply human novel. . . . Concerned with what it means to make a life in a place where so many systems and institutions are designed to make you feel precarious and, in some way, permanently unrooted."   —Omar El Akkad, *BookPage*

"Thoughtful and quietly suspenseful. . . . With understated grace and without sermonizing, Cásares brilliantly depicts the psychological complexity of living halfway in one place and halfway in another."   —*Publishers Weekly*

"In this gentle novel, Cásares has done a beautiful job . . . creating a vivid portrait of a boy caught between two worlds. The story is a necessary exercise in empathy at a time when there is too little. . . . [A] heartfelt story about an intensely timely subject that demands attention."   —*Booklist*

OSCAR CÁSARES

Where We Come From

Oscar Cásares is the author of *Brownsville*, a collection of stories that was an American Library Association Notable Book, and the novel *Amigoland*. He is the recipient of fellowships from the National Endowment for the Arts, the Copernicus Society of America, and the Texas Institute of Letters. Originally from Brownsville, he now lives in Austin with his family and teaches creative writing at the University of Texas at Austin.

www.oscarcasares.com

ALSO BY OSCAR CÁSARES

Brownsville

Amigoland

Where We Come From

Where We Come From

OSCAR CÁSARES

VINTAGE BOOKS

A Division of Penguin Random House LLC

New York

FIRST VINTAGE BOOKS EDITION, APRIL 2020

The Library of Congress has cataloged the Knopf edition as follows:
Name: Cásares, Oscar, author.
Title: Where we come from / Oscar Cásares.
Description: First edition. | New York : Alfred A. Knopf, 2019.
Identifiers: LCCN 2018043234
Subjects: BISAC: FICTION / Family Life. | FICTION / Literary.
Classification: LCC PS3603.A83 W47 2019 | DDC 813/.6—dc23
LC record available at https://lccn.loc.gov/2018043234

Vintage Books Trade Paperback ISBN: 978-0-525-56492-8
eBook ISBN: 978-0-525-65544-2

Book design by Cassandra J. Pappas

www.vintagebooks.com

Printed in the United States of America
10 9 8 7 6 5 4 3 2

For Becky, and for Adrian and Elena

Solemn's the night, but man
has disposed his fraternal signs,
and groping my way along roads and shadows
I reached the lit doorway, the little
point of star that was mine,
the bread crumb that the wolves in the forest
had not devoured.

—Pablo Neruda, *Canto General*

Prólogo / Los rules

No kicking the ball against the side of the house. Not the pink house in back and not the big blue one in front. She promises Orly that if later he eats all his dinner, she will take him to the field behind the school to make exercise, so he can practice all he wants kicking the ball. Allá, Nina tells him, you can kick and chase after the ball all you want, for as long and fast as you want, until the sun goes down, until they turn off the lights and leave you in the dark, until you get so tired of running back and forth you fall down, there on the ground, dead. She adds that last part to make her point, to exaggerate and maybe be funny, but when Orly doesn't laugh or at least smile she wonders if she said it wrong, because when she repeats the words to herself, in her mind, as they occurred to her—¡Hasta qué caes muerto!—it sounds funny, at least to her—the idea of a young boy wanting to play so much, having so much energy on a summer day that he keeps running and running and running until his legs and body give out, y saz he falls down and dies. Nina considers explaining to him that what she said was only an expression, something people say, help him understand how she meant to be funny—she probably said the same thing to his father when she used to take care of him—but sometimes what people say in one language sounds different in another and maybe if she says it the way she heard it in her head he'll get the joke and they can both laugh.

But instead she changes the subject and tells him that her mother
used to rent the pink house, but that was before the accident and
now her mother only sits in bed watching her novelas and *Judge
Judy*. Nina tells him the foil on the windows of the pink house is
for when it gets hot. This last detail in case he is curious. Foil on
the windows is the best way to keep a house cool and save money.
Who doesn't know that? She has it on the pink house in back and
not the blue one in front because she doesn't need everyone who
drives by seeing how they live. Pink and baby blue, those were
ideas of her mother. The foil is there to protect her makeup boxes
from getting too hot. Orly listens, but he wonders why she can't
put the boxes in the blue house, if the closet in the room where
he sleeps is almost empty. That, plus the blue house is really only
big if you compare it to the pink house, and every time she calls
it a big house he wants to say they could probably fit three of her
"big" houses into the first floor of his dad's house, not including the garage, but he keeps all this to himself because of the
next rule.

Have respect. Orly might talk back to his father, but not here, not
to his Nina. No, señor. Here is not Houston, a place where people spend all day driving in their cars, nobody looking at nobody
unless they want to say something bad, una cochinada, blaming
God for their bad luck, because they can't cross from this lane to
that lane, like He was the one who made the light turn from yellow to red. Sí, porque He has nothing more to do than to control
all the traffic lights in Houston. Who told them to go look for
work that was so far away they would always be in a hurry? Who
said that if she is driving a little slow it's okay to honk their horn
and raise their finger at her, a woman already in her late sixties?
Here Nina only wants there to be love. She gives Orly a hug and

a kiss on the cheek first thing in the morning and then again at night, como el sol y la luna. And so when she says, Mijito, do not be sad, he needs to stop being sad. Things are going to get better. He is not the first boy to be sad, he won't be the last one. It is sad what happened, but that was last year and now he's here with his Nina and she wants him to be happy. Orly tells her he's okay, but "okay" isn't enough when she wants happy. The first day she took him to the zoo, which was fun even if he had to take turns holding the umbrella or pushing Mamá Meche's wheelchair, and later at the herpetarium—the one exhibit he was most looking forward to—he had to go in alone because Mamá Meche didn't want to be in a dark room looking at the faces of so many snakes and later have ugly dreams. The second day to the beach, but there Mamá Meche said that in her life she had already felt enough sand and dirt and mud between her toes, and besides Nina was afraid for him to get into the water by himself, so he actually only saw the beach from the backseat of the car, and later they stopped by the Dairy Queen for lunch. The third day to the mall. But she must have forgotten that a mall in Brownsville is not a mall in Houston. Here there's no ice rink, no Apple Store, no Smoothie King, there isn't even a Starbucks. Seriously. How do you open a mall without a Starbucks? He imagines this is what it's like living in a developing country, Cuba maybe, only in this case with air-conditioning and a Chick-fil-A. There's a movie theater, but he hasn't been to the movies since the last time he went with his mom and his brother, Alex. On the way home from the mall, she mentioned Mata-moros but only to say it wasn't safe enough to be taking him across the bridge. Days four and five at the house, reading and taking screen breaks every thirty minutes or so, which is probably what he would be doing if his dad had let him stay in Houston. But to Nina it doesn't seem right for him to be stuck inside, same as it doesn't seem right for a twelve-year-old boy to take medicine for his feelings. And not just because of what happened to his mama, because Nina remembers Orly was taking the medicine already two or three years ago when she went to visit him in Houston. She has more opinions, but she keeps these to herself and for now is just thankful his daddy brought him. If he let her, she would keep him for the whole summer.

Always pray before eating. At first Nina was saying the prayer in Spanish, but now at the table and even when it's his time to sleep she says it in Spanish and then again in English, because she worries Orly might not really know what his father says he knows. It doesn't matter that he and his brother go to a private school where they teach them Spanish, because here, in this house, she has heard him speak it only to Mamá Meche and then just two or three words, a Buenas noches or a Buenos días, before he goes quiet again. His father claims Orly understands everything but just prefers to respond in English. That they shouldn't force it on him. But this is coming from a man who speaks less and less of it each time he comes to visit her, like Spanish wasn't his first language, like he never grew up here so close to Mexico, like now he is more from Houston than from Brownsville, like people in this country are not allowed to speak more than one way.

Eat all your food. Not just the parts you like best, tus favoritos, but the whole plate. This is not the Luby's, where you can point to what you want them to put on the tray and then pass up the rest of the food like you're driving in a neighborhood where you don't know anybody. He has no idea how many people live with so much less. If he knew how people went without food he would not be asking if he needs to eat everything on his plate. If he can eat only half of what she serves him. If he can eat the arroz but not the calabacita. Eat and be thankful, Nina tells him. She doesn't want to know about his favorite and un-favorite foods. All foods need to be his favorites. He needs to make them his favorites for today, and tomorrow have a new favorite and another one for the next day. Like that. And not just the tortillas. They are not for him to eat as fast as she or Rumalda, the one day that Rumalda comes to help around the house, can make them and then for him to say he's too full to eat the rest of his food. She doesn't want to hear that she is serving him too much. At first she thought Orly was just chiflado, the type of boy who is used to getting what he wants, but then she remembered all the things his father told her about his diet. The skim milk, the orange juice with calcium, and no Cokes, no sweets after seven o'clock, nothing of what he calls junk food, no potato chips, no cinnamon rolls, no donuts, and the pan dulce maybe just for special occasions and not during the week. Then for what are the panaderías open every day? For that Orly's father has no answers. He makes it sound like his life hasn't worked out because she gave him these foods when he was growing up, like it made all his teeth fall out and now he walks with a limp because when he was little she served him a taco de barbacoa with some Hawaiian Punch. Even if now he has money and drives a car so big it barely fits under the carport. All that money from making the advertisements they show on TV. Yesterday he called to remind her about Orly's chewy vitamins and the nasal spray for his allergies. She has never known a man to be so concerned about his child, but then it occurs to her that this list of foods and vitamins and medicines is something the boy's mother must have left behind.

Stay away from the canal. Even if it's usually not very deep and you know how to swim, that's not the kind of water for you to be playing in. Sometimes people throw away old tires and other things they're not supposed to be putting into a canal. Sometimes there are spiders and scorpions and even snakes and other animals you don't want to see. When it gets so hot like it is now they go to drink the dirty water and then look for a place to stay cool. They might be hiding in the shade of the ebony tree, they might be hiding in the grass where you step, they might be hiding under the pink house, especially the other side where the bottom of the house is open and easy for them to slide and crawl into the dirt, and then you don't see them until it's too late. Better just to stay away from the little house and the backyard. If you want to be outside, go sit on the front steps and look up at the parrots flying this way and that way, up and around the sky, all together like a little boy trying to hold a big green kite on a windy day. They come from across the river, but to them it is all the same. They only know to fly and sing and drop cacas on the roof of people's cars. Nobody asks them what they are doing here because a bird is a bird, and no matter where they are that's their home. Los inocentes.

Pick up the seat. She shouldn't have to say this one. She says it because there is only one small bathroom for the three of them. Her mother has a bedside commode she never uses and wants nowhere near her bed. And if Orly forgets to pick up the seat, then he needs to wipe. Because even a little wet is still wet. Nobody likes surprises in the middle of the night. If she wants surprises she can go buy a lotto ticket. He should go in and do what he needs to do but not take one of his books. Find another place to read. It's a bathroom, not a library. Her mother never knows when she's going to have an urge, and they can't be waiting for him to get to the end of the next chapter. Nina tells him to knock because the lock on the door is hard to unlock and so she doesn't lock it and neither should he. If he gets locked inside, his tío Beto will have to come with his tools to let him out.

No computers at the kitchen table. Even if it is just the two of them eating breakfast and she's busy scanning the pages of the *Bargain Book*, her reading glasses up to her face and a ballpoint in hand, or later reading the *Herald*, the whole time complaining about the things people try to get away with, taking advantage of the ones who have less and don't know any better. The police, the sheriffs, the politicians, the judges, the teachers, the coaches and principals, even some people from the church who are supposed to know good from bad. Aprovechados is what they are. Nobody cares anymore, they let those selling las drogas go free. Or they think building a wall will solve all the problems, that the poor ones will stare up at it and forget their children are hungry y que los malos are trying to hurt them. Orly nods, half listening to what she says, but also waiting for her to finish so he can explain that it's actually a tablet, an iPad Air 2, and not a computer. That a device like this can do some things a computer can but really he's limited because it's harder to do things like load videos onto YouTube or play *Minecraft* with any of his friends on the server, but still Carson keeps sending him screenshots on Instagram of the super mall he's building, and then his dad is always changing the password on the parental restrictions, more than even his mom used to, so there's no updating anything. And really he only has his iPad to get messages and see what other people are doing for fun over the summer. He skips the part about Nina not having an Xbox because they've already been over it, how she can't afford to

be buying this Xbox he keeps bringing up, especially not for the
three weeks he's going to be here.

No playing with La Bronca. La Bronca is not a dog to play with, for
her to chase you in circles around the grapefruit tree, for you to
throw a stick so she can bring it back in her mouth, to rub her belly
and then put her on your lap so she can lick your face and leave
babas everywhere. La Bronca looks old and slow but that only
makes her meaner. She is part Chow, with patches of her rust-
colored fur missing from her dark haunches, and part something
else that makes her head look like a block of wood with ears and
a wide jaw. The dog stays chained to the pink house and lies in
the cool dirt just under the wooden steps, next to where the last
people who rented the house years ago, a shrimper and his wife
from Nicaragua and their three kids, grew roses and hibiscuses
in some old Folger's cans. La Bronca used to be tied to the álamo
tree in front, but then one night last summer somebody crossed
the canal and got into the backyard and from the pink house stole
Nina's makeup boxes. Which is only half true—the dog was in
the front until recently and now is in the back but for different
reasons having nothing to do with anyone stealing the makeup
that Nina doesn't even sell anymore—reasons she can't get into,
won't say, and wishes she hadn't brought up because it only makes
Orly want to know more. Why? Because here in this town, if they
could get away with it and make some money, they would steal the
makeup off her face. Which is an exaggeration, obviously, but still
true. Why? Because here they steal anything they can—your trash
can, your lawn chairs, your water hose, your shirts and pants off
the clothesline, your Christmas lights and your Baby Jesus from
the manger. Which she only wishes were exaggerations. Why?
Because here there are more poor people than almost anywhere

else in this country. He can look it up on his computer, see if she doesn't know what she's saying. The few people that come from money stay just because there are so many poor ones to do all their work. These are not poor ones Orly thinks he knows, the ones he sees pushing shopping carts and begging for money. But that doesn't make them less hungry. You don't need to see them living squeezed together on top of each other, amontonados like the puppy dogs they keep at the pound, but at least there somebody cares and they give them something to eat before they put them to sleep. The only reason they haven't stolen the dog is that La Bronca would make picadillo out of them and have them for lunch there in the shade. Los mendigos. Infelices. For that reason Nina put the padlock on the door and tied La Bronca to one of the foundation blocks, where she just waits there under the house. The chain looks short, but it always turns out to be a little longer than people think.

≽ I ≼

Un favor

I

It bothered Nina that Rumalda looked her same age, like they might have been classmates in grade school and now had come to be reunited every Friday morning when Rumalda walked across the bridge to clean the house. Sixteen years younger was not nothing, yet Rumalda hobbled like an old mule with a bad leg that never healed. Bunions. A bone spur. A bad hip. Only God knew. The woman refused to see a real doctor, terca that the salve the curandera had prepared for her needed time to do its healing. Maybe leaving it on more than just overnight. Nina wondered who actually looked her true age, she or her maid. If she had been spared only by being born on this side of the river. If she shouldn't go back to coloring her hair, like she did when she had more time, before she moved back home to take care of her mother.

When the gray showed up she convinced herself she looked more her age, but then the gray began turning white and she didn't know what age she was anymore and if it mattered, as little as she left the house these days. But how much older would the Matamoros Nina look? Would her feet be as calloused and scaly, as misshapen with bunions from walking six days a week for however long to the bridge to wait in line with the rest of the men and women coming to this side to work? How many shades darker? How much more haggard and spent from walking home on the other side of the river, where you never know when Los Mañosos, as Rumalda calls the narcos, might decide today is a good day to start killing one another in the streets?

Two months earlier, before Nina's nephew Eduardo asked her to take care of her godson Orly, Rumalda had asked for her own favor. She had arrived like every other Friday and set down her purse, removed her flats, and put the first load of laundry to wash. She came back to the kitchen when she was called over a few minutes later. Maybe this was the only house she cleaned where she was invited to sit and have coffee. Maybe she had coffee everywhere she went and never mentioned it out of modesty. It was a small gesture to pass the time, to treat her like a person and not some criada, as Nina's mother sometimes called her. They paid her the standard forty dollars to do the laundry and clean the house. Even on a fixed income, Nina always set aside enough money for this expense. It was her only break from working around the house during the week. If Rumalda had extra time, she prepared the lunch and made tortillas so she could fill the rest of her workday.

When she did finally sit, it was close to the edge of the seat cushion and avoiding much eye contact, instead staring into the black, unsweetened coffee before her. Other than Nina's brother Beto occasionally coming to visit and the doctors and nurses they saw when she took her mother to her appointments, Rumalda was one of the few contacts Nina had with the outside world. Adelita Morales from down the street had died two years earlier and left her husband behind, who by that point was already going blind from the diabetes and now stayed indoors, afraid to venture even to his front gate. Most of her friends from work had moved on with their lives. Nina had tried to meet them for coffee or lunch, but this only happened on Fridays, the one day a week she could stray from the house knowing that Rumalda was there to keep an eye on her mother.

Rumalda wasn't much of a talker. But Nina was just happy to see someone else's face, to see her smile or grimace when she shared some small detail about the last seven days of being here with her mother. And perhaps this is how it would've continued if Nina hadn't been asking Rumalda so many questions, inquiring about her husband and the younger daughter and then the older one and her husband and their baby, instead of letting the woman sit and enjoy her coffee.

At first, Rumalda had claimed no, everything was perfectly fine with her family, as always. Gracias a Dios. Then a moment later the story changed. She confessed that in truth she had a small favor to ask.

She had started cleaning houses not long after her second daughter was born. This second daughter was a grown woman now, but born with Down syndrome. She stayed locked inside the one-bedroom apartment while her parents came across to work. Nina had only seen dated pictures of Paloma, ones that made it seem as though she hadn't advanced beyond the age of eleven and still wore pigtails while her mother's braided ponytail dangled past the middle of her back like the tongue of an old church bell, discolored with age and use. But the favor was for the other daughter, Noemí, the one married and with a four-year-old. The husband had crossed and found work with a plumbing company in Fort Worth, and now, after more than three years of being separated, he was sending for them. The plan was for next Friday morning Noemí and her little girl to walk across the bridge, pretending like they were only coming over to shop, and then wait on this side for a time when they could be taken from the border up north to Fort Worth. To do this they needed a place to wait until someone came for them.

If la señora would concede her this one favor and allow these guests at her house, Rumalda promised they would be picked up as soon as possible. Waiting on this side would be safer than paying a coyote to pass them in the middle of the night, with the risk of getting across the river and then over or around the wall without being seen by the authorities. And imagine, with a four-year-old. Even on this side of the river, they would still have to worry about how to get past the interior checkpoints that the Border Patrol had set up some eighty miles from the border, forcing many of the immigrants to walk through an untamed and merciless land where hundreds had died. But for that Rumalda's son-in-law already knew who to call, someone who could drive her daughter and the child hidden in a trailer to get through the checkpoints. She was asking Nina because of all the houses she cleaned this was the only one where she could ask in confidence. La señora wouldn't have to do anything other than allow her daughter and granddaughter to stay until the ride came for them. Before Nina could consider the question and how this would work, what type of people would be coming to her front door, Rumalda suggested they could stay in the little pink house. Only for a night. Two nights at the very most. "Por favor, señora."

Nina felt like she did when she used to drive across to shop or eat in Matamoros, back when it didn't feel like she was risking her life, and as she approached the bridge the blind and maimed beggars would come to her with their cupped hands, pleading just outside the car window. Only now it was happening at her kitchen table.

This was the favor the woman wanted. For her to hide people behind her house? And not even her house but her mother's. Her mother who she had to remind practically every Friday to stop talking about los mojados when she knew the word was offensive and more so because to her they were all mojados, rich or poor, legal or illegal, whether they floated across the river in an inner tube or drove over the bridge to bring their kids to the private school. And then for her maid to plan out the entire mess before she even asked her. To have visitors, papers or no papers, was one thing. To hide them so they could be taken—smuggled, to say it more clearly—was something different.

To Rumalda it was just a little favor, but who would land in trouble if someone reported them? The young woman and her little girl would be taken away, processed, transported back across to Matamoros, where they had started. Nothing gained, nothing lost. And meanwhile Nina locked up. Nina calling a lawyer. Nina with nobody to take care of her mother. Nina on the front page of the *Brownsville Herald*. But that's how they were, these people from across. For them everything had a simple solution. If there was a problem that could be fixed, by whatever means, then there was nothing to worry about. They were geniuses of the world when it came to finding another way. And if it turned out the prob lem had no solution, no way of it being mended or substituted with something else, no way of being glued or duct-taped, then there was nothing to worry about either. Ni modo, they said and moved on. They never stopped to consider what would happen next, after the solved or unsolved problem brought a whole new set of problems. Then what? For that they had no solutions They came with so little it was only ever about today, and tomorrow was tomorrow, another day to worry about when it arrived, if it arrived. Life, when one lived on this side of the river, was almost never that easy. But try explaining that to your cleaning woman.

Nina didn't answer her question one way or another, not even to say maybe or that she needed more time to consider it. All she told Rumalda was she had errands to run, the same as she told her every Friday.

She lost no time at the Walgreens. No lingering at the cosmetics counter, no gazing at the magazines she liked to flip through but rarely ever bought. They had a special on Ensure and she loaded two six-packs and a few other items into the shopping cart. She had to veer to the edge to avoid two little boys, barefoot and rolling hula hoops down the aisle, while their young mother sat nursing another child in the waiting area next to the prescription counter and blood pressure machine.

After the store, Nina drove to the bank to get money. If possible, she paid Rumalda with a combination of smaller bills, fives and tens and ones, so it looked like she was paying her more than she was. The three lanes of the drive-thru were full, each with at least two cars waiting in line. She pulled up behind a small truck on the far right. She was searching her purse for the checkbook when an SUV came up behind her. Without fully looking in the rearview, she knew it was him. She sensed Jorge's presence the way she had grown to sense when her mother was about to call her to come lower the bed rail or find the remote or bring her water in the middle of the night. Her one excursion from the house, other than taking her mother to her appointments, and this is who she saw. The last time had been at the Oyster Bar a year ago for her mother's birthday. He'd walked by their table like he hadn't recognized her, which may have been true but either way was probably for the best.

The wife was with him this time. Her visor was down, her face up close to the vanity mirror as she applied her makeup. In the rearview, it almost looked like he was alone.

Jorge was born on this side, but most of his family still lived in Matamoros. After retiring from the navy, he had settled in California and then a couple of years ago talked his second wife, a gringa originally from Dallas, into moving down here so he could be closer to his mother. That was the chisme, anyway, what Nina had heard from a friend who knew another friend whose cousin knew his sister. Not that she was asking, but people liked to talk. Even almost fifty years later people liked to talk.

She and Jorge had gone around in high school. He was two years ahead of her when they met her sophomore year. Only she had to be careful with her brothers, who at first had paid little attention to her but then when she got to a certain age were always following her, on orders from their father, especially when he learned the boy was from across, which he wasn't—it was his mother's family—but it didn't stop them from referring to him as her mojado boyfriend. Her father's father had actually been born in Reynosa, but that didn't mean her father had to approve of his only daughter going out with someone from that side of the river. After Nina was born, the family had stopped following the crops up north and her father got his commercial license to work as a long-haul trucker, which meant he was on the road for weeks and sometimes months at a time and during these stretches her two oldest brothers, Raúl and Luis, were in charge. One night they caught Nina talking to Jorge in his car, nothing more, outside a dance at the Civic Center, and pulled him out through the window by the lapels of his tuxedo. Her little brother, Beto, only eleven years old at the time, was there too, in the front seat of the car where he could watch all the action and later remember who was meant to run the family. When a couple of policemen happened to drive by the parking lot her brothers backed off, pretending they were just playing around. She had to promise Raúl she would get in their car if they just let Jorge go.

Later, after Jorge was back from Vietnam but still in the service, it was only Luis following them around because by then Raúl was married and starting a family. Luis wasn't so brave as to try anything alone, but he still followed his sister, waiting outside the Majestic for her and Jorge to come from watching a movie or sharing a burger at Rutledge. But not always, because after a while she learned how to give Luis the slip, paying for a matinee but then skipping out the back exit just as the lights turned off, or walking out of the restaurant without Jorge so it seemed like she was leaving on her own and then down the block she'd step into a fabric shop and her brother would decide to leave rather than waste half an hour waiting for her to come out. Most times she and Jorge just went down the street to Washington Park or someplace else where they could talk without being watched. It became a game for them, how to make the friendship look inno-cent enough that Luis would never suspect they might be walking a few blocks in the other direction and crossing the new bridge to Matamoros where they could be together at his tío's house. She loved Jorge—he was all she thought about during the long stretches he was away. She wanted nothing more than to be alone with him those few afternoons when he was back in town, and at the same time she didn't. She was afraid of what might hap-pen, not if Luis caught them but, rather, if he didn't and she kept crossing the bridge with him. She told herself, then and still now, that the situation would've been different if Jorge had been living here and not just coming back for short visits and if each time he didn't feel a tiny bit more distant, and not because he was adjusting to being back in his hometown but because he was adjusting to being away from his new home, and if she didn't feel the need to hold on to him in some way that lasted a little longer, even if that meant feeling guilty for their afternoons together.

It startled her when she heard the bank teller's voice thanking her over the intercom and a moment later the canister arrived in the chute. She removed her money and stuck the envelope in her purse. Behind her, the vanity mirror was still down. She pulled forward and tried to imagine herself as the one being driven and not the one driving to run someone else's errands. It wasn't until she was halfway home that she realized she had forgotten to ask for smaller bills to pay Rumalda.

With the left side of the carport blocked from view by the neighbor's wooden fence, the property was hidden from anyone not standing in front of the house. She had to pull in all the way before she could see into the backyard. Sometimes she forgot the little house was there. Tried to, anyway, because Beto was always bringing it up, telling her how they were letting good money go to waste when they could be renting it and making something extra to cover expenses. What he really meant was to cover the expenses so he wouldn't have to pitch in. He had already taken advantage of her kindness by having her be the only one taking care of their mother since Raúl had passed and Luis had moved thousands of miles away. Beto reminded her that she was the only girl in the family and had to do it. So when it came time, yes, she had left her work to come care for her mother, but not to be a landlord to strangers living behind her, hearing their problems about what needed to be repaired or replaced, collecting their late money. She didn't need more headaches every month. The headaches she already had inside the main house.

She was setting down the shopping bag in the kitchen when she heard her mother banging her drinking cup on the overbed tray.

"Until finally she came back. The one who likes to be in the streets."

"Less than an hour. You say it like I was gone for a week." The room was brighter now than when she left.

"As soon as you left I needed to go sit down."

"I asked you."

"Bah!" She flicked her hand. "You think my body is only waiting for you to say when? And with these bars on the bed, when I told you to leave them down."

"You could have called Rumalda to come help you."

"Esa mojada, you think she is going to know more than me about how to lower the bars?"

"Let me help you now." She lowered the railing.

"¿Ya pa'qué?"

"Then to clean you."

"Clean yourself," she said. "It passed. I had to go then and not now. But it almost happened and with me just thrown in the bed like a sack of flour." She turned away.

"Maybe I should call Dr. Robles."

"Yes, your answer for everything. Call Robles, call Robles. The man's going to think you want something more than pills from him."

She turned from her mother and took a deep breath and released it. This was a technique she had taught herself to do when she first started teaching second grade. After more than thirty years of working at Canales Elementary she had had her share of misbehaving kids who spent a couple of days at the principal's office every week just so she could focus on the other twenty or so students she had to teach. She was better than most teachers and teacher aides who didn't particularly like kids and did it only because they couldn't find another major and knew that this way they would always have a job.

"If you're mad we should talk later, when you feel better."

When she turned to walk out, her mother threw the plastic cup at her, missing altogether but stopping her all the same.

"You don't tell me when I can open my mouth to talk," she yelled at her. "You forget who is the mother and who's living here for free."

"Only to take care of you."

"That's what daughters do, and more the ones that stayed alone and have no one else to take care of." She looked away again. "And now she wants to go after the doctor, offer herself to him."

Nina turned to leave and bumped into Rumalda standing in the doorway. She wasn't done with the cleaning, but right then Nina wanted to pay her so she would go away and Nina wouldn't have to see her face or anyone else's for another seven days. The woman must have overheard at least some of their exchange, and she looked at Nina now as if she was the one in need of a favor, the one to be hidden and smuggled off to some more forgiving place.

After things had ended with Jorge, she became more careful with her money, saving all she could after giving her mother most of what little she earned working as a cashier and at the same time taking classes at the college. It took her close to a year to save enough to pay her part of the deposit on an apartment for her and two friends. It was nothing fancy, this first apartment near the airport, but she was on her own, and most importantly she was away from her family, who thought she was making a big mistake, trying to support herself while living with these two other girls she hardly knew. Her mother let her go, convinced she'd be back soon enough, if not to ask for money, then to move her things back into her old room. But she preferred to work extra shifts or find part-time jobs rather than go back home and ask for help. It took her more than ten years to get her degree and do her student teaching. By then she had her own place, a tiny studio apartment, off Boca Chica, and was saving up to buy a house.

Her kids, as she called her students, were mainly from the neighborhood but she suspected that a few of them were from Matamoros and walking across the bridge every morning to attend school in Brownsville. By law, the school wasn't permitted to ask about their or their parents' citizenship. Not that it had mattered to her—where they were born, where they slept at night, where they celebrated their birthdays didn't change the fact that they needed an education just as much, if not more, than the students born on this side of the river. Occasionally she would hear or read about one of her kids from one side or the other, all grown up— an accountant, an RN, an attorney, an engineer, a pilot, a police officer—and know that she had played some small role in their success. She had cared for them like they were her own.

This wasn't why she started teaching, but after the first few years it made her wonder if it wasn't meant to be some consolation for passing up that experience when she was young enough to have a family. She'd dated other men after Jorge, but in one way or other she never let them get close enough for it to last more than a few months.

The house she bought was tiny, in ways smaller than some of the apartments she'd lived in, but then again it was just for her. She had a small yard and a driveway, and wasn't sharing a wall with strangers who were up at all hours of the night. It was a yellow clapboard house with an off-white trim, close enough to work but also not so far from her mother's house. She wasn't sure about the color, but thought she could live with it for the time being.

She had been in the house six years when Beto asked her the question that eventually led her back to the house she had grown up in: Will you do me a favor and check on Mom on your way home from work? Just stop by for five or ten minutes, make sure she's eating and taking her medicines. Nina was tired after work, but it seemed like a small sacrifice to make for the family. But then later it was also her summers and school holidays, when she wasn't doing much but running errands, and why not take their mother to the cardiologist's office or the urologist or to get her hair fixed if her birthday was coming up. Until one afternoon she walked in the back door and found her mother lying on her side in the kitchen, unable to get up and the burner on the stove still on, the kettle screeching above her cries for help. She hadn't broken anything, but the scare was enough to tell them that from now on their mother shouldn't be living alone. And right then Nina knew there'd be no question who should be living with her mother and no question that Beto had had this in mind when he asked her for a little favor.

And now another favor, this one for Rumalda. Nina didn't know when it was that she became the person everyone thought they could come ask to do this and that, as if she didn't have her own life, as if her life only came after theirs. Can you do me a favor and check on Mom on your way home from work? Can you do me a favor and take her so they can check her feet, make sure they're not swollen again? Can you do me a favor and just retire a couple of years earlier than you were planning? Can you do me a favor and just sell the house you saved up for years to buy and go live with Mom? Can you do me a favor and give up your life for her life? Can you do me a favor and never sleep the whole night because she's always calling you to bring her water or calling you to go to the bathroom because thirty minutes earlier you got up to give her water? Can you try to help Mom and then let her say ugly things and throw a cup at you? Can you? Can you? Can you?

The following Friday, Rumalda arrived with her daughter and granddaughter in tow. Noemí helped her mother where she could with the cleaning, mainly in the kitchen and hanging the laundry to dry, but made sure she and Briana stayed away from the front of the house where la señora's mother might see them. Then later that afternoon, after bringing in the last of the towels

from the clothesline, Rumalda, Noemí, and Briana walked out
the back door carrying clean sheets and the small backpacks they
had arrived with in the morning. La Bronca was still chained to a
tree in the front yard, so it was easy for the three of them to slip
into the pink house unnoticed. Less than twenty minutes later,
Rumalda walked back to the main house alone.

*Five hundred and forty miles to the north, Juan Pablo, the husband of
Noemí, was helping load the jackhammer and pickax into the bed of the
work truck. He had received a text from her at noon letting him know
she and Briana had crossed the bridge that morning with her mother
and would be waiting for their ride. Juan Pablo barely had time to reply
with one of those heart emojis Noemí liked to send him, the ones he never
knew how to respond to, but in the moment, it was easier than trying to
tap out a message. He and the four other men in his crew had spent the
day digging out a seventy-five-foot-long trench to replace a corroded sewer
pipe, continuing to work while the owner of the house came outside to
observe their progress. The man claimed his mother's side of the family
was from Mexico—he couldn't remember from where exactly—and he
knew just enough Spanish to try to start a conversation each time he
came outside in his short pants and T-shirt and then make at least one
of the men feel like he had to put down his shovel to respond, when in
reality it was their boss he should be asking his questions to. They were
already behind schedule. Horacio, one of the other workers, hadn't shown
up for work again that morning. They had hired a day laborer to take
his place, but the man seemed to spend more time drinking water than
he did working. Horacio had gone back to Michoacán to see his family
for the first time since leaving seven years earlier. After all the equipment
was loaded and they were inside the truck, one of the workers wondered
out loud if he had been turned back or if something worse may have
happened. Horacio had left his car keys with Juan Pablo to hold until*

*he returned, which he had said would be a week earlier. Horacio was
supposed to have contacted the same coyote who had brought him across
the first time. Though no one was asking him, the day laborer mentioned
that he was from Honduras and last year his cousin had it bad because
first one of the gangs had killed her husband and she had escaped with
her fourteen-year-old girl, but then, after the coyote got them to this side,
the ones hiding them in the mobile home wanted more money before they
would release them to the next one, who was supposed to get them to
Houston. The day laborer hadn't said as much, but Juan Pablo wondered
if the cousin and her daughter might have been violated. Most of the
women and girls crossing alone were. People knew it but preferred not to
mention it, as if the omission might somehow prevent the memory itself
from crossing to this side of the border. Juan Pablo hadn't come out and
told Noemi this was the other reason she and Briana had to wait as long
as they had, that it was so he could save more money to pay the extra cost
for them to be brought up north by people who had come recommended
to him, and so later he could worry just a little less about what might or
might not happen to them on their way here.*

If she didn't already know better, Nina wouldn't have guessed
anyone was staying in the other house. The weather was cool
enough this early in the year that they didn't need to turn on the
air conditioner. They didn't so much as open the door or raise
the vinyl blinds or turn on a light or open a window—at least not
where Nina would have seen from her kitchen. She had promised herself not to step into the backyard, much less go up to the
little house and check on her visitors. On the news, she had seen
what happened when the immigration authorities found people
hiding in a house or apartment or trailer home. Twenty or thirty
of them, sometimes over fifty of them, all sitting on the floor
with their backs against the wall. And these were just the poor

ones who had paid to be taken. The other ones who took their money and sometimes were also smuggling drugs, those ones covered their faces when they got arrested, like they didn't want their families to see what they had been doing all along for their money and cars. Those were the people who would be coming to her mother's house.

The next night the phone rang close to eleven o'clock. At first she thought it might be Beto. Her brother liked to call at the most random hours, like she was operating a twenty-four-hour phone line for whenever it occurred to him to check on his mother. She sat up in bed without answering, letting it ring a second time to make sure she wasn't dreaming. Nothing good came from calls at this hour. This was the time of night when people called to inform you of car accidents and people who had died long before their time. Eight months earlier, Eduardo had let her know the afternoon after his wife died suddenly, but in her mind her nephew had called in the middle of the night. What was true was that she hadn't been able to sleep the next two nights because she was thinking of the boys without their mother, especially her godson, Orly.

She let it ring a third time. She wished she had a phone that showed her who was calling. She grabbed the receiver just before the fourth ring.

"¿Bueno?"

The line was silent.

"Hello?"

And then the line went dead.

Rumalda must have given them the address. This made sense, but Nina hadn't thought to ask if she would be sharing her phone number with these people. Somehow sharing her number seemed worse, as if these arrangements were premeditated and not something that simply occurred in the moment.

Half an hour passed without anything else happening. She

could hear the chatter of the young men who hung out at the twenty-four-hour car wash down the street, no more than four houses and an empty lot between them and her front door. Starting late in the afternoon they leaned against their shiny cars and trucks, cocking their chins to those they knew, giving mean-faced looks to those they didn't. What little traffic there was on the street at this hour was usually because of them.

She thought it might be one of them when the car dimmed its lights and parked across the street, idling just beyond the glow of the streetlight. She left the house lights off so she could watch the driver without his knowing. A blue flame flared close to the driver's face until it bit the end of a waiting cigarette. Barely audible over the sound of the engine, La Bronca grunted as if she was annoyed that someone had disturbed her sleep but still wasn't sure whether this called for lifting her anvil-sized head and rising from her place in the dirt.

She wished Rumalda had told her what to do: *When the phone rings but the caller doesn't say anything, do X. When he parks his car across the street and is waiting, like he has nothing else to do, then do Y.* She hadn't said anything other than thank Nina repeatedly, as if her appreciation made the rest of the details clear enough. La Bronca was sitting on her rump, her front legs kneading the dirt until she could engage the back ones. All Nina needed was for the dog to start barking and wake people. She stepped outside and just as swiftly the car drifted away, its lights still dimmed.

The next night the same car. Instead of opening the front door and scaring the driver off, this time Nina walked out the back and down to the carport, passing into and out of the shadows in her housecoat and chanclas. That afternoon, to keep the dog from barking and calling attention to anyone pulling up to the house, she'd moved her to the backyard and chained her to a foundation block under the little house.

By the time she opened the driveway gate, the driver had lowered the passenger window and angled the front tires toward the driveway.

"Maybe you can help me," the driver said, leaning against the armrest. "I'm looking for a friend."

Three weeks from now, this is the moment Nina will remember and wonder why she ever got involved with these people, why she didn't just say no, that she didn't know anything about any friend, and leave it at that. Why she couldn't figure out another way of helping Rumalda's family, a way that didn't involve her own family. But right then Nina was trying to make sense of the driver being female. Her dark hair was tucked into a hooded sweatshirt. She had on French nails and was scratching at the leather on the steering wheel. There had been no Buenas tardes. No I'm so-and-so, even if so-and-so was probably a made-up name. Maybe it was best this way, as strangers.

"This friend is expecting you?"

The girl looked at her like it might be a trick question. She seemed barely old enough to be out of high school. Young enough to be Nina's granddaughter.

"Two friends," she corrected herself. "And if not, then maybe I'm in the wrong place. They just told me it was the blue one at the dead end of the street. But then the light isn't so good."

"It looks more blue in the day," she said. "And this is the only one with people at the very end."

She stepped aside for the girl to pull into the driveway, then the carport.

"Wait here," she said when the girl was getting out of the car. In the halo of the light from the back door they could see the shape of the little house in the distance.

"First I have to see them. To know if these are the right friends."

"How many friends could there be waiting for you, already at this hour?"

The girl stood to one side, looking over her shoulder at the street and then back at the gate for Nina to open it. She was shorter and heavier than it had seemed she might be when she was slouched inside the car.

As soon as the gate creaked open, La Bronca came tearing out from under the pink house, snarling like she had been waiting all day only for this, saving up the energy and swiftness she possessed in her dreams when her paws and hind legs twitched her younger self back to life.

"Kind of a mean one, no?"

"She's not there to make friends." Nina blocked the dog's passage so the girl could climb the steps. "We like to know when somebody comes into the yard."

"We?"

"I take care of my mother," she said. "She stays inside, resting."

The girl pursed her lips, nodding. She seemed to be doing the math inside her head, calculating how old an old woman's mother could actually be.

"The dog belongs to her, but I am the one who feeds it." La Bronca strained against the chain, struggling to move forward as if she might dislodge the little house from its foundation blocks and drag it with her. Nina shushed her, but this only seemed to infuriate the dog more, and she finally had to threaten to fling one of her chanclas at the animal before it relented.

"Looks like a dollhouse."

Nina stared at her, unsure what she meant, if it mattered.

"I say because of the color." She tapped on the door with her nails, like she was dropping by a neighbor's apartment to borrow a cup of sugar.

"My mother used to rent it," Nina said, wondering why she kept bringing up her poor mother. What did it matter, the history of the little house or that she lived with her mother? What did it matter now that this wouldn't be happening if she'd listened to Beto and just rented the house?

She needed to be done with the girl already.

When there was no answer, she rapped on the door. This time the little girl, Briana, cried somewhere inside the house, from the bedroom or the living room, wherever they had decided to bed down. A few seconds later the blinds crinkled and Noemí peeked out. She and Briana had been inside for two days, and it took a while for her to figure out how to release the dead bolt. Finally the door unsealed itself from the frame like an abandoned refrigerator taking its first gasp of fresh air.

Nina waited outside, as if she were the one visiting and the driver and Noemí and Briana were the ones who lived here. A couple of minutes later the three of them exited the house, the mother carrying the daughter and both their backpacks, and walked out to the car. Briana was wearing jeans and a pajama top and her head was tucked into the crook of her mother's neck. The driver opened the passenger door and told Noemí to strap her daughter in the backseat and for her to take the front. They weren't going very far and she wasn't running a taxi service. Before they left, the driver put her hand out to shake Nina's and pressed a folded fifty-dollar bill into her palm.

"For your help."

Nina held the bill for the girl to take back. If she didn't accept the money, they couldn't say she had done anything wrong. "It was just a favor, to help a friend."

She felt the need to explain how this had come about, that it was nothing she planned or expected anything for in return. Until the words came out of her mouth she hadn't considered Rumalda her friend; the woman worked for her and they were friendly but not friends. There was a difference. They both knew it without anyone ever having said it. Still, if she hadn't done it for the money and they weren't friends, then why was she doing it?

The girl backed away, her hands held open in front of her chest.

"Keep it," she said. "There might be more friends who need favors, now that we know where you live."

2

The entire exchange—the driver asking for a friend, Nina walking her back to the pink house, Noemí and her little girl getting into the car—hadn't taken more than ten minutes and yet it was enough for Nina to immediately recognize the young woman's voice when she called two nights later.

"We need another favor?"

"What do you mean, another favor? What I did wasn't for you."

"The people I work for want to use the little house. They'll pay you."

"It's not for rent."

"One, maybe two months, that's all."

"Already I said no."

The line went silent for a few seconds and Nina thought she'd gotten rid of her.

"Mira, it's that you don't understand. If I tell them you said no, after you helped us the first time, these people might want to stop by to talk to you themselves."

"So now you're doing me the favor?"

"In a way, yes."

"And if I tell the police?"

"Tell them what, that you did one favor, got paid for it, but now you don't want to no more?"

"You're the one that took them."

"That's right, but you don't know where I live and these people I work for know where you and your mother are."

"You called my house to threaten me?"

"No, señora, I only called to tell you what's going to happen next."

She looked it up the next time she was at the Walgreens.

Favor \fa-ver\ n. 1a. friendly regard shown toward another person (2): approving consideration: b: AID, ASSISTANCE, KINDNESS . . .

It was a pocket-sized dictionary, abridged, the letters in large print, and still it took a minute before her fingers helped her eyes find the entry she was looking for. As if locating the definition would somehow make it all right, because there it was in black and white, and who could argue with that?

So maybe it had been a favor that first time, some kindness she extended to another person she felt friendly toward. The second time Nina barely saw their faces. All of them had jumped out of the camper and were led in a single row from the carport to the pink house, the backyard lights off, walking in the passing glimmer of what little moonlight there was. Shadows passing into shadows. Shadows with no outlines. Shadows from as far away as Panama and Honduras and El Salvador and Guatemala. Shadows prodded into her backyard, shadows locked inside, shadows that ate and slept and shat in the little house, shadows that moved about but in truth she didn't want to see or be seen by.

Los pollos, El Kobe called them, because like chickens they kept their heads down and followed the leader. El Kobe was as dark as his pollos but with a shaved head. He carried an aluminum bat with him everywhere, tapping the end on the heel of his boot as he walked, the clinking sometimes arriving before his shiny head came around the corner. The six men and two women, one of them with a small child sleeping inside his mother's rebozo, came with no names, no pasts, no futures. None shared with her, at least.

The driver from the first time, Sandra, had set things up and then the next day the Border Patrol pulled her over with a carload of crossers that had just made it to this side. From then on it had been El Kobe and Rigo, stockier and with the hazel eyes, who looked like he might be related to Sandra, a brother or cousin.

El Kobe paid her up front, $50 a head, with the expectation they would be gone in a day or two. The fat wad of twenties that neither of them counted in front of the other amounted to more than the rent her mother used to charge for an entire month. She understood part of the money was for the house and the other part was for her to keep quiet about the house. El Kobe phoned her a day or two before they thought they would be arriving and then again when he was on his way. *We stay only as long as we need to, you make the food, and then when we get the call we leave.* He got to the house first, just to make sure it was still safe, and Rigo showed up later with the load. That he described these people as the load, la carga, like a shipment of vegetables or lumber, should've been her first clue that this wasn't about doing favors.

It was only supposed to be a night or two, until they got word and would pack them up again. El Kobe stayed inside the pink house watching the pollos, but he'd also attached a padlock to the door so he could lock it from the outside in case it turned out he and Rigo had to leave for a short while. The back door, facing the canal, they had sealed off with some old planks they found under the little house.

Aside from providing the house, her other job was to prepare the meals and leave them outside their front door. The trouble of making some simple food, something easy to bag up and carry across the backyard, was better than her worrying that they might turn on the gas and accidentally set the little house on fire. In the morning, she brought them a dozen or so tacos de frijoles refritos, each half-moon wrapped in the foil left over from covering the windows. If she had extra time and was feeling generous, she might add some scrambled eggs. It was nothing she would've made for herself, store-bought flour tortillas and beans from a can, but she wasn't spending half her morning making all the food by hand, not with her mother down the hall calling her every few minutes to bring her this or that, a cup of fresh water or find the TV remote that had fallen under the bed again. For dinner El Kobe told her to just make them sandwiches, baloney or ham or whatever she had available. Later he sent Rigo to Stars to bring hamburgers for the two of them. This was Thursday and the same for Friday.

They left sometime early the next morning. She heard La Bronca let out a couple of dispassionate barks before retreating to her spot under the house. Nina managed to get to her window as the last two were climbing into the camper of Rigo's truck, the chassis dipping as the others made room and they all crammed in before El Kobe shut the hatch on the camper shell. They left without stopping to close the gate behind them.

She didn't know what she had been expecting. A light knock on the back door to say good-bye and see you next time? For them to excuse themselves after being on her mother's property for two nights? For it to matter to them what she was doing, the risk she was taking, and not just because it helped their business? She had to remind herself that these people were nothing to her, not family, not friends, not anything. Strangers that had moved in one night and then drifted away early one morning, unannounced.

They weren't going to all hug her in the driveway and promise to call when they reached their destination. They weren't going to pull away slowly as she made the sign of the cross and wished them a safe journey.

No one else knew. Not even Rumalda, who had started her down this road and might have understood. She didn't want to worry about word somehow getting out. If the crossers never saw her face, all the better. She was nothing to them and they were nothing to her. Nada y nada más. If someone reported her, she would claim she had rented the house to the young man and from there knew nothing about how he lived or who he chose to stay with him, to bring as his guests. The rent was the rent. Her family had been renting it for years—they could ask her brother—and never had any problems. Yes, maybe she heard noises, she wasn't deaf, but she wasn't the type to stick her nose in what her renters did. She had her own life, her own problems. Checking to see who was and wasn't supposed to be here, in the country or anywhere else, that wasn't her job.

Rumalda noticed a padlock had been added to the door of the pink house, but she knew not to open her mouth about what she found or didn't find in the houses she cleaned. The stories she could tell if someone paid her to sit around talking about other people. The paper bags stuffed with money she found in the bedroom closet of the restaurant manager's house. The two guns, one with diamonds on the handle, in the underwear drawer of the dentist's wife. The baggies full of pills in the teacher's nightstand. She went on like she never saw these things, but she knew the lock wasn't there when her daughter came to stay. Maybe la señora meant for the lock to say she should never ask for another favor, that the little house was no longer available. Last week when she was hanging the sheets to dry in the backyard she happened to look over her shoulder and la señora was watching her from the kitchen window, as if she were worried that Rumalda was too close to the other house. It was bad enough having to keep an eye on the menacing dog—now she was being spied on. The days of la señora inviting her to sit for coffee passed from one week to the next. After Noemí and Briana had arrived safely in Fort Worth, Rumalda shared with her the good news that they were with her son-in-law, Juan Pablo, but la señora only looked at her like she had mentioned some strangers she met one day on the bus. After that, Rumalda made it a point to simply do her work and not bring up her family, much less the pink house.

Nina shouldn't have been surprised with what she had found the morning after they left with the first load. There was no deposit, nothing El Kobe or Rigo had signed that said they would leave the place clean and in some reasonable order. The back cushions to the sofa were lined up in the bedroom, end to end, making a small bed in the center of the floor. The middle cushion looked damp from sweat or some other release. The material at the base of the sofa was ripped lengthwise, exposing the webbing and several of the springs. The coffee table stood upright in the corner, leaning against the wall near the air conditioner. One of the kitchen chairs lay on its side next to the sink. A used Kotex, its adhesive tabs curled like the clipped wings of a flightless bird, bloomed from beneath the cushionless sofa.

But what she couldn't even begin to figure out was the door-knobs. The bathroom and bedroom, even the closet, all of them missing their doorknobs. Who stole doorknobs? And why? Maybe there were some things she was better off not knowing. Besides, by then the stench had hit her. At first she assumed the rank odor was from the eleven bodies living in close quarters, all but El Kobe and Rigo having traveled for days if not weeks atop trains and wooden rafts and on third-class buses and offered rides and often simply on foot, in fields and across rivers and valleys, over and under fences. She wondered if she wasn't to blame for not leaving them more than two towels and half a bottle of shampoo, the same as she had left for Noemí and her little girl. Then she pushed open the bathroom door and whatever guilt she felt faded. The wastebasket lay on its side, toppled like a gorged animal, crammed beyond capacity with smeared and yellow-crusted toilet paper. When the wads overflowed the container, they had tossed them on the other side of the toilet, on the floor next to the tub, leaving darkened streaks alongside the fiberglass.

As upsetting as it was, she understood they had done this as a courtesy, perhaps their own favor to her, because in the ranchitos that many of them came from, flushing toilet paper might clog the sewer system. And it would take only the first one to do it before the rest followed. When she was still in high school she had visited her tía Manuela in Valle Hermoso and been scolded because she forgot to stick her used toilet paper in the wastebasket and instead kept flushing it. Her tío Efraín had to come with a borrowed plunger, complaining the whole time porque esta gringuita, as he called her, born north of the river, didn't know any better and somehow couldn't learn, already the third day in a row. Was she so delicate that no one could see what she left in the basket?

But here they were on this side of the river and at least El Kobe or Rigo knew better and should have told the rest of the group that this commode wouldn't back up. Later, after cleaning up the mess, she made a small cardboard sign telling them to throw the paper in the toilet and taped this above the tank. TIRA EL PAPEL EN EL ESCUSADO, she wrote in large block letters, at first wondering if she should include POR FAVOR or GRACIAS and then deciding to forgo the niceties, stick to her message, and hope they knew how to read.

3

It was the middle of the afternoon on Friday, a couple of days before Mother's Day, when her nephew Eduardo called to ask if his son Orly could come stay with her for a few weeks that summer. Nina had been inviting her godson to come visit her for years, but more so since his mama had died, a year ago. Of course Orly could come stay with her. Of course. She wanted nothing more than to have her special boy come stay with her. Bringing him in a few weeks was fine, or sooner if he wanted. Whenever it was, she would be waiting for him.

She had just set the phone back in its cradle when it rang again and she thought it was Eduardo calling to tell her something else about bringing Orly. Maybe he could bring him sooner.

"Did you forget something?" she said.

But there was no reply, no one breathing.

"Hello?"

She'd picked it up so fast she wondered if she had only imagined the ringing.

"Bueno?" she said a little louder. "Is anybody there?" It was quiet except for a faint clinking sound.

"We're going to need the house again, tomorrow," El Kobe said, then hung up.

It felt like she had been slapped across the face, slapped because she needed to wake up from dreaming that she was free to invite people to the house. What was she thinking, saying a twelve-year-old boy could come stay with her? It had all happened so quickly. First, Eduardo's call to say she was about to have a special guest, then El Kobe reminding her she'd already agreed to have another twelve or so other guests on the property. There was no chance to tell him that the pink house wouldn't be available anymore, that she had made a mistake saying he could rent it. She barely had time to register the sound of El Kobe's voice before the line went dead.

It had been only two weeks, but Nina was exhausted from tending to her mother, from making tacos in the morning and sandwiches at night, from calling Beto for no good reason but to give him an update on their mother and make him feel like he could stay away for another week. From cleaning up after El Kobe left with each load, from gazing out the back window at night to make sure nothing looked unusual, though she wasn't sure anymore what unusual might look like after weeks of seeing rows of men and women and sometimes children, once even a young man who looked to be from India, darker than any Mexicano she'd ever seen, and another time an older one with short kinky hair, shuffling through the yard. She was ready to go back to seeing nothing, same as it had been for the last eight years she'd been caring for her mother. She had no way of knowing whether any of these men and women made it to their destinations, to the wife or husband or child waiting for them somewhere up north who was praying that they arrived safely and could be reunited, and other times, if it seemed too risky or if they hadn't heard from them in days, praying that they had been turned back before it was too late.

The next evening she heard La Bronca barking and hurried out to the backyard. She found El Kobe as he was unlocking the little pink house, the aluminum bat tucked under his arm like a parasol.

The sun was dipping beyond the canal and it would be dark within half an hour.

"I need to talk to you," she told him.

He cocked his head, which meant talk already.

"Things have changed. The little house is not available anymore."

"Since when?"

"Since now." The bat was down at his side now and she heard it thump against the doorframe.

"And for why?"

They were standing only a couple of feet from each other and she took half a step back. "Because I said."

"Because you said."

"Because I said." She wasn't about to bring her godson into this.

"Somebody saw the truck, a neighbor?"

"No."

"You sure? Not even the one that comes to clean?"

"She hasn't seen anything," she said and hoped this was true.

He looked at her as if he were weighing the truth in her voice.

"If we go down, you go down, and you don't want to go down. Remember that."

"Nobody knows, nobody's going to find out."

"And then?"

"Nomás."

"We barely have two weeks using the house."

"Pero ya, you have to leave. You can have back all the money. I only spent to buy the food."

"That's not how it works. You don't tell me, I tell you." He rubbed the bat against the side of his jeans, twisting it one way and then the other as if it were important to keep all sides of it clean.

"But in my house."

"I give you money for the place, for this other house, and for

you to make the sandwiches. The deal was we could use the property for the payment, made in full before we came to occupy the
space. Both parties agreed to this. You do whatever you want in
the other house, me vale. If you wanted things your way then you
should have said no. I told my bosses that it was all good, that I
paid you, y no iba haber ninguna chingadera. And now you want
me to go say que no, she changed her mind, nomás porque you
didn't want to anymore? When already I got a load waiting to
come later tonight? That shit don't fly with me."

"How much longer, then?"

"Pues, how long did we say?"

"A month to start with and then we would see."

"Then we'll be in there for the whole month." He struck the bat
against the heel of his boot as if he had issued his verdict. "Unless
it turns out to be more."

If anything, there were more people the following week. If at
first there had been eleven or twelve in the loads, this time it was
at least fifteen or sixteen of them. Maybe because it was getting
harder and harder to cross them into the country and transport
them north, but this group stayed longer and before she knew
it three days had passed. She wondered how many sandwiches
these people could eat. Rigo would bring food from outside for
him and El Kobe, but the others were left to eat the baloney sandwiches, which she was now alternating with ham and cheese, and
tuna and potted meat. The van came back the fourth night and
dropped off another seven crossers, which brought the count to
over twenty not counting El Kobe and Rigo. What she witnessed,
she witnessed from inside her mother's house, peering out the
crinkled venetian blinds as the single file of men and women, and
even a young boy, snaked from the carport through the backyard.

Then one after another after another they stepped into the small house her mother had never rented to more than a family of five.

It worried her that she hadn't spoken to El Kobe in almost a week, since their talk outside the pink house. She had no idea if he was still mad or had let it pass, but she knew they weren't leaving on their own. She thought if things were better between them then maybe she could convince him to leave before the end of the month, when Orly would be showing up. For them to leave a few days early wasn't that much to ask. It was almost all of what they had agreed to, what El Kobe had paid her for. If she did something nice for him, maybe he would do something nice in return. She wanted to believe this.

Just after she had run her errands and Rumalda left for the day, she knocked on the pink door. She waited a full minute with no answer and then knocked again.

"¿Qué fue?" he said without opening the door.

"La comida."

"La comida?"

"The food," Nina said. "To eat."

"The food." He said it as if "food" meant something other than food.

"I didn't want to leave it outside."

"And for that reason you knock, para dejar unos pinches sánd-wiches?"

If she hadn't been trying to smooth things over, she might have left right then with the food. Talking to her that way. El Kobe cracked open the door, bracing it with his left foot, and glared out like she might be a bill collector. Then he glanced over her shoulder, toward the back gate that led to the carport and the street. His eyes were puffy with sleep or lack of.

"Something else this time." She lifted the bag of Church's and the deep-fried aroma wafted between them.

"That wasn't part of the agreement. We pay for the house and the food you make, not for anything from outside."

"Did I ask you to give me more?"

He looked her in the face.

"Nobody saw you coming with so much food?"

"I went in the car, not walking in the middle of the street."

"And the one cleaning the other house?"

"She left on foot, but without seeing the bag I had in the car."

Another glance over her shoulder and El Kobe pulled open the door.

Six, maybe seven, men sat huddled on the floor with their backs against the opposite wall, arms crossed over knees and heads hanging low between them, as if riding in a boxcar and only waiting for the train to reach its destination so they could hop out and find their next ride. The two women were on the sofa, one sitting, the other lying down. An older man sat on the floor next to the sofa, near the feet of the woman who was upright. Another five men were sitting against the wall nearest the bathroom. Four more were playing a card game in the bedroom, the rest were watching or not watching along the walls. The boy, his blue cap pulled low over his brow, sat alone next to the air conditioner they wouldn't be turning on for another four hours. Like the other men, he kept a hand on the water jug on the floor between his legs.

Other than El Kobe motioning for her to come in, no one greeted her or so much as raised a head to acknowledge her presence. With the door shut, the front room was dim except for the razor lines of dust filtering in from the top of the foiled windows and a small lamp clipped onto the edge of the kitchen counter. A thick workbook lay spread open, facedown, on the counter next to a legal pad covered with notes.

The only mattress in the house was bare and flopped over on itself, one corner keeping the bedroom door open. The pillows and the sheets were tangled in a tight ball. The toilet flushed and a few seconds later Rigo came out of the bathroom, a San Judas pendant on a gold necklace jigging across his V-neck undershirt as he shook his hands dry. He had a handgun shoved into the waistband of his jeans, the black grip clear to see even in the dim room. El Kobe probably had one under his untucked shirt, along with the bat down by his side.

"Pollo for the pollos," Rigo said when he saw the three family packs of chicken. He repeated it a little louder in case no one had heard his joke, which apparently they didn't the second time either.

Nina placed the plastic bag on the kitchen table and removed the wad of paper napkins she'd grabbed from the dispenser. The paper plates she brought from the other house. Rigo set aside one of the three boxes for himself and El Kobe, then called the men and women to come grab a plate. The smell of the chicken had been lost in the rankness of so many bodies that had been holed up for almost a week. She turned away when the older man, wearing only dingy red briefs, the elastic loose around his scrawny thighs, rushed forward to grab a plate and then held the line so the two women could serve themselves before the men. At first she thought the man had been changing his clothes and didn't want to miss out on the food, but everywhere she looked half-dressed people were walking toward her.

"Maybe you heard the barking last night," El Kobe said.

She might have, but then again the dog barked every night.

"One of them tried to take off without paying the new price, but Rigo caught her before she got to the gate. So it doesn't happen again we had to take some of their clothes, like for a deposit."

"Now the pollos have no feathers," Rigo said and laughed.

"Ya güey, con tus pinches pollo jokes," El Kobe snapped. "Just give them the food."

Only one of the women on the sofa had walked over, an arm crossed over her small chest and green-colored bra, but still wearing faded jeans. The other one stayed curled up on the sofa, her legs crossed at the ankles, her face buried in the seatback as if she had lost something valuable and irreplaceable between the cushions.

After the woman and the old man had served themselves, the rest of the men jockeyed for their place in line and the boy with the blue cap managed to sneak to the front. El Kobe slammed the barrel of the bat against the counter, making them rear back. He stabbed the dented tip of the bat into the boy's chest, shoving him back a few steps to show exactly how far he wanted him. If they fought, nobody would eat. Two pieces of chicken and a piece of bread, nothing more.

The boy slunk into the middle of the line before the men in the back room could come around. By the time the rest had served themselves, the old man in the red underwear had already polished off his first drumstick and the cartilage and started working on the marrow.

El Kobe, whose real name was Omar, had been given the nickname El Kobe by Parra, who was the one in charge and gave out the names, but only to the ones he liked. Rigo, for instance, who was Parra's nephew and had worked for him longer, was only Rigo. Sometimes El Kobe thought Parra wanted him there not to watch over the load, make sure they didn't run off, but just to keep an eye on Rigo. Six months earlier, at a different house, out near the port, El Kobe stepped outside to get his phone from the truck y el puto de Rigo had pushed one of the girls, maybe thirteen at the most, into the bathroom and tried to lock the door behind him. The girl was screaming but not as loud as her mother, who was straddling the doorframe, refusing to let him close and lock the door. El Kobe had to pull her and the girl out. *From then on, anytime they took over a new drop house, El Kobe showed up first to remove all the doorknobs before Rigo came around with the load. He didn't need las pendejadas de Rigo. It was bad enough the shit Parra did to the crossers when they couldn't pay the extra money for the rest of the trip, what he told them they had to do to earn it, especially the women and girls. El Kobe tried to stay out of it, let Rigo handle his tío's orders. After this load he figured it was maybe two more and he was out, done. He already had his first hundred hours of the class time he needed to get his real estate license. He had a primo named César who was a broker on the island, selling and leasing condos to all the rich Mexicans coming in from Monterrey. César, who worked only four or five days a week and drove a black Hummer, loaded with leather seats and a badass sound system, told him he could hook him up at his leasing office. He just needed to take care of getting the license and he'd have it made. You show the properties, get the maintenance guys and cleaning women to prep the home, make sure you have your numbers right, and close the deal. Easy work. A lot easier than sitting in a little pink house with twenty-three crossers and Rigo.*

Nina was halfway across the yard when she looked back at the pink house. She had done her part, done something nice for them, something she hadn't been asked to do and wouldn't be repaid for, same as with the doorknobs, which she hadn't bothered to bring up. Without exactly reminding him of her gesture, she had thought she might ask El Kobe about possibly leaving a couple of days early, but after seeing how they treated these poor people, especially the women and the boy, she realized Rigo and El Kobe weren't the type you did nice things for and expected anything in return.

4

Beto liked to surprise her, like not returning her phone calls and then one day just showing up like they had planned it all along. This surprise happened on a Sunday afternoon. Him and his twin boys, all three of them dressed in Astros T-shirts and blue-jean shorts with elastic waistbands. He only brought the boys around when they didn't have tee-ball or whatever else might seem more important to him at the time.

"For Mother's Day!" he said, all proud because he had given his wife, Melba, the day off from watching the boys and dressed them himself. "You act like I need to call you first or something, make an appointment to see my own mom for Mother's Day." The front door was open, but they were speaking through the grating of the security door.

"She's resting in bed. She had trouble sleeping last night. And anyway, Mother's Day was last weekend."

"We got busy," he said and left it at that. His sister was always trying to put the guilt on him for not coming more often, as if he didn't have his own family and a business to run. He cocked his chin at the yawning trash can next to the ramp. "Looks like you had a get-together. It didn't get that full when we all lived in the house."

"I forgot to put the can out on the street for them to take it."

"A family pack, just for the two of you?"

"They had a special the other day. What we didn't eat I saved in the freezer."

"Still, it looks like you had a party or something."

"Yes, that's all we have around here, every night one pachanga after another. That's why she's so tired." For the last two weeks she had managed to keep him away from the house. She blamed herself for not being more careful with the trash.

"And then what, are you going to open the door or not?"

She jiggled the lock like it was stuck. "You couldn't even stop by for a few minutes last week, on the real Mother's Day. She was asking for you."

"Melba wanted to go to the cemetery to see her mom. She's all the way up in McAllen and we had to leave early because after we saw her mother Melba wanted to try the Olive Garden over there."

Earlier, Mamá Meche had been sitting outside, getting air; her wheelchair was still parked between the front door and the ramp, but now the two boys were playing with the locking mechanism on her chair, trying to figure out how to release the brake. "Ya, open up," Beto said, yanking on the door. He could feel the sweat rolling down his back and the Astros shirt clinging to the underside of his belly. "It's hot out here and we can't stay all afternoon. I have to take the boys to get ice creams."

She pushed open the security door. He was walking into the house when one of the boys—either Roberto Jr. or Rudy, she could never tell them apart, always dressed the same and with their crew cuts showing their dark scalps—climbed into her mother's wheelchair and the other one pushed the chair down the ramp, making his brother collide with the railing at every sharp turn. When they reached the driveway, the one pushing turned the chair toward the carport and then disappeared around the side of the house.

"Tell them to bring it back," she said.

"Leave them, they're just playing around. Why you have to ruin their fun?"

"Yes, but that's not a toy for them to play around with."

"Roberto," his mother called out from her bedroom. "¿Eres tú? I wish this woman would tell me you were coming. And with my little boys this time, I hope. I could have gotten dressed nice, and not the way she has me here, just thrown in the bed."

She was about to tell her mother that "this woman" has a name, but right then she heard the gate squeak open and the twins push the wheelchair into the backyard. Before she could reach the kitchen to get outside, La Bronca had risen from the dirt like some mythical creature drawn to life from the center of the earth. The little boys, not having been in the back since the animal was moved there from the front yard, where they knew not to go near the meanie dog, were so startled that the seated one tried to jump out before his brother brought the wheelchair to a full stop and the chair toppled over into the grass. All while the dog lunged repeatedly against the chain, a motion that seemed to both strangle and energize her.

"Bronca," Nina shouted from the middle of the yard. "Ya, Bronca!" Half a dozen more barks for good measure and the dog eventually retreated into her lair, her back legs again used up and rickety after the sudden exertion.

Beto scooped up Rudy, the one closer to the back door and still on the ground crying; his brother had run off and was whimpering near the gate. Between the sobs, Beto could feel his boy's little heart galloping in his chest. He carried him over to the gate and there knelt down to also hold his brother, soothing them both with promises of later ordering an extra scoop of ice cream for each of them.

Then he turned to his sister. "And you, why the hell didn't you say something about that animal?"

"I told you to not let them be playing all wild. If you had paid attention to what your boys were up to."

"What do you need that dog back there scaring people for? You're lucky it didn't get loose and bite one of them, give him the rabies."

"If you would've been watching them like a father."

"And if you were watching them like a tía." He was shaking his head at her. "Good thing you never had any kids."

He gathered up his boys, one in each arm, and walked back inside to see his mother.

"They would've been better taken care of than those two," she stammered, fighting for the words to rise beyond the tremble in her voice. "That I know." But now she was saying it only to herself.

After the boys calmed down some, the rest of the morning was taken up with their grandmother spoiling them in her own way, letting them pick through most of the Whitman's Sampler they had brought her for Mother's Day and then delegating who would hold the remote control and for how long while she visited with their daddy.

Nina busied herself in the kitchen, washing and drying dishes, sweeping the floor she'd swept earlier, all near the kitchen window. Across the yard the little house was still, but in the middle of all the barking and screaming and crying she could've sworn she heard the click of the second dead bolt.

5

Early the next morning Beto let himself in through the back gate. No more dealing with his sister trying to control him, saying when he could come inside the house to visit his own mom. He was still upset about the dog scaring his boys half to death. Little Roberto had woken up in the middle of the night screaming that he was being chased by the dog, which startled his brother and made him think the dog was in the room. And because it was both of them crying and because it involved the afternoon they'd spent with their dad, Melba made him get up too and hold one of the boys in his lap until he finally fell asleep half an hour later, after which Beto had to sleep there between the two beds, on the floor, like some refugee. On a work night.

Nina heard the barking before she knew they had a visitor. The sun barely up and there he was in the backyard again, two days in a row, walking toward the other house but also trying to avoid the lunging dog.

"First you show up late for Mother's Day and now you show up when people are just waking up." She pinched the neckline of her housecoat into a knot.

"I told you, I don't need to call to come to the house." He spoke in the direction of the dog and not his sister, who was coming up behind him. She had rushed outside barefoot and could feel the dew between her toes.

"Did the boys drop something in the grass?"

But he wasn't paying attention to her. He was trying to figure out how to get himself from point A, where he stood, to point B, the front door of the pink house. When he reached the house he faked going right and then rushed left, toward the steps, but there discovered the chain was long enough for the dog to block his path, her snarl that much more menacing when she realized he was trying to trick her.

"I don't know why this dog has to keep barking and barking," he said. "You should train it. I used to live in the other house. This was my backyard, where we used to play."

"That was before she came to live here. Maybe if you came around more the dog wouldn't think you were a stranger."

She waited for her brother to back away from the wooden steps and face her before calling the dog off. Today he was wearing blue-jean shorts that covered his knees and a khaki work shirt, the tail untucked and billowing in the breeze.

"It's funny how the weather changes." He gazed up at the sky and then over to his sister. "They say it's supposed to rain later, close to noon, but last night it was clear with a full moon."

"You came to give me the weather report?"

"Yesterday when we left I kept asking myself, 'Why does she have that animal back there, if she's not trying to protect something and doesn't want people to get close?'"

She fought her impulse to turn and look at the driveway. She had parked on the street so the truck and then the van could back up all the way to the gate.

"So last night I came back just after dark and stayed watching," he said. "I wanted to make sure I was seeing what I thought I was

seeing. I counted eight or nine of them getting up into the back of
a truck with a camper shell and then another bunch of them into
a van. There might have been more—it was hard to see anything
but shapes."

Other than the first time with Rumalda's daughter, this was the
one night she had come out of the house. It helped that they had
left early, when she was still watching the last of the ten o'clock
news. She remembered seeing a car parked across the street, but
thought it was someone else working for them.

"I said, 'What are so many men and two women, one of them
a gordita who needed help climbing in, and some kid behind her,
what are they doing in my mother's backyard so late on a Sunday night? What business could they have there?' I was going to
call 9-1-1. But then I saw they were carrying backpacks and water
jugs, but nothing you would steal from a house. And who brings
so many people to break into a house? They were coming from
somewhere behind the house and there's only one place to come
from in the backyard. And then I saw you come close the gate."

"Y qué, you want a prize, a medal for spying on my house?"

"Not yours."

She thought about arguing back that it was her house as long as
she was here to take care of their mother, something no one else
was willing to do, but instead she only glanced over her shoulder
at the back door. For the last three weeks she had gone out of her
way to avoid the chances of his stopping by unannounced—calling
him just before the weekend and having him speak to their mother
so he wouldn't feel obligated to come visit, pretending that she
and her mother had a busy schedule running errands, anything
to keep him away—but her brother was about as metiche as they
came, always wanting to know her business, always putting in his
opinion, always thinking his way was the best way, as long as his
way didn't mean any extra work or money from him.

"Go home to your family and leave us alone, like you do most of the time anyway."

"How long?"

"You should be more interested with what happens in the other house, with your mother, and not what you think is happening behind it."

"Hiding mojados."

"I wasn't hiding anybody," she said, not stirring from her place in the yard. "It was something for a friend."

"And then you want to take care of Eduardo's boy." He shook his head. He couldn't imagine what would have made her do this. "You think he's going want to bring him, with all this trouble you made here?"

"You let me worry about my godson. You stay out of it, Beto."

"I followed the van a little ways, thinking I was going to call the police, but then I got worried you were going to land in trouble if your friends talked."

"I have to go inside now, Beto," she said. "To make the breakfast for our mother."

"¿Y eso?" He cocked his head toward the foil on the windows of the little house. "It looks like you're making a baked potato."

"I can have the windows how I want. You don't tell me the way things are going to be. Go be the boss at home." She hadn't liked it either when she first saw what El Kobe had done to all the windows, including the small glass panels on the front door. He claimed it would keep the house cooler, so they wouldn't have to turn on the air conditioner, but she suspected it was just to keep what they were doing a secret, no one looking in, no one looking out.

"You need to stop it already with these mojados." He motioned back over his shoulder as if they were all standing there at the front door. "How many more you got in there?"

"I just have what you see inside the other house, no secrets, no other life. Like you and everybody else. What other life do you see?" She was in his face now, close enough to smell the VO5 in his hair. "And now you come to tell me how I have to live the way you say, who I can help and who I have to send away, because you tell me to, because you think your words matter."

"Don't be getting all mad at me for saying the truth. You're just mad because you got stuck taking care of Mom. But what'd you think was going to happen, if you were the only girl and didn't have no family? The rest of the boys are gone, and me, what do I know? And even if I did know how to take care of her, how would I do it? With those two mocosos at home. I'll be working until I'm seventy-five. Eighty if she makes me give her another one. Already I told her que ya, párale, no more." He stretched his arm out in front of him with his palm raised like he was standing in the middle of an intersection directing traffic after an accident. "And who takes the chinga for all this? You don't see me crying. I accept it."

"That was a choice you made. Who told you to find one still young enough to have babies? That's what you get for not looking for one your age."

"The ones my age are grandmas," he said. "And anyway, I told you to rent the house to make some extra money for the bills, not this trouble you went and found."

"You never can be happy, that's your problem."

"For what, if they catch you. Doing something illegal, and you know it." He stretched out the *eeee* sound as if her illegal was much worse than someone else's illegal.

"For wanting to help," she said.

"And what, you think they're going to let Sister Teresa go free? Les vale madre, you trying to save all the hungry ones." He flicked his hand at her. "Let somebody else save them wherever they're going to, Houston or Dallas, New York. They didn't come across to eat fried chicken behind our house."

"Mother Teresa, not Sister Teresa. Shows how much you know," she said. "And giving them something to eat is not saving them."

"Call her how you want. All I know is you have to tell them que ya, no more. If not, I tell Mom what you been doing at night. See if she doesn't call next time she thinks she hears noises."

"And then?"

"And then they take them away, and you with them, lock you up with all the other people who say they didn't do nothing wrong."

"And you look after her."

It took him a few seconds to respond; he looked like she'd just told him Melba was pregnant again.

"We hire somebody, lots of people looking for work."

"With or without papers?"

"What's it matter, as long as they do what we pay them to do?"

"And so now you don't care if they're mojados or not?"

"Not if it looks like they work hard and save us some money."

"But ones you can trust? You don't think I would've hired somebody if it was so easy to find people? You think I couldn't use the help, that I don't like to sleep the whole night like everybody else? Let's see who you find that is going to be patient with her and brings her all she needs and helps her to take a shower. Let's see how you pay for them."

"Then we take her to the nursing home, y ya."

She stared at him a long while to make sure she'd heard him right, if he was serious or just moving his mouth.

"When she had her accident you said she had to stay in the house, that you would never send her to one of those places."

"That was before."

"A place full of people just waiting to die. That's what you want for your mother?"

"I'm not the one who opened a hotel for mojados in her back-yard." He jabbed his finger in her direction and held it there. "You should've thought about those things before saying yes to them."

That night, after her mother was asleep, Nina sat in the living room with the television on. She stayed watching a singing competition and then a cop show, anything to take her mind off her brother and the fact that she now had only nine days before Orly would be here. Later, she flipped through the channels, then landed on *Primer Impacto*, where they had a report on another mass grave uncovered somewhere in Mexico, and finally she switched over to the local news. She was waiting for the weather report when they announced there was a NEWS UPDATE. She wasn't interested in hearing more sad stories right before she went to sleep, but she stayed watching because the news had happened last night at Las Brisas, a run-down motel close to the flea market where she sometimes took her mother on Sundays to pass the afternoon if the weather wasn't too hot. Men and women were sitting in a motel room with their backs up against the wall, against the beds, against the dresser, against window and curtains. So many of them crammed together, almost sitting on top of one another. Like a dream, the faces were cloudy so nobody could recognize them, not how they showed their faces on the other channel, where it wasn't news unless you could see the people who were suffering. At first it was hard to make them out, but then there they were, El Kobe and Rigo in their mug shots, like bad high school photos no mother would ever want to carry in her purse.

She called Beto. "Turn your TV to the news on channel four. It's over," she said and hung up.

*   *   *

It was two nights later, close to midnight, when she heard the back door rattle. She was in the kitchen, putting away the last of the dishes, and heard something that sounded more like a tap than a knock, faint enough to be taken for the wind shaking the screen door that led to the back steps. The temperature had dropped to almost sixty, but with the gusting wind the air felt colder. Whether or not she was imagining the noise at the back door, there was no mistaking the dog's incessant barking. La Bronca wasn't the type of dog to bark at nothing, to bark because she heard a police siren blaring somewhere across Brownsville or because some other dog decided to bark for no real reason except that was what dogs did in the middle of the night. La Bronca was too old and tired to waste her energy on anything except what entered her backyard.

Nina peered into the river of darkness that separated the blue and pink houses. The glow coming from the kitchen window barely reached the back steps. She turned on the outside light, but it didn't help and in fact seemed to make it harder to see what she sensed was lurking out there. It had been a couple of days since El Kobe and Rigo were caught. She couldn't imagine they would have been released so soon and come back here.

"¿Quién es?" she shouted over the barks. "¿Quién es?" She stepped onto the small enclosed landing, but stayed this side of the security door, still far enough away where no one could reach her between the black iron bars extending from the top to the bottom of the threshold. But with no response, as if she and the dog were crazy to be crying out in the middle of the night.

"Come out now, o si no I'll call the police." Then she repeated herself in Spanish, her voice now quivering less than it had the first time.

She turned off the outside light and suddenly he appeared before her, first as a shadow and then as a boy. He couldn't be more than twelve or thirteen years old. Too young to be out at this time of night, knocking on people's back doors. He reminded her of Orly and how he would be here in another week.

This boy was shorter and not as filled out. It looked like he hadn't eaten since she'd seen him in the other house, in line for the fried chicken. Even with the cap, his hair was still long enough to cover part of his forehead and ears, the same as her Orly's.

Without his saying it, Nina knew there had to be a story behind what had brought him back to this place. But the story would have to wait until after she fed him and later took him across the yard to the other house, where he could turn into a shadow again.

II

De camino

6

This is the year after Orly's parents had made plans to separate and then his mother died unexpectedly, but not from a broken heart or anything like that because he's pretty sure the separation, or the almost-separation, was her idea, though this isn't the sort of detail his father is going to share with him or Alex.

The other bit of information his dad is keeping to himself is why Alex gets to go again to Camp Armadillo for three weeks this summer, but Orly instead is going to spend that time with Nina in Brownsville. His dad said he had missed the deadline for Orly at Camp Dry Springs, that he had meant to send in the deposit sooner and it was something their mom had always taken care of and now all the spots were filled at the camp.

At first, Orly thought not going to camp meant he could just hang out at home for those three weeks, but then his dad said he had to be in San Francisco to shoot a commercial for one of the agency's new clients. Last year, Orly had tagged along to a shoot in Houston and spent most of the time grazing at craft service, munching on bagels and M&M's and ordering smoothies, so he figured he would do the same in San Francisco, but his dad said this time he'd be too busy with the pre-production meetings and client dinners. Orly would be bored waiting for him in the hotel room. Besides, afterward he was planning to take a little downtime and do some traveling with Kayla, who used to be an intern at the agency but was taking some time off to figure out if she really wanted to go to graduate school. He said it like this was still part of her internship, this downtime he was planning.

Anyway, his dad thought it'd be better if Orly just went to stay a few weeks in Brownsville, where his family was from. His dad told him that this way he'd get to spend part of the summer growing up on the border, the way he himself had, and Orly would see things he never would come across if he was at camp with a bunch of other twelve-year-olds just like him. But Orly doesn't think being around a bunch of other kids who go to the same kind of school and live in the same kind of neighborhood and go on the same kind of vacations is the problem. He knows the real reason for sending him to Brownsville is because his dad wants him to grow up more like he did and less like a boy who was always closer to his mother. His dad tried to do the same thing with Alex a few years ago, but by the time his mom got wind of it, she had already scheduled every minute of his summer vacation with one camp or another. It was something their parents had argued about often—their dad saying both his boys were growing up soft, with everything handed to them and without knowing where they came from, and their mom saying that their boys weren't actually from Brownsville, only he was. The "soft" part came up when Orly didn't want to sign up again for tae kwon do, which his dad thought he needed to stick with, not be a quitter, and his mom said not wanting to hit another boy in the face didn't make him a quitter. Alex was actually working at his summer camp this year; otherwise his dad might be sending them both to stay with Nina. In Brownsville, Orly would toughen up some and learn to be more independent, while still being with someone who loved him and would take special care of him.

Nina is Orly's great-aunt and his godmother, but of the two he prefers to think of her as his godmother, especially since his grandmother passed away before he was born. Nina is also close to his dad and helped raise him. She and his tío Beto are the only ones of his father's family still living in Brownsville, the rest of the Diaz and the Hinojosa sides of the family having died or moved as far away as Fresno and Chicago and Grand Rapids, looking for work or love and staying when one or the other kept them long enough that it would have cost more to leave again and come back home.

Orly remembers seeing Nina maybe once or twice a year, not including the first year when she drove up a couple of weeks after he was born and then a few months later for his baptism, which he doesn't count because he was still in diapers and knows it happened only because there are pictures to prove it and a cross she gave him hanging over his bedroom door.

When Nina comes to visit his family in Houston, she mainly sits on the couch and asks him about his school day or his piano lesson or tennis practice and each time he says it went "okay" and then not much else, because, really, what's there to say? Ms. Engleton wants him to work on a new song for the holiday concert? Kevin called Truman a bitch, like a million times, and Truman finally called him one back, but Mr. Domínguez only heard Truman say it, so he's the one that got sent to the principal's office? Coach wants him to switch from a one-handed backhand and go with a two-handed backhand? Zack, the new kid, puked on the field trip before they got to the museum, and then, even if he was better and all, nobody wanted to sit by him since he might do it again on the way back?

Because Nina hates driving in Houston, his father always drops her off and picks her up outside the same door at Macy's. After that, she waits around the house for the boys to get home. She was visiting a couple of years ago when Carson called the house and left a message for Orly to call him back, which she relayed to him when they were out at dinner.

"That took long enough," Carson said when Orly called him back later that night. "I thought we were going to talk about our booth at Culture Fest."

"I had to go out to eat with my family."

"Whatever, dude. I was just worried your maid had totally forgotten to give you the message. She said she would write it down, but I could hear the TV going, so who knows if she was even paying attention."

Before then, Orly hadn't thought their real maid, Maribel, who was more like a nanny, sounded anything like his godmother. Sure, Nina had a little bit of an accent, but that didn't mean she spoke like a maid. And besides, a lot of people had accents but still spoke perfect English. Maybe he never paid attention to Maribel's accent because she had been with them so long and they considered her part of the family, enough so that they didn't have to say hi or bye when they arrived or left the house because she was always there, like Pepe, who did actually require you to stop and pet him or he wouldn't stop with his yapping. Then again, maybe Orly hadn't compared his godmother's accent to his nanny's because Nina and Maribel only ever spoke in Spanish to each other.

Your maid? He didn't know what to say back in the moment or the moment after the moment days and weeks later. Was there even something to say? He let the comment slide, like he did with most things Carson said about other people, which weren't exactly slurs but weren't exactly not slurs either and floated somewhere in between irreverent and offensive, depending on how closely you were willing to listen and then, if you did happen to say something, how willing you were to listen to Carson ask why you had to be so sensitive, so PC. Either way, from then on, Orly told him and the rest of his friends if they wanted to talk to him it was better to text or just call his cell phone.

* * *

"Nina" looks like "niña," but it's a different word, sounds different, too. The second way is how you say "little girl" in Spanish, which his godmother is definitely not and wouldn't like being called. Orly knows this without her saying so or making any rules to remind him. In world history class, Mr. Domínguez told them that *La Niña* was the name of one of the three ships Columbus used when he set out for the East Indies, or what he assumed was going to be the East Indies but later was known as the New World—at least that's what it was to the great explorer and everyone back home. Mr. Domínguez, who sometimes adds stuff that isn't in the book, also said *La Niña* was the ship Columbus used when he sailed back to Spain to show Queen Isabella some of the "Indians" he had found on his voyage. That's how he said it, with his fingers curled in the air like quotation marks, the way he does when somebody in the back of the room might not get the joke.

When Orly was in third grade he sat next to a girl named Nina, but she was named after her grandmother who had grown up on an apple farm in Minnesota and now lived in a nursing home and didn't remember she had a granddaughter, so in a way each of them was the only Nina in the family. Her mother sometimes came on field trips and they had the same platinum blond hair and probably her grandmother did too, since she was her mom's mom and the girl was named after her, and it'd be weird if she didn't look something like her granddaughter. Back when she still had a clear mind, the grandmother had given Nina a gold charm bracelet that she wore every day to school and refused to take off, even during P.E. or the end-of-the-school-year bouncy house party, which is where one of the charms came undone, either on one of the inflatable slides or in the foam pit, and she lost the first *N*.

The only other Nina he knew of was a singer his mom used to listen to at night. One night, back when he was still in fourth grade and couldn't sleep, he stretched out on the carpet outside his room and watched her from between the stair posts. His dad was out of town for work and she wasn't doing anything but looking out the window at the patio light lapping off the pool. She looked sad, the way she did when she told the boys she needed to go lie down and then closed the door to the bedroom for most of the afternoon. She was sitting at the far edge of the sofa and had the music turned down low, playing as softly as the lullabies she used to sing to him every night at bedtime and sometimes still did, even if he was older now and knew this was kind of babyish. After she sang the song he would keep humming the melody under the covers long after she kissed him on the cheek and said her last good night. The recessed lights were on their lowest setting and Pepe, who wasn't supposed to be on the furniture but refused to sleep in his kennel in the mudroom or on the pillow by the picture window in the sunroom, was on the ottoman, curled into a tiny ball next to her feet. She liked to say Chihuahuas were very particular about what they wanted and weren't shy about letting you know it. She had taken a quick shower and changed out of the T-shirt and black leggings she was wearing when she picked him up from school, half an hour after all the other after-care kids had already gone home and the teacher had started calling her cell phone, which she didn't answer until she was leaving her Pilates class.

Now his mom was wearing lounge pants and a T-shirt from their trip to Colorado. She was leaning back on the sofa, holding a glass of white wine from the bottle she'd opened after dinner. She sipped from the glass like she was trying to make it last the whole night. Sometimes she would swirl it around and notice there was hardly any left and then go to the kitchen to get more. Each time she came back she had to readjust herself and Pepe in their original positions, then place the glass on the end table so he didn't knock it over with his tail. It was sort of boring, just watching someone else who looked bored. More than an hour had gone by, and he wondered if she would be rushing them in the morning. Sometimes if they were running late and missed the car line drop-off she had to walk him to his classroom. He wanted to go back to his bedroom to check the time, but he was afraid Pepe would hear him and start barking. After a while he realized that all the songs sounded familiar, because the music on her iPhone was on repeat. He didn't know what he was expecting to see her do, but he kept watching, thinking something was about to happen in the next moment, maybe before the song ended. But the only thing that happened was he dozed off and when he opened his eyes a little later she was gone except for the wineglass with her lipstick mark on it. He could still hear the music playing softly in the background, but he couldn't tell if it was real or just inside his head.

Later, after his parents announced they were separating, Orly thought his mom might change her mind and not move out. Sometimes she said one thing and the next day changed her mind. She did it at least twice when they were all planning to drive to Brownsville to visit family and then that morning she said something had come up with a case at work, though when the boys and their dad were pulling out of the driveway it didn't look like she was headed to the office that day.

At their first parent check-in after the news, Dr. Nancy told his mom that he was upset about the impending separation, obviously, but that it was better to wait until he was ready to talk more about it at home, since pressuring him to open up might just cause him to shut down and make things worse. Which was true, because then he wouldn't be able to tell his parents or anyone else how part of him felt sad because things were changing even while he was doing everything he could so they wouldn't change. His thoughts were jumbled up inside him in a way that he couldn't figure out how to say what he was feeling or if he was feeling anything other than crushed. He wouldn't be the first of his friends whose mom and dad didn't live together, but he wasn't sure if this was good or bad or if it just made him like a lot of other kids.

Orly hadn't wanted to go to Dr. Nancy's office and sit on the floor to talk or draw or play games or whatever they did for the fifty minutes he was there every week, but he did it anyway because his mom wanted him to and he thought it might make her happier and if he could make her happier it'd be easier for her to change her mind about moving. Maybe if he and Alex didn't fight as much or if he did his chores without her asking so many times or if he wasn't always losing his coat or water bottle. He wondered if it was his fault they were separating and probably divorcing—he hadn't heard of anyone separating and then not divorcing. Dr. Nancy explained to him that his parents loved him and his older brother, but they also had their own relationship, one they'd had before he and Alex were born, just like he had his own relationships with his school friends, which he understood on some level, though until recently he hadn't had a reason to really think about what his parents felt when they were away, with just each other or with other people.

Alex had a different reaction to his parents separating, or taking a "time-out," as their dad called it. Two nights after they broke the news to him and Orly, their mom caught Alex trying to climb out his window and told him he didn't have permission to be climbing onto the roof, even if it was only to go out to the tree house. So later that same night he deactivated the security system and set the alarm on his phone with enough time to be back inside the next morning before his mom started calling him for breakfast.

Orly knew he was sneaking out because he could hear his brother's moccasins padding around on the part of the roof that connected their rooms to the pergola Alex used to climb down. Before the news of his parents separating and his mom moving out, Orly would have definitely told on him; now it felt like saying anything was only going to make things worse. Alex wasn't hurting anyone by sneaking out, he wasn't drinking or smoking in the tree house, not that Orly knew of, so why say anything? Their parents might have been none the wiser about the nightly escapades if one night Alex hadn't found it reasonable to take a dump on the roof, all of which rolled down into the rain gutter, and because of the lack of rain it stayed stuck there, nestled between a thatch of pine leaves and cones, where Carlos discovered it a few days later when he was clearing leaves off the roof with his blower.

"Sorry," Alex said, dragging out the word like he couldn't understand why his dad was making such big deal out of the whole thing. "It was an accident. Can we just stop talking about it now? You're embarrassing me."

"I'm embarrassing you? And what do you think I was when Carlos told me he had something to show me but wouldn't say what it was and so I had to climb the ladder to see it for myself? We can stop talking when you tell me how that was an accident."

"Why do you even make him clean the roof? You have the poor guy risking his life up there. Like anyone walking by really cares if there's leaves on the roof."

"We care, and we ask Carlos to tidy up because we want our home to look nice. Anyway, I'm not the one who needs to be explaining things."

"That's only because Mom doesn't want anyone to see you

mowing the grass after that woman pulled over to ask how much you charged."

"She stopped to ask for directions. And don't worry about what your mom thinks and doesn't think."

It was midmorning on a Sunday, and Alex and his father were standing outside, near the pergola but still far enough away from the curious flies hovering near the rain gutter. Orly was across the yard, lying flat on the trampoline, staring up at the hazy sky through the pine trees. He could hear bits and pieces of what they were saying, mainly when his dad raised his voice, and he wondered if he should have threatened to tell their parents, if that wouldn't have stopped Alex from sneaking out, but then a second later remembered his brother never paid attention to him anyway.

Carlos was back on the ground plucking leaves off the mulch since he couldn't restart his blower until the man had time to speak to his son, help him recognize right from wrong, though it didn't seem like a father would need to explain that making cacas on the roof was no good. He couldn't say now why he'd told the man. What child hasn't caused extra work? There was the morning he took Carlitos, only ten at the time, to help him around the ranch he worked at just outside of Téguz. They were about to feed the horse when the boy suddenly poured the oats into the basin where the hay was supposed to go, where he'd been shown over and over. Without thinking, Carlos backhanded him across the face, leaving the mark of his knuckles seared on the boy's temple and cheek. So he'll learn, he told himself as he cleaned out the oats, a task that took him less than a minute to complete. But how many times had he told him how? How many times had Carlitos seen him feed the animal? The boy wasn't paying attention, wasn't using the mind God had given him. But as the boy's father, Carlos also knew his hand had gotten away from him and once it did there was no way of pulling it back.

"What was I supposed to do if I had to go but was already outside?"

"But you weren't supposed to be outside in the first place."

"Sure, and if you want to give me a consequence for that, fine, go ahead and give me a consequence. I shouldn't have been outside and I broke Mom's rule. But the other part wasn't anything I planned. It just happened. And you can't punish someone because they have to go and can't get to the bathroom."

"She isn't the only one who makes rules around here. And being outside with or without permission still doesn't make it okay to undo your pajamas and squat down on our roof."

"I was afraid to wake everybody up if I opened the window and came inside."

"So you're telling me you were being considerate?"

When there was nothing left to say, his dad made Alex help Carlos dislodge the mess with a trowel and the pressure washer, and then made him pay Carlos, from his allowance, for his day of work, even if only a tiny part of it included cleaning out the rain gutter.

Years later, Carlos paid for Carlitos to be brought from Honduras and across the border and then to Houston, paying extra to hide him in the back of a refrigerated trailer that on this particular night was not cooling and so the refrigerated section turned out to be more like an oven. Seventy bodies trapped inside for five hours with temperatures over a hundred degrees until the driver abandoned the trailer before getting to Houston. Nineteen had died, including a five-year-old boy, before they could be rescued. Carlitos was treated in the hospital for severe heatstroke and later dispatched back to his mother in Honduras, where he remained, the brain damage having affected his short-term memory and making it difficult for him to hold down a steady job, much less attempt another trip north. Carlos thought of him often. Wondered what, if anything, his son remembered of him and if what he remembered was the father he was at first or the father he tried to be later.

7

Orly's dad packed the Suburban on a Saturday morning. Alex had left for camp the day before, the bus departing from the Methodist church parking lot down the street. For Orly's dad this would be only an overnight trip, 725 miles down and back, because after he drove back to Houston he had to fly out to San Francisco two days later. He considered putting Orly on a direct flight to Brownsville, but thought they could use some father-son time, especially with Orly still wondering why he couldn't just stay in Houston. When they were done bringing all their bags out to the car, his dad told him to ride up front with him.

"But Mom said I had to wait until I was a teenager."

"It doesn't look like there's any room in the back, buddy." His dad had tossed the bags in the backseat instead of in the cargo space in the very back of the Suburban, where they usually stored the luggage. "Plus it's a long ride. I could use the company."

"She always said it was against the law for me to sit in the front and we might get in trouble."

"Not really," he said, "and you already look thirteen to me." He mussed Orly's hair in that way he did when he meant to say it was a private joke, some caper between the two of them.

*　*　*

Until that grayish Tuesday afternoon when he learned she died from one, Orly had never heard of an aneurysm. It was already weird, their dad picking him up after school two hours late when it should've been Maribel picking him up on time. Alex was in the car and still sweaty from his basketball practice.

This was the day their mom was supposed to be moving into her townhouse.

Oct. 4: Mom moving to Condo.

There it was on the dry-erase board for everyone to see when they were at the refrigerator getting a cheese stick or filling their water bottles at the dispenser; she'd even peeled off the magnetic stickers to Vincent's Doggy Daycare and the poison control center so they could see her note more clearly on the board. After the first or second week, though, the words had become more of a blur to him, seen but not read, recognized but no longer processed, no different from a reminder about an upcoming chimney sweep visit or Pepe's heartworm pills. It didn't help that she had run out of room to write "townhouse" and instead had settled for calling it a condo, when all along she had only called it a townhouse. There were probably similarities between townhouses and condos, sure, but in his mind he associated the word "condo" with the times they had gone as a family to the beach, which were fun and worth remembering and he knew this condo wasn't going to be either of those.

Her notes usually ended with two exclamation points, but in this case, because it wasn't exactly a happy day, not like a birthday or anniversary, she had settled for underlining her words. Underlining wasn't the same as exclaiming; underlining meant this is important, don't forget because sooner or later this is coming around and you'll want to remember it; an exclamation point meant PAY ATTENTION because something's about to happen, something you'll probably regret missing for a long time. And so yes, as soon as his mom had mentioned it that morning Orly remembered the date, of course, even if he tried to act like he thought it was next month or at the end of the summer, and anyway by then she'd pulled up to the front of the car line and Mr. Domínguez, who happened to be on traffic-control duty that morning, opened Orly's door and said, "¡Buenos días, Orly!" in his chipper voice and waited for him to exit, as did the other two dozen cars behind them. From there, his mom had rushed back to the house to wait for the movers, who were the ones who found her passed out next to the boxes she'd been storing in the garage. Weeks earlier she had started taking the packing boxes out of the house so Alex and Orly wouldn't have to see what they already knew but didn't want to believe.

Their father had planned to wait until they were home before telling the boys anything, but with the summer heat and stop-and-go traffic and the tightness in his chest building like it would only be harder to say the longer it took to finally circle into their driveway and sit them down in the living room, he instead pulled into the first open parking lot he saw. He undid his seat belt so he could turn around and face them, then signaled for them to turn off their devices and remove their headphones, but told them not to open the doors because they weren't getting out.

Then why pull into Star Pizza? For as long as the boys could remember and way before their parents ever mentioned separating, they used to come here as a family on those Friday nights when Maribel had the night off. It was the place they used to order the garlic bread from, with the deep-dish pizza that Alex used to get all over his shirt, the place that looks like an old house and has tiny restrooms, with the busboy who looks like their cousin Eloy, only older and with a gold tooth, where their parents sometimes let the kids sit outside on the patio while the grown-ups ate inside looking at their phones. Why that place?

"I need to tell you something sad that happened today."

Orly's hand shot up. "You got a new job and we're all moving somewhere else together?"

"No, it has to do with our family, with Mom."

"She changed her mind and isn't moving out?" Alex said.

"Why would that be sad?" Orly asked.

"I'm just saying. Maybe he's the one moving out now."

"But Mom said she had to be the one or else it might not happen."

"Just let me finish, okay? Me first, then you." Their dad had twisted around in his seat but was still gripping the steering wheel with his left hand. He stared at both of them for a couple of seconds, as if he wanted to remember what their faces looked like in this moment before he said what he had to say. "Your mom had an accident this morning."

Without knowing what exactly was coming next, Orly covered his ears and buried his face in his lap. He was humming so loud that it should've blocked out the sound of his father's voice, but he heard enough to know the accident, as he suspected, was more than an accident. He heard it in his father's voice before he finished and the words made any sense.

After their father gave them the details of how she had died but they still had no idea what an aneurysm was, he told them it was a brain stroke, thinking this might stop them from asking so many questions, but of course it didn't because neither Orly nor Alex knew what a stroke was either. Even with his seat belt still pressing against his chest, Orly felt as if everything he had inside him, his heart and lungs and liver and kidneys and stomach, was slipping from his body, down his legs and onto the floor mat where he'd just dropped his iPad.

Their father tried to explain that a stroke was like a heart attack but to her brain and the damage it did to her brain was what killed her. They knew heart attacks because their dad's mother had died of one years earlier, but a heart attack was something that happened to old people and their mom was barely forty-one, which was old but not old-old, like grandma-old, not like heart-attack-old, even if hers was more like a brain attack. None of it made any sense. Their dad was seven years older. So why was she the one who got sick? Alex had stopped with all his questions and was staring out the window at something in the bushes. Then he started slowly bumping the side of his head against the glass over and over until his dad opened his door and went around the car to hold him in his arms, and a couple of minutes later did the same with Orly.

Even going against traffic, it took almost half an hour before they passed every Marshalls, Target, Walmart, Chili's, McDonald's, Academy, Subway, Home Depot, and Bed Bath & Beyond it seemed there could be in the world. The drive down to Brownsville usually took about six hours, but this time Orly knew it would feel a lot longer, more like seven or eight hours, maybe because on this trip he would be staying weeks and not days, or because his brother and his father wouldn't also be there with him. When he sat in the backseat he always had a movie or game to play on his iPad and basically, unless his mom or dad told him and Alex to look at some random cows in a pasture, he never had to deal with how utterly boring it was to look out the window.

They were only an hour from the house when his iPad dinged with a text.

[Where r u?]

[In car w/ dad, just left HTX.] Orly responded.

[Tell Eduardo I said hi!]

"Alex says hi," Orly told his dad. He knew better than to say that just between them Alex liked to refer to their father by his first name. Or that he insisted on calling him Eduardo, the way he was addressed in Brownsville, and not Eddie, the way he was everywhere else.

[D says hi back. Says he heard there were no devices @ camp.]

[Fake News!]

[D says ur going 2 get into trouble 4 breaking the rules.]

[Tell Eduardo to chillax, it's a summer camp not a prison.]

[D says he should've made both of us go to Brownsville.]

[AKA Camp BS (Boring Summer)]

It wasn't long before what they saw out the tinted windows turned to miles and miles of dreary coastal plain, dull enough that Orly could nap for twenty minutes and after opening his eyes feel like they'd been moving but were still in the same place. Before, when he used to sit behind his mom, he thought the boredom had to do with only being able to look out at the side of the road and not the road in front of them, but as it turned out, with the exception of spotting some roadkill, he really hadn't been missing all that much. Still, he liked sitting up front like they were in a buddy movie, just the two of them traveling cross-country, even if it meant he had to talk more or listen to his dad's news station and couldn't just put on his headphones or play another round of *Clash Royale* on his iPad, which he had planned to do for most of the trip. Close to noon they stopped at a Whataburger for lunch and a pee break.

"But what if I get bored and there's nothing to do?"

They had already ordered at the counter and were waiting for one of the table servers to bring their meal out to them.

"That's why you're taking your summer books and your iPad. But you should really be outside doing stuff."

"Like what?"

"Lots of things. Taking chances and doing fun stuff, not just the things some camp director plans out for you and a bunch of other kids."

"But doing what?"

"Whatever there is to do," his dad said. "Your own ways to spend your time and have fun, different from mine. Give it a chance and you'll have a good time. Just wait and see."

"Were you ever bored in the summer when you were growing up?"

"All the time, but then I found things to do. You'll have fun in Brownsville and get to do things on your own. You'll see how different it is down there and how good you and your brother have it where you live and the schools you go to, stuff I never had growing up. It's just three weeks to try something new. Your Nina will take good care of you and keep you safe."

"What if I hate it or if she's mean?"

"Has she been mean to you before when we've gone to visit or she's come to see us in Houston?"

"No, but maybe she'll get tired of me being there."

"I doubt it—she's been begging me for years for you to go stay with her."

"She looks like she could be mean."

"Because she's older?"

"Maybe." He took a sip of his soda.

"You should've seen her when she was young."

"What was she like?"

"I've only seen pictures, but everybody used to say she was even prettier. I heard that one time she was in the parade and a photographer from San Antonio walked the whole route, like more than a mile, just to give her his phone number and ask if she wanted to be a model."

"Wait, seriously, she was a model?"

"Not really. She was still in high school and her parents didn't let her."

"What about after she graduated?"

"I guess she changed her mind."

"How come she never got married?"

"Who knows? It just didn't work out that way. Not everybody's supposed to be married."

When the food showed up there was some confusion about who had ordered which cheeseburger. This was actually the first time Orly had ordered something off the regular menu, which he did only because his dad had invited him to sit up front in the Suburban with him and Orly wanted him to think he was older. His dad had even let him get a soft drink, an orange Fanta, something his mom never let him do.

The most frustrating part for Orly was not knowing what happened to her, not having a way to understand why someone would have an aneurysm. Even later that same day, in his room at home, he couldn't immediately look it up on his laptop because he didn't know how to spell the word, which in a stupid way made the whole thing that much worse, his mother dying of something he didn't know how to google.

"The doctor said nobody knows why this happened now. Sometimes it happens this way with aneurysms." They were eating dinner at the time they were usually already in bed. Their father had reheated the chicken and pasta soup Maribel had left for them.

"No warning at all?" Orly said.

"Sometimes, or the person feels like something is wrong but keeps it to himself until it's too late."

"Herself," Alex said.

"Right," his father said. "Herself."

The doctors did all they could to try to save her. At least she hadn't suffered long. This last part was meant to make them feel a little less sad. And of course Orly wouldn't have wanted her to suffer, but he also wasn't sure about her leaving so suddenly, about his finding out when it was already too late, about having to wait until after school because his father needed time to figure out all the things he needed to do next, the arrangements with the funeral home, the death certificate, phone calls to family and certain friends, to her law firm, to his office, before the next thing to do was tell the boys what had happened to their mom.

A good twenty miles after the stop at Whataburger, they reached the stretch of Highway 77 that sliced through the middle of the King Ranch, all 825,000 acres of it, and were now more than two-thirds of the way to their destination. The Border Patrol checkpoint stood off in the distance, the American flag whipping high above the mesquite and huisache that filled the wide median separating the south- and northbound sides of the highway. A fleet of green-and-white SUVs parked and at the ready sat under what looked like a huge carport. The line of northbound cars and trucks and buses and 18-wheelers extended for more than a quarter mile. On earlier trips, when he and Alex were sitting in the backseat of the Suburban, this was the part of the trip when their usual refrain of "Are we there yet?" turned to "How much longer?" because what followed was an interminable hour of driving past nothing but barbed-wire fence, cactus, acacia, mesquite, grazing cattle, empty train tracks, a couple of radio towers, the occasional pump jack, and on this particular afternoon an empty water jug lurching across the land like a tiny tumbleweed.

It was an easy detail to overlook across the otherwise desolate landscape. For the last two days, a northwesterly wind had propelled the plastic jug miles and miles, past trees and fence lines, from the last person to carry it, Odilia Hernández, an undocumented immigrant from Guatemala. Three days earlier she and fourteen other immigrants had been smuggled into the U.S. and then kept in a safe house in Donna, a few miles from the river. At that point she was only an hour from the interior checkpoint that everyone driving north from here had to stop at. But the coyote warned her that to get beyond the checkpoint they would be dropped off and have to walk around it, across the surrounding ranchland for hours and hours in the dark and in the sun. Hundreds of people had died on this part of the trip. He told Odilia that in truth she should find an easier way to go. She wasn't falling for it, though. She knew these coyotes would lie to your face to take more money from you. She was an older woman—only sixty-two, she said when asked, though she was closer to seventy—her years showing in her weathered hands and unsteady gait. He laughed when she claimed she had been exercising for weeks to prepare for this. But it didn't matter how many times he told her she was too old and should find another way to go; she had only enough money to be taken this way. Her daughter and grandson, Roger, and his baby sister, Zena, were waiting for her in Missouri. The boy was entering the sixth grade soon. Odilia carried his school picture in the front pouch of her backpack and pulled it out to show the two other women also traveling north. The last time she had seen her grandson was the day they left as a family, when he had barely two years. Now her daughter's husband had been deported months earlier and had tried to

get back to Kansas City but never arrived. She was the only other family
her daughter and grandchildren had. Late the next day, the coyote led
the group through the dark as they began the long slog across the sandy
terrain. Odilia kept up with the group for most of the night but then later
started falling behind and delaying their progress, until the coyote eventu-
ally came back around and told her they couldn't wait around anymore
and that she was on her own. She begged for a little more time to rest, she
begged for him not to be so mean, she begged because she had a family that
was waiting for her, she begged until he and the rest of them were too far
away to hear her. From there she walked another three or four miles, most
of this in the wrong direction, before her legs cramped up and she had to
rest again. Then she continued, repeating this routine as many times as
she could, until there was nothing left in the water jug. After the sun came
up she crawled under the shade of an enormous huisache, dehydrated,
her pulse racing, close to death. Before leaving, one of the other women,
who had once lived in the U.S., told her to call 9-1-1 for help, but when she
did that, the dispatcher said it would take at least four hours for them to
reach her, maybe longer. They had two other calls before hers. She wanted
to contact her daughter to tell her what had happened and maybe speak
to Roger, but her phone battery was running low and the dispatcher said
she might call her back, which she did, closer to noon, though by then it
was too late to save her. Later that same afternoon, the coyote reached
a clearing off the main highway, where he and the fourteen other cross-
ers were picked up in a white panel van, far beyond the checkpoint that
separated them from the rest of the world to the north.

Orly knew they were close because of the swaying palm trees, the
fruit stands that lined the northbound side of the highway, the bill-
boards that were in Spanish, and the occasional car with Mexican
license plates. People drove slower here, he remembered. That,

and sometimes it felt as if everything was moving in slow motion, like they were underwater and just didn't know it. Eventually, the side of the highway entering Brownsville was dotted with the same Chili's, same Academy, same Chuck E. Cheese's, same La Quinta, same Golden Corral, same everything, so if he squinted it almost looked like Houston or anywhere else he might call home.

Then his dad was taking the exit and a minute later stopped at the intersection next to another Suburban, this one white with a green stripe and marked BORDER PATROL, also in green, on the side. They were now less than five miles from Mexico and the Rio Grande, the river in places no wider than two hundred feet from its northern to its southern banks. The agent driving was alone in the vehicle, or least it seemed that way; the back passenger and cargo-area windows were tinted dark enough that it was hard to tell if anyone else was inside the vehicle. The reflection of their black Suburban glimmered off the windows of the white Suburban. Orly's dad looked over and nodded at the agent, who nodded back and lifted a couple of fingers off the steering wheel.

"You know him?" Orly asked.

"Nah, I thought he was somebody else, this guy I went to high school with."

"But he waved and you waved back."

"So, you don't need to know somebody to say hi. There's no law against it."

When the light changed from red to green, his dad took a left and then a few miles later a right that led them into Nina's neighborhood, past the dollar store and raspa stand and self-serve car wash. A mound of brushwood, higher than the mailbox, lay at the curb in front of one of the houses. Next door a man was in the driveway changing his oil, only his feet and hairy legs extending from beneath his car. Nina's house was at the end of the block and easy to spot with the aloe vera plant fanning out from the front corner of the lot and the bougainvillea blossoming above the barbs of the chain-link fence.

She'd left the driveway gate open and parked her car on the street. His dad pulled the Suburban all the way into the carport and Nina came out the back door before he turned off the motor. She and his dad were hugging at the gate now and calling for Orly to get out of the car already so she could give him the biggest hug ever, show how much she loved him and how she had been counting the days until his visit. But he knew his three weeks in Brownsville would officially start as soon as his opened the car door and he wanted just a second to take it all in. The baby blue house, the long ramp from the front door, the tire swing, the faded sheets on the clothesline, and beyond all that, the barking dog chained to the little pink house.

❧ III ❧

La madrina

8

After dropping Orly off near the field, Nina makes a huge U-turn, stops twice for a pair of speed bumps and another time for a gaping pothole brimming with yesterday's rain, and finally parks at the other end of the lot beneath the wispy shade of a mesquite.

He carries the ball under his arm, careful to sidestep the still muddy trail, until he reaches the gravel track. A young couple is taking turns running and pushing their little boy around the track in a stroller that can't go any faster than a fast walk without a pebble choking the caster on the right front wheel and bringing everything to a skidding halt. So the man jog-walks a lap while his wife pushes the stroller, and when he catches up to them again they switch places. The man, skinny with a slouch to him even when running, is wearing blue-jean shorts, black socks and running shoes, and a wife beater, which down here is just an undershirt, mainly to be worn in that manner, under a guayabera or any other dress shirt, for church or work or a night out, but also, depending on the weather, worn alone if the man happens to be cutting the grass or barbecuing on the weekend or even taking an early-evening jog around a high school track. His wife is twice as heavy as he is and has on spandex tights, a loose T-shirt, and pink high-tops; the little kid, maybe three at the most, sits in only his Pull-Ups, his plump legs, pecked with mosquito bites, dangling over the edge of the stroller. The boy has his father's face, same broad forehead and chinito eyes, a mini version of him except for not having a faint moustache draping the edges of his little mouth.

When Orly has crossed the track and reached the soccer field, Nina honks to let him know she's still there, watching him, and he responds by dropping the ball and shielding his eyes with one hand and with the other, raised high, waving back. She tapped the horn only once because she's afraid of startling her mother. The dark green tint of the wraparound sunglasses the ophthalmologist gave her at her last visit makes it impossible to tell if she's gazing in the opposite direction, out toward the tennis courts, or resting her eyes, as she calls it whenever she dozes off throughout the day. She hasn't uttered a sound since her last "Ay Diosito" when the boy was wheeling her out the front door and down the long and angled ramp and she claimed he was going too fast and she didn't know what all the hurry was for—if the house was suddenly on fire—if she was having a heart attack and didn't know it—or if they were just trying to give her one, here on her own ramp—and then he finally helped her stand and position herself between the car and the door, preparing her for her slow, precarious descent into the front seat.

Nina wants to turn off the engine, but the sudden lack of cool air from the air conditioner might disturb her mother. Mamá Meche's breathing is steady and she looks comfortable. Then again, she's liable to wake up complaining that it's too cold, ask if Nina's trying to freeze her to death by making it like an icebox in here, the same as it is everywhere else, the house, the grocery store, the pharmacy, the lobby of the cardiologist's office, the elevator to the urologist's office, the bathroom of the rheumatologist's office. There is no lack of places where she might feel a chill, and so regardless of the weather outside they don't leave the house without her brown knitted cap, her purple fleece jacket,

, and at least one of her rebozos draped over the backrest of the wheelchair.

The little boy has begged off his stroller so he can run onto the field where Orly is kicking the ball. His mother is trying to put shoes on him, but he insists on running barefoot.

"He can play with you?" the father asks.

"I'm just kicking it," Orly says, pulling the ball from the goal and rolling it to the boy.

"He likes to give kicks to the ball and yell, real loud." Then the kid demonstrates, kicking it once, twice, and on his third kick makes the ball go far enough to piddle into the net.

"Goooool!" the little boy yells until he falls down and his father laughs.

Orly scoops out the ball and the boy does the same thing a couple more times, yelling a little louder with each goal and running down the field a little faster.

"Like I said, no?" the father gushes.

Orly nods, unsure whether to answer him in Spanish, which he suspects might be easier for him but might also suggest he doesn't think the man speaks very well. If he switches over, the man might think Orly's Spanish isn't so good either, even if it's no worse than the man's English. It's complicated. He probably doesn't think Orly knows Spanish. He has his mom's light skin, and so most people assume he doesn't. And if it weren't for his last name being Diaz no one would expect him to speak anything other than English.

His godmother says his name in Spanish, calling him "Orlando, mijito," like she's speaking to someone else, another Orly, a shorter and darker version of this one who all along has been following right behind him, lurking in his shadow, but who only she can see.

She and his tío Beto are always saying he should speak Spanish, but as soon as he does someone is correcting him, saying he mispronounced a word or messed up the conjugation. It happens enough to make him not want to respond in Spanish and sometimes not even in English. Like when he goes up to his dad's office in the evenings and the cleaning people wave to him and he waves back. He could be friendlier, but he keeps his headphones on even if he has the music turned off. If it wasn't for his dad saying hi to them they might not be so friendly. The guy vacuuming the conference room might be from Michoacán or he might be from the Northside. He might have showed up just last week or it might be his great-grandfather who showed up first. Does it mean something that he's named Orly and the janitor guy probably has a name like Javier or Servando? Or that they might have the same last name? Sometimes he wishes they didn't say hi to him and that he didn't feel like he had to respond. Hola or Hello? ¿Qué tal or How's it going? Buenas noches or Good night? Better to wait and let them make the first move.

Nina wants to honk again just to make sure he's okay and the man and his little boy aren't bothering him. Her mother is still dozing behind the dark glasses, her breathing altered now and then when her nose twitches like she has an itch or might need to sneeze.

"For that reason, if you would listen," she says, recovering some frayed thread of a distant conversation. "Nobody listens anymore. They forgot how to listen, how to open their ears."

"Mamá," she says, tapping her knee. "Mamá, can you hear me? It's me, Nina."

She lowers her sunglasses. "¿Y quién es Nina?"

"Tencha," she corrects herself.

"Then say it right and stop trying to fool me with other names." She nudges the sunglasses back onto the bridge of her nose.

It's true. Nina's not her real name, it's just what Orly started

calling her back when he was learning to talk and couldn't pronounce "madrina," the proper word to say godmother. His father
calls her Tía, or says, "Your Nina called today," or "It's your Nina's
birthday today, we should call her." Or even "I bet your Nina
would like it if we called her for Mother's Day." After a while,
Nina was the only name Orly knew her by, and even if she isn't
his brother Alex's godmother, he calls her Nina too.

She was happy to be a Nina. She had never been happy being
an Hortencia, an old family name handed down from her great-
great-grandmother who had arrived as a baby when Texas was still
Mexico. Even shortened to Tencha, the name fit like a borrowed
dress that was tight in all the wrong places. "Nina" to her sounded
younger and more fun to be around, the type of woman who
sometimes forgot to use her seat belt and had her hair done once
a week, maybe even colored it, the type who had been married
but was also happy alone, who had traveled to other countries and
had a home full of trinkets and photos, each with its own story,
the type of relative a young boy would be eager to see around the
holidays or his summer vacation.

"And the time?"

"Still early—look at the sun."

She leans toward the dashboard for a better look, but the seat
belt's locking mechanism restrains her. She tries to press the
release button and undo the buckle.

"Ya, we're leaving in a little while."

"In how much?" her mother says. "Because your little always
comes out longer than my little."

"I told him seven thirty."

"All day waiting and you want to make me lose my program."

"Only for a little more, until the boy finishes and we can go
back."

Her mother stays silent, thinking of the few boys, if any, she knows the names of. There has been a young one in the house the last few days. He comes every morning to give her a kiss and say Buenos días, and later, after her novela, Buenas noches. Earlier today she played a game of Lotería with him. She couldn't believe it was his first time ever playing. She had to show him how and after the first game, which she won handily, she let him read the cards for the next two games, just to hear him say more in Spanish.

"Orlando," she says suddenly, as if a leaf with his name written on it has just floated in through the crack at the top of the window and landed on her lap. "The one who is the son of Eduardo?"

"Yes, his boy," says Nina.

"Because there is also a Rolando they call Rolly, verdad?"

"That one that belongs to Ramiro, in Michigan."

"Michigan," she repeats. "Mich-i-gan," like it's another name to remember.

"Far away."

"You think I don't remember? I was the one who was there, not you. We went every year to work in the fields until when you were born. After so many years I told your father, 'No more. Find other work to do or go alone, but no more working in the fields, living like animals in those shacks.' You should thank me that you never had to live that way."

"I tell you each time you say it."

"You could have brought him, este Orlando, and left me at home to watch my novela."

"And if you needed me?"

"I can get down from the bed and walk to the bathroom without you there to watch me. You just think I need you helping me for everything or I will fall down going from here to there."

"If you mean at night, then yes, you need to be sleeping in the bed or call me to come help you."

"I could be dead and the noises would wake me up. People coming and going, people walking in circles, talking in whispers."

"Remember that Orly stays up later than you do. Maybe you're hearing me talk to him in the kitchen."

"Sí pero, this has been since before el Orly came to stay. And not in English, like he likes to talk."

"I used to have dreams where I could hear my father's voice in the next room."

"Now you think I am imagining it? Me lying in bed hearing the voices of strangers, first outside and now like they are inside, there in the very next room."

"Then maybe I'm more tired than you are when the day ends." Nina checks the clock on the console. The couple with the little boy have left the track and are walking toward the far end of the parking lot. "We should ask Dr. Robles, see if he can give you something more to help you sleep."

"Your answer for everything," she says. "Instead of going to his office to get more pills, you should pay Robles the same money to come stand in the yard or outside my door, see what's making the noises. Pay him for that, not for more pills."

Nina will give the boy another minute before tapping on the horn; the fading sun has already made it difficult to see him in the distance. The novela is coming on in less than half an hour and the giant cicadas they know as chicharras have already begun their shrill evening concert. Inside the car, though, all she can hear is the scorn in her mother's voice.

The other boy knows they are home when the shaft of light passes through the slit between the top of the window and the aluminum foil. He stays crouched inside the pink house, his back flat against the front door, his ear up against the frame. He hears the engine turn off and a moment later one door opens, then a second and a third, and finally the trunk, where la señora keeps the wheelchair that belongs to her mother. He can hear la señora walking in the other direction, toward the front door of the other house, her voice faint like the murmur of a distant river he cannot yet see.

Earlier in the day there had been barking and then the windows shuddered, as it happens when the mean dog gets excited in the middle of the night and yanks against its chain and the little house begins to tremble. But in between the barking, there was also a pounding on the other side of the wall, as if someone was hammering just outside the window, but slowly, each blow delayed as if the carpenter had dropped his hammer in the grass.

The boy tried standing on the sill but couldn't balance himself for more than a few seconds. Then he pushed the old couch up against the window to see if he could reach the crack at the top of the aluminum foil. He was higher on the cushions but only enough to look straight out at the roof of la señora's house and not into the yard, where the pounding was coming from. Only when he spun the couch around and stood on the backrest was he able to look down and see the one who must be la señora's godson. He was standing in the middle of the yard, kicking a yellow-and-black soccer ball against the side of the little pink house. He lined it up and kicked it with his right foot, and when the ball came back to him he lined it up and this time kicked it with his left.

Then, from atop the backrest, the other boy heard the screen door of the blue house and a few seconds later there was la señora in the yard talking to her godson, scolding him for something. The other boy scrunched down on this side of the wall and then dropped onto the sofa, afraid she might have somehow spotted him through the tiny crack at the top of the window.

He knows the rules. La señora has told them to him for the last two weeks. Do not come out in the day, even those times when she happens to remove the padlock. Do not open the door to anyone but her. Do not be

*looking out the window. Do not be making any noises. Do not turn on
the air conditioner if you hear somebody in the yard. Do not even flush
the toilet. Do not let them hear any sounds coming from inside the little
house. And no matter what, do not let anyone see you.*

Later, after Mamá Meche has watched her novela and gone to
sleep, Nina goes to the hall closet and from the top shelf pulls
down an old photo album, the spine and cover as worn and speck-
led with time as her own hands.

"Mira, Orly," she says, tapping on the sofa for him to sit with
her, "I'm going to show you where we came from."

His hair is still wet from the shower she made him take after
coming home sweaty from the soccer field. He has on the only
pajama shorts and T-shirt he brought with him to sleep in.

"But closer, mijito," she says until he scoots over right next to
her so she can spread the photo album over both their laps. Then
she drapes her arm over his shoulder as if they're about to go on
a ride somewhere.

The photos are in no particular order, each spread onto a moldy
page and sealed with a crinkly plastic cover. There's one from 1914,
next to one from after World War II, next to one from a fortieth-
anniversary party in the 1970s, next to one of the reunion he and
Alex came to a few summers ago with their dad.

"He died before you were born, but this one is your great-
grandfather, your daddy's grandpa and my father. His name was
Orlando, like you."

Orly already knew he was named after him, but the only photo
he had seen of him was in a group shot taken at the fortieth
anniversary. In the photo that Nina is showing him now, his great-
grandfather is standing at the edge of a cotton field. He's wearing
a straw hat with a narrow brim, and the sleeves of his white shirt

are rolled up to his elbows. It must be a windy day—the cuffs of his khakis are billowing out from his ankles. Maybe it's because the image is in black and white that everything looks so clearly defined.

"Was he really that dark?" Orly asks and then remembers his mom telling him not to talk about people's skin color, but he figures it's okay in this case because he's named after the man and because the question makes Nina smile like she knows something he doesn't.

"It was from working outside all his life, from the time he was younger than you. Then he had to leave home to look for work when he was fifteen. But when he took off his shirt he was as light as you, maybe lighter."

Orly has a hard time imagining his great-grandfather's skin being anything like his, that they could be related by anything more than a last name, but he doesn't have time to turn this over in his head before Nina goes to the next set of photos. Each comes with its own story she has to tell before she lets him turn the page again, so many that they flood his mind with who was married to who, whose grandfather's land was stolen, which were the brothers who were hired guns, whose father was lynched by the Texas Rangers, who died in Korea, who died in a bar in Reynosa, who was shot in Vietnam and got a Purple Heart, who worked in a beauty parlor, who was a policeman and also played the harmonica and accordion in his own conjunto, who did time in prison, who left her boyfriend to marry the Jehovah, who raised six little ones on her own, who left to work the fields and stayed up north, who was the first to finish high school, who was homecoming queen that one year, who was the first girl in the family to finish college, who went away to school in Washington, in Boston, in California, who was the first to go to dentist school, who was the first to go to law school, who lived for years and years allá

solita in New York City, who was the first to own her own business, who was the first to move away and not come back. Most of
them dead and the rest living far from here. She turns one page
and there's the sepia photo of Mamá Meche when she was three
or four, standing on a large wicker chair with a huge bow in her
hair. As different as her hair and skin are today, the shape of her
little eyes and nose looks the same. The next page has one of his
dad when he was Orly's age and riding a horse. Toward the end
of the album they find his mom and dad's wedding photo. Nina
waits a little longer here because he's moving his finger along the
edges of the picture.

"Are there any more of them?"

"Only this last one," she says.

It's from his baptism, with his mom and dad and Nina, the
same one he has stored away in his closet at home. The priest has
just blessed him, and his godmother is cradling him in her arms,
smiling, beaming actually, lifting up the child she will help guide
through life by her words and deeds.

9

Orly sleeps in a small room next to the kitchen and the bathroom, which makes it easy if in the middle of the night he needs to pee or wants to go serve himself a glass of water. The bed is pushed up alongside the paneled wall and at night before falling asleep he likes to feel the grooves on it. Between some of the grooves he can stretch out his hand and barely reach the next groove; between others the space is only large enough for his fingers to stay scrunched up together. The actual grooves also come in different sizes, some of them as wide as a full inch, others more like three-quarters of an inch. He likes to know when there's a pattern. A pattern makes him feel there is some logic to the ways things are, someone has thought this through, whether he knows the reason for this or not. In the morning he'll ask Nina for a ruler and measure them. There's a mystery of some kind to be solved in the grooves and the distances between them and he has a sense that figuring out the pattern might lead to something bigger and this might lead to solving other mysteries. When he asks her for the ruler she'll say, Pero why, Orly? But he's learned that some questions, especially the more important ones, don't have answers.

Nighttime is the hardest part of the day for him, especially when he can't sleep and he's trying not to think about how he was bored most of the day. How Carson keeps posting pics on Instagram with the hashtag #AllTheShitOrlysMissing, today hanging out at his family's beach house with his older half sister and her boyfriend, who go to Tulane, yesterday at the Marble Slab in River Oaks taking a selfie with two unidentified girls, both blond, holding waffle cones with enormous scoops of ice cream, one of them dotted with gummy bears, the other with Skittles. It makes him miss home. Even the musty smell of Nina's sheets and quilt remind him of the old sleeping bag they keep in the tree house and how squirrels chewed through the lining and so no one had used it until Alex started sneaking out at night.

If Orly turns his pillow the other way, so his head is at the foot of the bed, or what he assumes is the foot of the bed—there's no headboard—and if he squints hard enough, he can make out the shelf with a Virgen de Guadalupe statuette and then behind it a few bowling trophies and a plaque Nina received in 1999, when she was Teacher of the Year. There's also a framed photo of her with a group of girls from the kickball team she used to coach. Like all the other rooms in the house, his bedroom door has a wide gap at the very bottom, as if the doorframe is too tall or the door was too long and they sawed off the last inch or so. When the light is still on in the hallway, the gap is almost like the night-lights he has in his room and bathroom at home.

He hasn't inspected the entire room, but at least near his bed the pattern is two narrow spaces, a wider space, and then another two narrow ones; it's the opposite with the grooves, one narrow groove between the narrow spaces, but all the rest are wide. He's guessing the spaces and grooves continue in the same pattern down to the floor, beyond where he can wedge his fingers between the wall and bed. During the day he hardly notices the paneling; it's only at night when he has nothing to do or look at that he reaches out to feel the grooves.

Though he can't see it at night, he knows the room has a popcorn ceiling, the kind his mom said she was going to have in the townhouse and was so '70s, whatever that means. She was still living at home with the family because the townhouse wouldn't be ready for a couple more weeks. Orly never got to see where she was moving to or even drive by it, but one night when she was cuddling with him in bed she told him about the popcorn ceiling and how it was the one part she wished she could change about her new place. She said it like the tiny bumps on the ceiling were the only thing that might keep her from being happy when she moved out.

"You know when there's something that really bugs you and every time you look at it, it bugs you a little more, but there's nothing you can do to change it right away, you just have to live with it that way."

"Sort of," he said, though nothing was coming to mind. He just liked the sound of her voice, the wisp of her breath on the back of his ear.

"You probably won't remember any of this, you were too young, but when you were a baby you used to ride in the backseat of the car facing backward. It's safer this way, for little babies, and then when you got a little older, it was okay to turn your car seat the other way, so you were facing forward and seeing what we were seeing, and we could look back and make sure you were doing okay or know if you fell asleep. But you hated looking this way, to the front. You'd cry and cry anytime we had to put you in the car and wouldn't stop until we pulled you out. At first we thought it was making you carsick to look out this way, the way we were, facing forward, and you kept twisting your little body in the seat to see what was behind you. We asked you what was wrong, but you were just learning to talk and we couldn't understand what you were saying and that upset you even more. Then we remembered you hated when things changed. You used to put up such a fuss at the day care if they tried to feed you in a different spot with all the other little kids. This was happening around Christmas and we almost didn't want to leave the house, especially not for any long trips. Your dad finally had the idea to turn you back around, since you still could ride this way and it was safer. But even this didn't make you stop crying when we put you in the car. Then one day I picked you up from day care and on the way home it started raining and this made you clap. Clapping was always good because this was how you told us you liked something, and this time what you liked was watching the windshield wiper go back and forth, the one that's for the back window, which was what you didn't like about facing the other way, because the front wipers were kind of blocked by the seat in front of you. Then I finally remembered your favorite song at the day care was 'Wheels on the Bus,' and your favorite part was when they sang about the wipers going 'swish, swish, swish' and you'd do the motion with your little hands." She grabbed his hand to show him how he used to do it side to side. "Swish, swish, swish . . ."

(He actually remembered hearing this story from his dad, but he didn't want her to leave yet and so he'd pretended this was the first time he'd heard it. The only difference in the two stories was that they each claimed to be the one who'd picked him up from day care that rainy afternoon.)

"But until this happened and we figured out what you needed, you were like me with the ceiling. So frustrated, you know?"

He nodded like it all made sense to him. Then he listened to her explain the difference between the smooth texture they had throughout their house and the popcorn texture at the townhouse, but the whole time he was wishing that instead of her being worried about the ceiling, she was worried about how she wouldn't be here every night to say good night to him. He couldn't bring himself to say these words because it seemed like his wish would mean she couldn't have her wish and this would make her sad again, which was the reason she was leaving them in the first place. So maybe it was better to say nothing and pretend the popcorn ceiling was the only thing on his mind right then.

Sometimes he'll feel the grooves on the paneling for ten or fifteen minutes before rolling over and falling asleep. If he wakes up in the middle of the night he might reach out for the wall as if he were a blind man steadying himself.

When he's fading is when one thought slips to another that leads to another that doesn't always make sense, at least at first. The popcorn ceiling, for instance, reminds him of real popcorn and how Nina said she would buy some for him next time she went to the store. And the popcorn reminds him of going to the movies, even if their dad never let them buy popcorn.

Before their parents ever mentioned the separation, they used to all go as a family to the movies on Saturday mornings. It was his dad's idea to save a few dollars by going to the matinee. He had worked as a movie usher growing up and didn't think paying the full admission price was worth it and never let them buy anything from the concession stand, especially not the popcorn, which he claimed was recycled popcorn, from the previous night, stuffed into large plastic bags and then the next morning tossed in with whatever new popcorn they made, so by looking at it you never knew if it was just made or had been sitting around from the night before or longer. He said it as if the ushers had collected the popcorn people left behind, under their seats on the sticky floor, and stuffed this into the plastic bag too.

Their dad also didn't think they should have to stay in a theater if it turned out they didn't like the movie they'd bought a ticket for.

"If you go to the store and try on a pair of jeans and they don't fit, they're too short, like high-waters, what do you do?"

"What's high-waters?" Orly asked from the backseat. They were on the tollway headed to their family time, as their dad liked to call these trips to the movies.

"You know, pants that are too short."

"We don't buy our clothes at the store," Alex said. "Mom buys them online and we try them on at home and she sends them back if they don't fit or whatever, or if they're the wrong color. She doesn't like going to stores."

This seemed like new information to their father and it was another exit before he spoke again. "But you don't keep them, that's the point. If they don't fit, they get sent back to the store. So if the movie you're watching isn't something you like, what you thought you were ordering, then why should you sit through two hours of it?"

"Sure," their mom said, glancing up from her cell phone, "but if the other movie is sold out, then you might be taking somebody else's seat."

"But only when the theater is busy, and it's almost never busy on a Saturday morning."

"You're teaching them to steal, Eddie. If you buy one ticket you can't just decide to slip into another theater. People don't do that here."

"So nobody likes to save money?"

"Not that way."

"All I'm saying is to get their money's worth, to see the movie they really want to see. Is that such a bad thing, to watch the movie you really want to see?"

It was quiet for a moment in the Suburban; they were about to exit and could already see the movie theater. She checked her cell phone one last time before sticking it into her bag. "Don't listen to your father."

But they did, except Alex made Orly promise not to tell about those times when they snuck into another movie. This meant they could see practically any PG or PG-13 movie they wanted, maybe even R-rated, unless Alex thought there might be something super scary that would give Orly nightmares and then the whole thing would blow up in his face because he was three years older and was supposed to be watching out for his little brother.

Later their dad changed jobs and was traveling more, mainly during the week to Dallas, where the ad agency had opened another office, but sometimes also to L.A., if they were shooting a commercial and he'd have to be back the next week for editing. So then it was just their mom, Alex, and Orly. That their mom was watching her own movie during their Saturday morning outings made it easier for the boys to sneak into the one they really wanted to see. The last time the three of them went to the movies was the weekend before their mom was supposed to move out. Their father was out of town, as usual, editing in L.A., and was due back on Sunday or Monday, depending how it went with the client.

All that week at school Alex had been hearing from Kyle about *Blair Witch*, which was supposed to be way scarier than the original *Blair Witch Project*, made back in the late '90s and which he'd seen one night in his room. Kyle's dad was still an undergrad when the first one came out and, because he wasn't always checking parenting websites or traveling for business, he had taken Kyle and his little brother to see it last Friday night, because who goes to see a slasher movie on a Saturday morning? What time of day he saw it mattered less to Alex than just seeing it already and not having to hear which character gets it first in the movie, when you're totally not expecting it. Which was all he had to hear to know he couldn't take Orly.

He let Orly know this only after their mom had given them their tickets and rushed off to catch a movie at the other end of the multiplex. Theirs was rated PG, and based on the reviews it was an inspiring movie about an underdog baseball team that wins a state title against all odds.

"But I don't want to see it by myself."

"You're acting like that's the scary one." His brother was already walking backward toward his own movie.

"You're going to make her mad, Alex."

"Not if you go to your movie and I go to mine and you stop being stupid about the whole thing."

"You're the stupid one."

"I'm not the one who thinks not making her mad might make her change her mind about leaving."

Orly flinched as if his brother had punched him in the arm.

"Seriously, stop acting like a baby," Alex said and then hurried off to his movie. Orly waited a few minutes before following him into the same theater.

The previews had just ended and they were announcing that the audience had to turn off or silence their cell phones. The theater was pitch-black now, and he held on to the railing until he was almost at the place where the corridor ended and he would've turned to walk up the steps to the stadium seating. There were only twenty or thirty people in the whole theater, and he thought he could make out Alex in the middle, instead of in the very back

row, where he normally wanted to slouch down when it was a
movie their mom had picked out for them. Orly was squatting
against the wall—low enough to where no one could spot him—
when he heard the first scream, but more like multiple screams,
one layered on top of another and coming from different directions. Only there weren't any people on the screen, just disem-
bodied shrieks moving, running from whatever it was they saw.
The person holding the camera was scrambling through an old
house, up stairs and around corners, away from the screams and
thunder in the distance, away from the pounding on the doors
and windows, and later, still in the house but now in more like an
underground tunnel or secret passage, searching for a light, some
escape from what was coming for them. Then the person holding
the camera stopped suddenly, locked a door, looked at the other
locked door in the dim room, looked back at the first lock, and
that's when the door busted open and the screams started again.
All before Orly could rush out of the theater.

And then he was beyond the door, in the glow of incandescent
lights, the paisley carpeting in the hallway. He felt unsteady, like
he had been the one running to get away. The floor was calling
him to sit for a while. But he was afraid to draw the attention of
the usher coming this way, so he walked in the opposite direction
and slipped into the restroom. He splashed cold water across his
cheeks and into his eyes, like this might dilute some of what he
had just seen.

Orly found his mom's theater at the very end of the multiplex.
He planned to tell her that he had a stomachache and needed the
car keys so he could lie down for a little while. At first the theater
looked empty, as if he'd walked into the wrong movie. Then a
moment later he spotted her in the back-right corner of the room.
He wanted to wave to get her attention and make her come down
to talk to him, but something told him not to, to just squat and

wait, same as he had in the other theater. His mom hadn't seen him below, in the corner, and neither had the person sitting next to her. He was leaning over, whispering in her ear, and she laughed at whatever it was he said, nudged him with her elbow. Then her hand went down into his lap but with their eyes still on the screen.

She hadn't mentioned meeting anyone, so maybe it was by accident. Someone she just ran into from work or her Spin class, what a coincidence and isn't it a small world and why sit alone? He and Alex got to go to the movies together, why shouldn't she have someone to go with? It was dark, though, and he was looking up and across the stadium seating, clear to the other side. That's what he was basing this on, some sort of superhuman vision across a dark theater. Like he was an owl or wearing infrared binoculars. His mother sitting with some stranger.

Some part of him felt as though he was still in the other theater hearing the screams and didn't know which way to turn. His heart was racing as much as if he were being chased. Even if he could've stood up and walked to her, he didn't know what he would've said, if he could open his mouth wide enough to get the words out, to release the scream coursing through his body.

The man had his arm over the back of her seat, a hand resting on her shoulder as he whispered again in her ear. Like it couldn't wait, whatever he was telling her that was so incredibly important. And her hand was still down there somewhere, lost in the stranger's lap, but then when he turned toward her she reached up and put a piece of popcorn in his mouth.

Sometimes when Orly finally drifts off to sleep, he dreams of his mom, but never about going to the movies or what might have been on her ceiling. Usually it's just the two of them and sometimes Alex is there too, in a park or at the beach, though when he's awake he has trouble remembering the last time they all went to the beach together. The dreams are happening less and less now, not like in the first couple of months after she died; then it was once or twice a week. He wonders if this is good or bad, keeping her alive this away. If waking up a little sad is worth the price of not letting her go completely.

IO

In the morning Orly is standing at the kitchen sink pouring himself a bowl of cereal when the reflection off the window across the yard catches his eye, as it has the last two days. This time, though, the aluminum foil shimmers as if the window might open on its own. Then a few seconds later it happens again. He wonders if the wind is rattling the window and causing the foil to move. The rest of the yard looks as it has every day for the last week, the glistening grackles conferring in the grass, the swollen papayas dangling from way atop the spindly trunk, the dog tamping down the dirt before it curls around and lies down.

The foil actually makes it seem as if there is no glass in the window. He imagines kicking the ball against the side of the house again and this time hitting the window but the glass not shattering and just a gash opening and then closing up on itself again. Weird. Like he's watching a sci-fi movie about extraterrestrials that have taken over a small pink house and need to cover the windows with aluminum foil to keep the atmosphere inside the house habitable, free of ultraviolet radiation and whatever else might threaten their well-being and force them to unleash their wrath on mankind. The kind of movie his brother would sneak into. Now, with the sun high above and bright, the window's aluminum surface looks like a hologram, quavering as the light sifts through the passing clouds.

He eats a few spoonfuls of his cereal before he realizes he served himself too much—this was his second bowl—and he has to pour the rest of his Froot Loops down the drain. But a second later he remembers Nina doesn't have a garbage disposal, which means he has to scoop all the bloated rings and hold them in the palm of his hand and then toss them in the trash can in the corner, next to the two-by-four she uses as a crossbar for the back door.

He's plucking out the last of the Froot Loops from the sink when his iPad chimes and it's his dad on FaceTime from San Francisco. They're finishing up the shoot today, and tomorrow he and Kayla head to Napa for the weekend. She leans into the frame wearing a fluffy robe and says, "Hi, Orly! Are you having an awesome summer?" then leaves the frame again before he can answer.

His dad says he wanted to call yesterday but he spent most of his free time on the phone talking to Alex's camp director after they caught him using his phone. It took most of the afternoon to talk the director into not sending Alex home and only putting him on probation for the next week.

"So how's it going so far with Nina and Mamá Meche?"

"Fine," Orly is quick to say, which means the same as last time you asked, which means boring, which means sure, like you really care. And to keep his dad from asking more questions, Orly starts telling him about the zoo and the beach and the mall, but right then is when his dad says to hold on, he needs to answer the door. The phone stays on its dock and Orly is left looking at rumpled sheets and comforters on the bed. His mom died last year, but it still seems too soon for his dad to have moved on, to be calling from his and his girlfriend's room. Orly wonders how long it would've taken his mom, if his dad had been the one who died suddenly, and then he remembers she already had moved on.

In the background he can hear his dad speaking in Spanish, asking the room service guy where he's from and how long he's been here and how he likes it. This goes on for a minute or two before the room service guy switches to English when he uncovers the trays to present their food. His dad ordered the Denver omelet with hash browns and bacon and a cup of coffee; Kayla ordered the yogurt parfait and a glass of cranberry juice.

Orly can see the food now because Kayla grabbed the phone and tapped the camera icon to switch around to the back camera. His dad is signing the bill.

"Hi!" Kayla says. The room service guy, whose name tag reads FELIPE, smiles. "You're supposed to say Hi back."

"Hi," Felipe says and waves to her.

"No, I mean in Spanish. Like 'hola,' like you were earlier."

Orly's dad explains to him that they're speaking to his son, that he can see them from where he is in Texas.

"¡Hola, Orly!"

"Hola," he says and is relieved when he doesn't have to say any more.

When his dad is back on the phone Orly begins telling him he's caught up on his reading. He's in the middle of telling him about the book his teacher gave him when his dad shakes his head and tries not to laugh at something Kayla is doing on the other side of his screen, and then a minute later says he has another call coming in and needs to go, they'll talk again soon.

After they hang up, Orly hopes his dad stops calling every few days to check on him, ask how he's spending his time. The part about Orly being caught up on his reading is true if his reading only includes the book Mr. Domínguez loaned him at the end of the school year. It's a book of poetry by Pablo Neruda. Orly doesn't really like poetry, but he didn't want to be rude and say no thanks, especially since it was pretty obvious that his teacher hadn't asked anyone else to stay after class so he could give them a book to read over the summer. Orly doesn't understand most of the references to ancient civilizations and pyramids and temples and conquistadors and liberators and dictators and revolutionaries and fugitives, but he reads it over and over again as if reading it enough times might make the words mean something they didn't the first three times. Mr. Domínguez told him the book explains the story of the Americas, which means not just the U.S. In class, he'd talked at length about how the Americas were much larger and more diverse, with a longer history than most people stop to consider, something that got a major eye roll from Carson.

Felipe, before working his way up from dishwasher to room service, had come from El Salvador sixteen years ago with his wife and kids and settled in San Francisco, near his cousin Amalia, who worked in house-keeping at the hotel and helped him get a job in the kitchen. Felipe even-tually learned to speak English from listening to his son, Erick, now a freshman at Cornell, and his daughter, Mariah, a junior in high school. They started by teaching him to read the breakfast menu out loud. Gra-nola, Smoothie, Denver Omelet, Bagel with Smoked Salmon but without saying the "l" because in this country it was there but not pronounced. The Yogurt Parfait was the hardest. His brain and his tongue weren't cooperating and the "yo" kept coming out like "jo," and no matter how friendly he was on the phone taking their orders—"Good morning" and "Thank you for calling room service, how may I serve you?"—or how much he smiled when delivering the order to their rooms, he still had to read their orders back to them on the phone and again when delivering the trays and the guests wanted Yogurt not Jogurt for breakfast. When they were all at home, Mariah and Erick would use their mother's cell phone to call their father in the next room and pretend to order a full breakfast, which he then had to repeat back to them, starting over every time he stalled or stumbled over a word. It became a running joke in the Ramírez household. What's for breakfast? Erick would say. What's for lunch? Mariah would ask later that morning. What's for dinner? she would ask again in the evening. And the answer was always the same. Yogurt! Yogurt! Yogurt! Por Dios, YO-gurt! Felipe and Imelda brought their children to the United States when they were so young that all their education has been in the U.S., and now they still understand Spanish but speak only English, which Felipe thinks is good because it will help them make a life for themselves here in the only country they know as home, but not so good if someday they get sent back to the country where they were born.

Orly's rinsing his bowl when he takes another look out the kitchen window. The humid breeze resuscitates the sheets Rumalda hung earlier to dry on the slackened clothesline, the ends of which are attached to two corroding poles between the houses. Closer in, around the shade of the ebony tree, the thick grass gives way to the packed dirt littered with woody pods from the tree. Two of the three legs of the rusted barbecue pit are chained to the trunk. At the back end of the lot, in the shadow of the pink house, the creviced dirt slopes awkwardly toward the canal.

Yesterday afternoon he flung rocks into the water, which he reasoned wasn't the same as playing in the canal, and then went looking for something lighter that wouldn't just sink to the bottom. The dog had barked at him when he first walked outside but then quieted down when he curved around to the other side of the pink house, away from the front steps. Under the back end of the house, opposite from where the dog sleeps, he found some planks of wood like the ones nailed across the back door.

The leftover scraps were only a few inches wide and rotting, so it was easy to smash them in half with the heel of his sneaker and then use these smaller pieces to smash the ants scurrying around on the underside of the boards. Before pulling out the last plank, he heard a sound that made him scramble backward on his chest and belly, away from the opening.

Back in the sunlight and several feet away, he crouched and gazed into the murky underside of the little house, ready to sprint back to the blue house if he noticed any movement. At first he thought it might be a tlacuache, a word he had heard mentioned but it took him a few days to figure out it meant possum and only after his godmother pointed to one squashed dead in the middle of the street. The tip of its tiny tongue, no bigger than a pink candy heart, was sticking out just beyond the edge of its serrated teeth. The pallid tail lay curled like a pirate's hook and two baby tlacuaches were still alive and clinging to their mother's back.

Nothing stirred under the pink house. For a moment he thought someone might have gotten inside, but then he remembered the back door was nailed shut and there was a padlock on the front door. Earlier, when he was trying to avoid the dog, he had walked all the way around the house and none of the windows were broken. Then he heard it again, a faint creak like when Alex was sneaking around on the roof outside their rooms. He jerked back and tumbled into the grass, at the same time glancing up at the roof and halfway expecting to see someone or something looking down at him over the edge of the shingles. And suddenly it was quiet again, until a minute later when the chicharras began screeching somewhere beyond the canal.

"You can't be taking chances," Beto says and glances over to make sure he's paying attention. "They like to hide in exactly the places you would never think to look for them, old newspapers, paper bags, between the walls."

Orly sits on the front steps of the blue house and half listens to what his tío is saying and half listens to his squirts, counting them to see if there's a pattern to how many times he squeezes the sprayer before he stops to say something else. Usually it's four or five squirts. Other times he starts to talk and then stops suddenly to release another two or three good squirts.

"La cosa es que las cucarachas know where we are, but we don't know where they are." Beto runs his silver wand along the threshold of the front door. He stopped by after his last appointment and still has on his Ro-Ru Pest Control work shirt, only now it's untucked so he can get a little breeze. "Son bien sneaky. You have to train yourself to think like them, como una cucaracha. 'A ver, where am I going to run and hide this afternoon because the mean man with the sprayer is here to get rid of me and my babies?'"

The spray is hardly coming out now and Beto works the hand pump to make sure his squirts have enough force. "It's only later when the little bodies start showing up, with their legs in the air."

He stops to pretend he's a dying roach, leaning back with his eyes closed, his hands flailing above him.

Orly scoots down to the last step. "But I thought they were nocturnal."

"Eh?" His tío stops in mid squirt, a drip of pesticide falling on his work boots.

"No offense, but you said it like the cockroaches are awake and watching you right now." "No offense" being a phrase his mom taught him to say whenever he feels like he has to make a comment and the comment might offend the other person, especially if the other person is a grown-up.

"And how do you know they're not watching?"

"Because they're nocturnal and wouldn't be coming out right in the middle of the afternoon. I saw it on a website they let us use at school."

Beto narrows his eyes at him. This kid thinking he can tell him how to do his work, like he knows so much. Then he remembers this is Eduardo's boy. Eduardo who moved away to college when he was seventeen, creyéndose, acting like he was hot shit, and then Tencha treating their nephew like he was a prince or something, except the prince never came back—the jobs here weren't good enough for the prince. So now they only see him when he passes through to go vacation on the island or to dump off his kid so he can go on vacation somewhere else.

"Who said anything about coming out? I said 'watching.'" Beto swivels his head side to side to show him how, his hands above his eyebrows, fluttering, like a pair of antennae. "And anyway, here we just call them night animals or insects, the ones that come out at night. Not the way you said it. Or you going to be like your daddy, one of those scholarship boys? Then we don't see you again except for when you pass through on your way to the beach."

"Déjalo," Nina says from the front door. "He can say it how he wants in this house."

"And now you make the rules?"

"For my guests." She steps outside and Orly slinks away to ride the tire swing for the first time since he arrived. Off to the side, closer to the fence, there's a bald patch of grass where La Bronca used to lie.

"Still doesn't make it your house. This one thinks he knows so much, telling me what's what, like he's the one that went for the training and test."

"The one it took you four times to pass."

"Let's see you pass it, remember all those names of the different insects, not just the roaches, and then the chemicals. Dangerous ones. They don't give out those licenses just to anybody."

They stop arguing only because they hear their mother complaining about the bed rail being stuck again. Orly offers to go help her, but Nina tells him to stay where he is and goes herself to check on her mother.

He stops the tire swing to see if his tío will be going back inside too, but his tío only stares at him until he pushes off again, spinning it in the opposite direction. By the time the tire circles back around, his tío is already headed to the backyard.

La Bronca barks her head off before Beto has even made it past the gate, making enough commotion for Nina to hurry out the back door and intercept him.

"What?" He still has the pump and sprayer in his hands.

"What you?" she says and then turns to shout at the dog to stop its barking. "You didn't spray in there last time."

"Because I was in a hurry."

"Because you don't need to be spraying empty houses."

Beto looks over his shoulder at Orly, now standing at the back gate, and then turns to Nina. "Empty-empty?"

"You didn't hear me? Empty is empty."

"Doesn't matter if it's empty for them to lay eggs, then they come across to the other house. Just give me the key and I'll show them to you. So you can see the eggs, what I'm talking about." He steps to his left to get around her, but she blocks him.

"I don't want to see any eggs, Beto."

"Because you know I'm right."

"Because I don't want to see any cucarachas or their eggs. That's why I called you, so I don't have to see them."

"Then just give me the key. I can go in by myself and you stay out here, if you're so afraid of seeing some eggs in an empty house." He moves to the right of the wooden steps, but the dog is back on its haunches, waiting, making an ugly face at him.

"I lost the key," she says.

"And then what, you're never going to open it?"

"Not till I find it. Maybe by next time you come to spray."

"Next time won't be until the end of the summer."

"That's not that long."

"Not that long? Vas a ver que later you're going to be real sorry I didn't give it spray this time. Right now is the time of the cucarachas, when they hide with their babies."

"And since when have you cared what I'm sorry about doing and not doing?"

He looks at her for a long while and shakes his head. Then before walking off, he aims his wand toward the steps and unloads a couple of generous squirts into the grass, the way a dog would to mark its territory.

They walk out to his van, under the carport, and there they argue more, but not loud enough for Orly to hear. His parents never really fought, not in front of him and Alex anyway. Sometimes in the middle of the day they would just close the door to their bedroom for ten or twenty minutes and then one of them would come out, usually their dad, while their mom would stay in bed the rest of the afternoon and then later neither of them would say anything about it. This was before there was any talk of a separation or a townhouse and he thought if he could hold out for those two or three hours that he wasn't supposed to go into the bedroom, not ask her again if he could watch a video, not go ride his bike, not ask if he could have a snack but just get it himself, not do anything except leave her alone, then afterward it would be like none of it happened.

After Beto leaves, Nina takes Orly and her mother in the car to go buy raspas to cool off. She tries not to complain about how long it took Beto to finish because she knows her mother will only defend Beto, say he put the extra spray to las cucarachas to kill them, because he wants to make sure his mother and sister are safe. He cares about them, no matter what she says about her poor brother. The extra spray proves it.

The raspa trailer is just down from the car wash, in the parking lot of the dollar store. Her mother waits in the car while she and Orly stand in line behind three other sets of customers: two shirtless boys holding fishing rods, a little boy with his mother, and behind them an older man wearing cowboy boots caked with mud that flakes off every time he takes a step closer to the counter. A black SUV—unmarked but with government-issued plates—pulls into the parking lot. Everyone waits to see if he's here for someone, but then less than a minute later the car pulls out, back into the hum of the afternoon traffic. Even after it leaves, Orly notices Nina is still leaning into him, the way his mom used to when he was little and would grab his hand because they were in the parking garage at the mall.

It's hot but windy and so not as hot as it would feel if they were in Houston. Two women work inside the bright yellow trailer, taking turns scooping ice from the shaver while the other pours syrup from the neon-colored bottles that line the windowsill, the outside of the glass smudged with the tiny fingerprints of those who know what flavor or color they want but not the name. Outside, the bees hover above a rainbow of sweet puddles.

"I wish there was more time to take you places," Nina tells him when they're waiting for their order. He knows that by "more time" she means more free time from having to watch her mother, which she only has on Fridays when the maid comes to clean. Otherwise wherever they go she has to bring her mother along.

"Like where?" he asks.

"Lots of places," she says, and then she tries to think of one. "Like to where they have all the palm trees and people go watch the birds."

"Watch them do what?"

"Be with the other birds. People from everywhere, from far away like New York and Wisconsin and California, they like to come here just to see the birds all in one place. Where they have them protected, so they are safe."

"Safe from what?"

"From people trying to hurt them, safe from other animals."

He's never been interested in birds and doubts he would be even if they had the time to spend a whole afternoon watching them.

"Or if things weren't so bad now, I would take you to Matamoros, for you to see the mercado and later we could eat lunch or go to the plaza and I could buy you some of the calabaza candy they sell there and we could listen to the musicians."

"My mom wanted to go last time we all came down together, but my dad said we couldn't go across because it was dangerous."

"Your daddy knows. The ones with the drugs are trying to kill the other ones with the drugs and then all the rest of the people, the innocent ones, they get hurt too. Nobody I know goes there anymore, not like they used to."

"It sounds like the birds are safer than the people."

"Yes, something like that."

There's more she wants to say on this subject, but right then the little window of the trailer slides open and their raspas are ready.

12

Nina makes the sign of the cross on Orly's forehead and kisses him on the cheek, the same as his mom used to, except without the praying part. He stays still until she's done saying the Our Father, otherwise she'll start over again. She wishes him a good night and leaves. The slice of light at the bottom of the door will keep him company for the next nine or so hours.

Before he came here, the only praying he ever did on his own had to do with his mom not leaving. It started off as an Our Father, but halfway through it became more just him asking God to do something to make her not leave. His dad was the one who did all the traveling, so it made more sense for him to move out. That is, if anyone had to move out. He didn't want his dad to leave either, not exactly, but he'd be willing to trade them out, his mom stay and his dad go find someplace to live nearby. Maybe he could take Alex and that way he wouldn't be alone. His brother probably wouldn't like it, but this was his prayer not Alex's, so he could say it the way he wanted. He spent a few nights coming up with scenarios that would keep her from moving. The townhouse could catch fire and burn down before she moved in and then it might be a month or two before she found another place to live and she could change her mind by then. There could be a hurricane, which was about the only natural disaster he could think of, but even a hurricane wouldn't last forever.

He wonders if what he saw at the movies wasn't God's way of showing him why she wanted to leave or had to. If it isn't his fault for not figuring this out sooner. How much clearer did he need it to be? And still he wanted to believe there had to be a perfectly good reason why she would be sitting in a dark theater with another man on a Saturday morning, feeding him popcorn.

He went from praying for nothing to change to praying that the change, if it had to happen, wouldn't include someone else. He thought that with more time he could make her change her mind and want to stay, but he didn't know what it would mean for her and that other person. The way he imagined it, she just woke up one morning and changed her mind and their life went on pretty much as normal. His praying never involved anything actually happening to her. No sudden illness, no aneurysm, especially since he'd never heard of one.

It seems stupid to miss his water bottle, but after his laptop, this is the one thing he most wishes he had from home. It's the same water bottle he's had for years, so far back that it used to be called his sippy cup. The outside has the faded orange outline of Nemo lost in a murky patch of sea, discolored after going through countless cycles in the dishwasher. The inside is insulated to keep his water cool longer, especially in the summer when he likes his water with crushed ice. Sometimes he has to unscrew the top and fish out the attachable straw when it comes loose. After kissing him good night, his mother used to turn on his humidifier and leave the bottle on his nightstand, always in the same spot, where he could reach it without having to open his eyes. When she was working late or out to dinner with a friend, his dad sometimes forgot to leave it on the nightstand. Orly wouldn't remind him because he knew his mom would be checking on him later and he liked her leaving the bottle instead of his dad. If it wasn't too late, he might still be awake and she would lie down with him so they could talk about his day at school or where she went to dinner. Now that his mom isn't around, his dad says filling his bottle is one of those things Orly is old enough to do on his own. He's not a baby anymore. So he started filling the bottle himself and leaving it in the same spot his mom used to, the small hatch open so his lips can always find the straw no matter how dark it is in his room.

Tonight, after her prayer, Nina asked him if he wanted a glass of water. He told her no, but didn't mention it was because he's still a little worried about leaving the glass of water next to his bed and something crawling inside his glass while he's sleeping. He hasn't seen any roaches, but she talks about them like it's only a matter of time. Ándale, close the screen door so they don't come inside. Shut the trash can the right way, all the way down, on both sides, si no, olvídate, it's like you're inviting them to come have dinner with us.

It takes him almost an hour to fall asleep, but then thirty minutes later he wakes up feeling restless and thirsty. He figures going to the kitchen for a glass of water will help him fall back asleep. The drinking water comes from a dispenser she keeps in the corner of the kitchen that leads to the bedrooms.

By now he knows the nighttime sounds of the house. Mamá Meche messing with the rail on her hospital bed, trying to disengage the lock before Nina can rush over to help her get to the bathroom. Then his great-grandmother arguing that she could've made it on her own, without the walker, without Nina watching her every step, treating her like some baby. Then the toilet water gushing, followed by the faucet. The three bedrooms and one bathroom joined by one tiny hallway make it difficult not to hear everything, especially in a bathroom with no exhaust fan to cover up any sounds or odors coming from that region of the house. Earlier, just as he was falling asleep, he heard the dog barking a few times and a moment later go quiet again. But now, a quarter past eleven, what he hears are bare feet clinging to the linoleum and a second later the kitchen faucet. He opens the door expecting to see Nina, for her to ask him if he had a bad dream, but what he sees is a boy standing at the sink, his back to Orly, looking out the same window Orly looks out every morning, toward the pink house and its aluminum foil windows. The boy has on an old soccer shirt and long shorts that reach to just above his dark brown calves. At first Orly thinks the boy might be one of his cousins he saw at the last family reunion but whose name slipped away from him before they got back to Houston. But why would he be here now? Why to wash dishes?

The boy glances over his shoulder and then jerks around to face Orly, keeping his back pressed up against the edge of the sink. Orly waves and the boy begins to wave back but stops to wipe the edge of his soapy hand on the side of his shorts. He spun around so fast that he forgot to shut off the water running into the pan he was washing and now has to reach back to turn it off.

"Orlando," Nina says as she walks into the kitchen. "¿Qué haces despierto? Le voy a decir a tu daddy que casi no duermes," she rattles off and much more. She sticks to Spanish whenever she is anxious—returning something she bought at the store, talking to him about his mother, talking to Tío Beto about the pink house.

"I was thirsty."

"Te pregunté dos veces y me dijiste que no." She holds up the fingers to show him how many times she asked him if she could bring him water. "Mira la hora. Ya deberías estar bien dormido."

She goes on, speaking in a way that forces him to look at her and not at the other boy in the room, who is looking down as if he's imagining some way of sinking into the floor.

Orly wants to step back into the hallway, into the bedroom, under the covers, under the bed and so on, until he's away from here.

"I just wanted water," he manages to say, and looks over at the dispenser to make sure it's still there.

"Then go on," she responds, almost whispering now, as if one of them were still half asleep and should remain that way, lost in the fogginess of what has clearly been a dream. "Go with getting your water and then to bed." He looks away from the grip of her stare, but by then the other boy has unlocked the security door and slipped into the darkness that separates the two houses.

13

The next morning Orly stays in bed longer than usual, thirty minutes, an hour, two hours, as if the extra time will create more distance between what happened last night in the kitchen and this morning, and that distance will make it less real, not so unsettling that he wishes he could stay tucked under the covers until he hears his father's car pulling into the driveway. If this were a normal morning Nina would be coming around to check on him by now, ask if he's hungry or if he feels sick, something, but not leave him to stay burrowed under the covers, under the weight of what he saw last night.

He gets up only because he has to pee, even if the immediate need he had an hour ago has now dulled to a low-grade pulse that he feels only when he turns onto his stomach. Afterward, he wipes the seat he keeps forgetting to lift, washes his hands by passing them under the water, dries off some on the towel and the rest on his T-shirt, and heads to the kitchen. He pours himself a cup of orange juice, takes his meds, and grabs a bowl for his cereal.

Except for the doily curtain hanging on the window over the sink, everything looks the same from yesterday morning and even last night. The curtain is beige and gold with a pattern of red and green apples, the bottom rod placed high enough that he'll need to stand on his tippy toes if he expects to see over it and into the backyard. He doesn't remember the curtain being there before but maybe that's because it was open and he was looking past it and not through it. Now he can only make out the silhouette that he knows is the other house and next to it the looming shape of the dog.

It's funny, not ha-ha, but strange funny, like weird, the things you begin to see and realize when you can't see the one thing you most want to. He hadn't seen, for instance, the wall calendar for Capistran's Tortilla Factory hanging on the side of the cabinet right next to the window. He thinks he would've remembered the cartoon image of a bright yellow corn stalk with red tennies. The curtain, he can imagine her putting up last night after he went back to bed, but why add the calendar? To distract him, give him something to look at instead of out the window? His name is scribbled and circled on the 3rd, a Saturday, the day he arrived, more than a week ago now. The days leading up to the 3rd are marked with Xs.

It makes sense to him now, how he went through a new box of Froot Loops the first three days he was here, especially when she and his great-grandmother don't eat cereal. The next time they went to the store she bought two boxes so it wouldn't run out so fast. She said she'd forgotten what it was like to have a young boy in the house who wakes up hungry. Orly doubts he ate even half the cereal in the box. Maybe they don't sell Froot Loops where the boy comes from. He knows enough to know not every country has the same foods we enjoy in this country.

Last night, after he went back to bed, Nina came to his room and explained that the boy was the son of a friend she was letting stay in the other house for a little while until he went to live with his father. She said his name is Daniel and he came from a place in Mexico called Veracruz, but she hadn't told anyone because Mamá Meche and Tío Beto wanted to rent the house and would be upset if they found out she was letting someone stay for free. She was sorry she got upset when he came to get water; he had scared her. Orly didn't want her to still be mad or sorry—he wanted to change the subject and for things to be like they had been before he walked into the kitchen. If he could do it again, he would stay in bed the whole night and have nothing ever change. He told her his world history teacher, Mr. Domínquez, is also from Veracruz. He showed the class some images of it on the last day of school. Nina told him that was nice, having a teacher from Mexico, but right now they needed to talk about the boy in the other house.

"Can you keep what I told you a secret?"

"But how come he can't just stay here, like on the sofa?"

"Because my mother, she wouldn't like it, having more people in the house."

"Sometimes Alex and me and my dad stay here."

"But this one is not family," she said.

He wanted to believe at least some part of what she was saying was true, that it wasn't all a lie. He was almost sure of that, but which was which he couldn't really say. He wanted to be mad, but he couldn't figure out what part to be mad at the most, that she had been hiding something from him or that what she was saying was more of the same lies and she was trying to fool him again.

The boy's name made him think of Daniela, Maribel's fifteen-year-old daughter who sometimes came with her mother to stay with him and his brother when their parents used to go out. Maribel spoke only Spanish to Daniela and made her answer in Spanish, even pretending she suddenly didn't understand English, something that only made the girl say it more slowly in English, as if this might solve the problem. Maribel brought Daniela over one time when their parents were at a New Year's Eve party. The boys could stay up watching TV but not their screens, something Alex couldn't accept because the TV *was* a screen and what difference did it make if it was hanging on the wall or you were holding it on your lap? He'd done the math, and the TV was more than six times the size of his iPad. He was still complaining about it later when he walked into the kitchen for more popcorn and saw Maribel slap Daniela and then a second later try to hug her, which didn't work because the girl ran out the side door, slamming it behind her. The ball was about to fall in Times Square, but the slap sort of put an end to New Year's Eve for the boys, because after that Maribel, without mentioning what had just happened, told them to please go upstairs to watch the TV in the media room, which they did turn on, but then they immediately regrouped on the bed in the guest room where they could see Maribel's car along the cul-de-sac, the place she parked because she was afraid of backing out and the car rolling off the driveway and into the drainage ditch. They knew Daniela was in the front seat because of the glow from her phone.

Orly almost couldn't believe it when Alex told him about the slap. Before then they never would've thought Maribel had it in her to hit one of her kids. During the ten years she had worked for the family, the boys had done enough to frustrate her, but she never seemed bothered by their antics—the mad-science experiments in the kitchen, the underwear stuck to the ceiling fan, or one of them hiding her cell phone in the clothes hamper or inside a cereal box so it took most of the day for her to locate it. And then there were the fights she had to break up between them, the accusations about who started it and who did what to whom and who was making it up to get the other one in trouble when their parents got home. She'd sigh, shake her head, say something like "Son tremendos," and continue working. Sometimes she'd take her Virgen de Guadalupe pendant and rub it between her thumb and forefinger. No matter what they did, though, she never got as annoyed as their parents did. They figured Maribel for one of those parents who didn't believe in spanking and not just the kids of the family she worked for. But a slap across the face was definitely hitting, way more than just a spanking, and a lot more than raising her voice.

After a while Maribel went outside to talk to Daniela, who by then had locked the car doors. Alex cracked open the bedroom window so they could hear Maribel begging Daniela to open up, telling her she was sorry, she overreacted, it wouldn't happen again, she promised, even saying it in English. Across the street, Dr. Murphy, who was retired and generally asleep at this hour, New Year's or no New Year's, flicked on his porch light and stood by his picture window when he saw it was the Latin girl who worked across the street. He had his cordless tucked into the pocket of his robe, ready for the first sign that things might be getting out of hand. Alex said it was like watching a reality show.

"The Real Nannies of Houston," Orly said.

"La Súper Nanny," Alex said.

"Don't Mess with Our Nanny."

"Nanny No-no's."

"Nanny Bloopers."

"Who's the Boss in This Casa?"

"The Slapping Nanny."

Which got a fist bump from Alex. "Nice one, little bro."

The list went on for another twenty minutes, until Maribel came back inside and the boys headed off to their bedrooms. Their parents came home close to one in the morning.

Maribel and Daniela drove back to their apartment without saying a word the whole thirty minutes it took to get there. Four months later, Daniela gave birth to a healthy baby girl. After a short stay in the hospital, she returned for her final weeks of ninth grade and the end-of-year parties her friends were having before the start of the summer. Maribel and her husband raised the baby as their own.

14

The next night Orly hears them in the kitchen. The sounds haven't gone away and only become more obvious because now he knows it's not just Nina. He tries to sleep, runs his fingers up and across the grooves on the wall, imagines what hotel his father might be in tonight, what Alex is doing at camp, if he's done anything else to make the counselors call their dad, if this is the week Carson's dad is taking him to Paris, who his teachers will be in seventh grade, but none of it works.

There's another universe on that side of the paneling, close enough for him to smell the fideo they had for dinner being reheated in the microwave, the bubbling broth and noodles, the wafting cumin finding him, the ding when it's ready. When Orly asked for another serving at dinner Nina told him there wasn't any more, offered to make him a taco, with butter or refried beans, something to fill his belly. But that was just another lie because he knew there was more, knew why she was saying there wasn't any left, which was the only reason he'd asked for another bowl, to make her have to choose between him and the other boy. She only makes fideo once a week and it's his favorite of the foods she prepares for him. He's her family, her only godson. The other boy isn't even from here or supposed to be inside the house. Feed the tortilla with beans to him, not to her family.

Orly kicks the wall, pounds it with the outside of his fist, and waits to see if Nina responds, if one of the doors, the one directly to the kitchen or the one to the hall, opens. But nothing.

She thinks just because she made up the rules he has to stay in his room at night, in the house during the day, or maybe in the yard but only in the front and not anywhere near the pink house, which basically means not anywhere in the whole backyard. Nina and his dad think he couldn't leave if he really wanted to, that he always has to do what they say because they're the grown-ups and are always supposed to know the right thing for him to do. They think he would never open the front gate and just start walking. They think he'd be too scared and not street-smart because he hasn't grown up here, hasn't done the same things his dad did back when he was this age and younger.

He's the only one with rules. Not her and not the boy. They're the ones who need the rules. All he did was get up in the middle of the night that wasn't really the middle of the night and only to get himself a glass of water that didn't have anything floating around in it. For that he ended up with more rules—no going in the backyard, no staring out the window, no telling what he saw, no more getting up at night—when he should be making the rules for them.

No more lies. Because it's not like he believed her when she said the boy is the son of a friend. Who sends their son to hide in a little pink house?

No more saying the boy will be leaving any day now. Which might be true or might be another lie to make it sound like hiding someone behind your house for another night or two in the middle of the summer isn't such a big deal. Because that's what this is, just somebody else lying to him. Somebody telling him where he has to go but not why. Somebody doing something he isn't supposed to talk about. When none of it was anything he started or was looking for.

Eat in the pink house and only the pink house. If you don't want anyone in the house to see the boy, then don't let him come inside the house. She says he's only staying for a few more days. But she won't say how long he's already been here, how long she's been hiding him, how long she's been lying about the whole thing. If he's really about to leave, take the food to him so he can eat over there or stay with him while he eats so he's not alone.

Don't always be speaking in Spanish. Not because Orly doesn't understand, because he does, most of it, enough of it, but it makes it that much harder to hear through the paneling what they're saying, if they're saying something about him, about how he's too young to understand and that his easy life back home in Houston has nothing to do with what is happening here in this world, that soon enough he will be going home and put this out of his mind, that he'll forget about seeing a boy standing in his godmother's kitchen, washing dishes.

A little more than a month ago, before he knew what he was actually doing for the summer, he and Carson were in the backseat when his father put in his earbuds to take a call a from Nina. The radio was still on NPR, but Carson kept leaning forward to listen. Why's he talking in Spanish? He's speaking to his aunt, Orly told him, but left out the part about her being his godmother, the one Carson had thought was their maid. For the last twenty minutes they'd been stuck in traffic on the Southwest Freeway. They could hear the police sirens and ambulance but they were still too far away to see what the holdup was and how long it might last. Is she like in Mexico or something? Carson wanted to know. Guatemala? No, Orly answered, not exactly. What's he saying? I don't know. You don't know or don't want to say? Both. Which was sort of true because he couldn't exactly hear over the radio and Carson's questions, though less than a minute earlier he'd thought he heard his dad say something about wanting him, Orly, to have a real summer. Wait, seriously, Carson said, I thought all of you knew Spanish, like it was your native tongue or something. Not really, Orly replied. It wasn't clear if by "all of you" Carson meant "all your family" or if he meant everyone who happens to have a Spanish-sounding last name. Orly would've thought about it more, but he was still trying to figure out what sort of "real summer" his dad had in mind for him and how it involved his godmother. That, and how much longer he was going to be stuck in the backseat with Carson asking him questions.

He kicks the wall again and again until he feels the jolt rising from the ball of his foot. He wonders if Nina can hear him, if she's ignoring him, if he should just go to sleep so he can wake up in the morning and see what's on the other side of the gate.

15

Nina calls him, for the second time now, to come have his lunch. The chicken nuggets, tus favoritos, are getting cold. Orly didn't want to go with her to run her errands, he wanted to keep reading his book on the bed. Bueno, she didn't argue with him and left him in his room. She's trying to make him happy, so he won't be walking around so sad as if she took something from him. After her errands, she drove halfway across town to the Chick-fil-A because he doesn't like the chicken they sell other places. And when she was back on the highway she remembered he had asked her for the special sauce and so there she went back again. The least he can do now is come to the table when she calls him. "Orly, mijito," she says as she cracks open his door. "Ya, the lunch is ready." It takes her a second to realize no one's there. The bed is made, the comforter spread flat across the mattress like it hasn't been used in days. His backpack is gone from its usual place next to the night table.

The bus drops him off in downtown Brownsville in front of what looked like a movie theater when they were a block away, the green signage and marquee extending over the sidewalk, but up close four of the panels on the marquee are either cracked, chipped, or have fallen off altogether and instead of a movie theater he finds a mini-mall called Mercado Juárez, with Cookie Monster, Elmo, and My Little Pony piñatas hanging in the window. He passes a jewelry store where a neon-yellow poster announces they have precios bajos y garantizados. He understands most of the signs and the cumbia pulsing out of one of the stores but not the norteño music booming from a passing truck. Between the shuttered storefronts there's Casa Kevin and Tienda Del Dollar and Uno Plus and Minky and Para Telas and Los Chinitos and Lupita's Perfumes & Wireless and Eva Shoes, in the old Kress store, where today the high heels are on sale, from $7.99 to $9.99.

He steps in and out of the stores to look at the caps and soccer jerseys, but not to buy because he only has nine dollars and change left in his pocket, having spent a dollar on water and then another dollar on the bus, a quarter on a transfer ticket, and then almost two dollars on a Fanta and a bag of Sabritas at Mercado Juárez. This was just after he heard his stomach growling and knew it was past lunchtime.

He'd thought about leaving a note but wasn't sure what to write or if it mattered or why he had to explain himself to her. Let her figure it out. She didn't explain herself to him. And anyway there wasn't anything to explain since he hadn't really planned anything out besides getting to the bus stop. He didn't plan on boarding three different buses or sitting behind the driver or walking in and out of stores for no reason but to look around or even how all this wandering would lead to the very end of downtown and then to the bridge.

Nina checks in the carport and the backyard, even out by the canal behind the pink house, where she told him not to go. La Bronca follows her as far as the chain will allow and then crouches to look under the house and maybe catch a glimpse of Nina walking away.

Standing at the edge of the canal, she calls out to him as loud as she can, the panic carrying her voice clear beyond the other side. Her mother thinks she heard him in the bathroom about an hour earlier. Rumalda remembers asking him if he had clothes for her to wash and he said no and then stayed in his room. Maybe he's hiding? She works for another family and the little boy likes to play like that, making the poor mother look everywhere until she finds him under the bed or in the bathtub, behind the curtain. Nina can't imagine her godson, already twelve, doing something so childish, but she checks under the bed and in the closet before heading outside again, this time to the front. She stands in the middle of the street as if expecting him to suddenly materialize in the waves of heat rising off the asphalt. Where could he be? What does he know that is close by? He would have to take this street to get out to the main road, and then what? At the far end of the street she finds la señora De la Garza sitting in her drive-way, where like most days she is selling little girls' dresses, each hanging from a clothesline she strung up from her mailbox to the driveway gate. She saw the boy walking this way, but he was too much in a hurry to even say good afternoon. One of the women working in the raspa trailer says a boy like that stopped to buy a bottled water and then got on the bus. But which bus? What number? Nina has trouble even asking, getting out the words she feels have lodged themselves in her throat. But those questions the girl can't answer, nobody told her to be writing the numbers of every bus. All she knows is it was heading that way, rumbo al centro, toward downtown.

After passing the shuttered Payless Shoes shop on the corner, Orly crosses a mini plaza where two old men are smoking on the con-crete benches. To cross the bridge on foot he first needs quarters for the set of turnstiles at the far end of the plaza, next to the kiosk where people get change. To the left of the kiosk one lane of traffic is inching toward the tollbooth, which leads to the bridge. Opposite the tollbooth are the northbound lanes and pedestrian walkway for those coming from Matamoros and approaching one of several stations manned by U.S. Customs officers, whose job it is to ask for proof of their nationality.

The uniformed woman behind the Plexiglas takes Orly's crumpled dollar bill and gives him quarters. At the turnstile he has to wait behind a group of tourists, a pair of husbands and wives, somebody's grandma and grandpa from Wisconsin, who are also walking across to Matamoros. The men are dressed in cargo shorts, matching red polo shirts, and white walking shoes fastened with Velcro straps. Their modest paunches appear more pronounced with their fanny packs tucked under their shirts. The wives are wearing blouses, loose-fitting jeans, lace-up sneakers, and sun hats. One of the old men, the jokester of the bunch, walks through the turnstile first, pretending he doesn't hear his wife calling him to come back with her four quarters.

Orly pushes through the turnstile but worries that the guard's going to run up and grab him by the collar, ask what he thinks he's doing crossing into Mexico by himself, if his mother and father know where he is. While Orly was getting his quarters, the guard kept an eye on the five school-age boys who were passing through, just in case they tried to jump the turnstile. Now he's more interested in chatting it up with the young mother putting her baby back in the stroller.

The plastic awning and chain-link fence span the seven hundred feet that separate one country from the other. This covering is the only thing shielding the people from the sun, though there's still the heat radiating off the pavement beyond the safety rail. Traffic is heavier on the pedestrian walkway than it is in the driv-

ing lanes; most of those walking across are eager to get past the
puttering tourists and the young boy trailing them. They have
work and families and errands and clinics and pharmacies and
orthodontists to get to and have no interest in looking at the lazy
green river down below them. These are men and women, boys
and girls, who cross back and forth every day. What do they care
about the eighteen-foot-high wall and its rust-colored steel bars
rising up from the levee and extending out from the bridge? It'll be
there when they come back tomorrow and if not it, then another
one, higher and uglier. Who hasn't seen the Border Patrol agents
cruising back and forth along the levee in their SUVs, waiting for
some pobre desperate enough to swim across in the middle of
the day or later in the glare of the portable searchlights? Those
curious sights are for the tourists who come to see something different, something to photograph and later show their families and
friends and tell them about how interesting it was to travel across
the border into old Mexico.

Back at the house she dials the transit station, but the dispatcher
tells her he needs more information before he starts calling all
his drivers. The boy might have gotten off the bus anyway. If he
bought a transfer, he could be anywhere. Besides, he isn't the first
twelve-year-old to ride the bus alone. Is he a runaway? Because run-
aways don't usually take city buses. Maybe she needs to hang up
and call the police. She does hang up, but only because the thought
of his having run away has been lingering along the outskirts of
her mind and she doesn't need any help inviting it any closer.

Passing through the Mexican customs checkpoint, travelers have
to walk up to a short traffic signal and press the crossing button

before they are allowed to continue forward. If the traffic light comes up green, they are free to enter the country y Bienvenidos a México. If it comes up red, the traveler must pass through extra security. The jokester's wife wonders aloud why the heck the airport security people don't do this back home and save passengers the trouble of showing their feet in public. These people may be onto something, says the husband. Everyone nods in agreement until the other old man happens to get a red light and has to undo his fanny pack and place it on the conveyor belt so it can pass through the X-ray machine. Then one of the guards unzips the fanny pack to look inside but doesn't find anything other than traveler's checks, loose coins, a tiny pill case, and his and his wife's passports. He has his cash in another pouch hanging from his neck and tucked inside his shirt, but he shows the guard only what he asked for. Orly gets a green light and passes through without having to open his backpack. There's nothing in it besides the book Mr. Domínguez gave him to read over the summer, and half a bottle of water; he brought his backpack out of habit, of wanting to hold on to something of his own.

The tourists ignore the calls of the taxistas offering their services. To the mercado, mister. Very safe inside taxi. Good shopping, better prices for you and your beautiful wife. Do not believe what the people say, it is very safe for you. The best prices in all of Matamoros. But across the street they already see the signage for the only place they want to go. García's Restaurant & Bar. They wait for a pesero loaded with passengers and then its stream of noxious fumes to pass so they can hurry across to the median, barely noticing that the young boy is still behind them, tagging along for the trip as though he were an unclaimed grandson. The parking garage attendant rushes over to open the door for the group, hoping this might result in a tip, but they pass through like the door might have opened on its own.

*   *   *

And here she is on the other side of the river, chasing down bus after bus through the streets of Brownsville, like some crazy woman. She hasn't shopped downtown in years. She stopped coming sometime after things ended with Jorge. Every restaurant or movie theater used to remind her of how her older brother, Luis, would follow them and park outside. She and Jorge became experts on the alleyways and corners of downtown, on how to escape through the service door of Fisher's Café or slip into the lobby of El Jardín Hotel and wait until it was safe and then hurry the three short blocks to the bridge and across to Jorge's tío's place where they could be alone. But when she spots a bus, she pushes aside these memories, off into the back of her mind. She speeds ahead and waits at the next stop for the driver to pull over. She asks four different drivers before the fifth one tells her he dropped off a boy like that in front of the old movie theater, across from the old courthouse. But he says that was a couple of hours ago. The boy could be back on the other side of town by now.

He follows the tourists up the marble steps to the second floor and through another set of doors. The blast of air-conditioning feels good after sweltering outside most of the afternoon. The two American couples head into the bar to cool off. To his left, Orly finds a gift shop, brightly lit and filled with more American tourists. Most are browsing at the jewelry case, asking to see silver rings or bracelets, trying to haggle a better price from the clerk, who apologizes in near-perfect English that the prices are already set. Each display has a neon-orange index card indicating the price of the decorative sombreros, of the festive Mexican dresses and guayaberas, with long and short sleeves, of the various bottles of tequila and mezcal and rum, of the leather whips and bandoliers with shot glasses, of the Talavera plates and pottery, of the Aztec calendars and wooden chess sets, of the stuffed frogs playing the guitarrón or acordeón, everything with prices clearly marked in American dollars.

He doesn't know what his dad and Nina and Tío Beto are so scared of that they won't even cross the bridge. If it's really that bad, why would the old people he followed come across? Next time he talks to his dad he'll tell him that he came over by himself and even walked down the street and it was totally safe. Maybe that'll prove to him that he isn't soft, isn't a baby and can take care of himself and from now on he'll let him stay home alone, not send him to his Nina's just to show him how different things are down here, so he'll see how much tougher his dad's life was growing up.

"Looking for a gift, a souvenir for a friend?" asks the lady behind the jewelry case.

"Just looking," he answers, relieved to not have to respond in Spanish, as he did at the stores on the other side of the river. She has dark hair and wears it in a ponytail. Her thick eyebrows stand out against her light skin.

"You would like to see the necklaces?" She slides open the glass panel.

"My mom used to have one like that." He points to a square-shaped pendant with tiny diamonds along the edges.

"And she lost it?"

He nods. "I think she misplaced it," he says, not wanting to explain what really happened, how he ended up down here for the summer.

"Well, now here it is again," she says and smiles like she might have resolved all his worries. She pulls it from the case, holds it up to her neck and chest to show him how it looks on her, then lays it out for him on a black felt tray. He never held his mother's necklace, but this one feels heavier than he had imagined it being. He remembers her wearing it sometimes when she and his father used to go out at night.

"I can save it here for you, behind the counter, if you want to go bring your mother to show her what you found."

Orly nods again and drifts away like he might go look for her in the restaurant, but instead he heads down the marble steps.

The sidewalk in front of García's is empty, but the traffic is backed up from the bridge for several blocks; on the opposite side of the avenue, heading toward downtown and the mercado, the cars trickle by after passing through the Customs checkpoint. He wants to buy something small to remind him of his trip into Mexico. He'll go just far enough to find another gift store or curio shop and then head back so he can be on the other side of the bridge before it gets dark. He has taken only a few steps when two black trucks surge around the corner across the street, their hoods and doors marked POLICÍA FEDERAL. Aside from the driver, each truck has four heavily armed men in the back, leaning against the cab rack. They wear dark blue uniforms and what look like bulletproof vests, their assault rifles up and ready at their shoulders. The first truck stops directly across from him; the second one cuts off all traffic coming from the bridge. Orly has just enough time to ease back into the garage, where the guard has already taken cover behind a gray Jetta. The men's black balaclavas and tactical goggles get Orly's attention, remind him of a dream he had in the days before his mother was supposed to move out. And now he hears his father's voice saying it was too bad they couldn't cross over anymore. Nina saying it wasn't worth the risk anymore. Tío Beto saying it wasn't worth the risk even when there was less risk. But none of that matters at this very instant when he feels himself paralyzed to move in any direction. He feels that sensation that he feels when he's playing soccer and knows he's about to fall hard but there's nothing he can do to stop himself, to remain suspended between his reality and the pain that awaits him. On the street, the vendor grilling corn pushes his two kids to the pavement behind his cart, the paletero rolls his icebox several feet in the other direction, the women waiting for the late-afternoon bus crowd behind the taxista stand, all of them watching the federales' eyes and then turning in every direction to see what it is the federales might be looking for that they don't yet see. Close to two minutes pass before one of the men standing in back lowers his rifle and taps twice on the roof of the first truck and the driver pulls away, followed by the other vehicle, the tires squelching on the pavement. And then Orly takes off for the bridge.

Nina pulls out a school photo from last year to show the attendant. The man wipes his hands and the corners of his mouth with an already balled-up napkin. She caught him eating his dinner. Orly's tie in the photo is the same dark blue as the man's tie, though the bottom half of his is tucked between the buttons of his uniform shirt. He leans in, then picks up the photo for a closer look. But no, no güeritos like that leaving town on one of his buses, he would remember him if he came through. Nina doesn't think of her godson as so light-skinned, but looking again at the photo and then back at everyone else in the bus station, including the two Border Patrol agents lingering near the exit, maybe the man has a point. Ask to the other counters, he says, but she has, even in the sandwich shop. Then maybe the police can help you, if the boy is lost. He picks up his plastic fork, takes another bite of his carne con papas. Everybody with ideas for her, nobody with answers.

In the car, she flips open her phone. Seven different bus counters, half of them said she should call the police. But she can already imagine their questions. Was your godson mad or upset about something? Has anything happened at your house in the last week that would make him want to leave? She can feel her blood pressure rising with each question. And if they come around to the house to ask more questions, to look for clues? She might as well just drive over to the police station and turn herself in, confess to them she lost one young boy and has another one, without papers, hiding behind her mother's house.

Now almost four hours since she left her mother with Rumalda, promising to pay her extra to wait until she got back. Telling her not to say anything if her brother Beto calls or comes by. She still has her cell phone open when the screen suddenly lights up. Orly's father has called only once or twice since he left him. And now of all times to be checking on the boy. She lets it ring and ring, ten, twelve, fifteen times. Then it stops, but a few seconds later it begins to ring again.

"Hello?"

"Tía, they just called me from the bridge."

16

Nina sits on the hard plastic chair in the waiting area, her ankles crossed under the seat. She waits in a room full of people they didn't let enter the country. A little boy crawling under the row of chairs trying to scare his younger sister, who's sitting on their mother's lap. The older man at the other end of the row dressed in a dark suit and white socks with no elastic. Two men, younger, with thick beards, speaking quietly in a language that sounds like nothing she's ever heard.

There's the story of what's happening at this very moment, which amounts to nothing more than waiting to be called in so they can ask her a few questions about her godson and how he ended up in Matamoros. And there's the other story that she imagines unfolding. Some people might call it a worst-case scenario; she calls it the only thing left to happen. In this second story, Orly lets it slip about the other boy he saw in her kitchen, that he's from Veracruz but stays hidden in the little house behind his great-grandmother's house. That, or Nina herself just breaks down and tells them everything, about the boy she's hiding, about El Kobe and Rigo, about Noemí and Briana. She tells them about the money she accepted and how she hid this from her family, how it started as a favor and then one day it wasn't a favor anymore, how she couldn't make herself turn the boy away, all of it. She

imagines the immigration officer reading her her rights, asking
her if she has a lawyer. Then she gets handcuffed and taken away
without even saying good-bye to Orly. And Orly having to stay
with her brother until Eduardo can come get him and take him
back to Houston. And then when they find her guilty and send
her away to the penitentiary, her mother gets sent to the nursing
home, where she stays the rest of her days with no visitors except
for when Beto remembers he still has a mother. And worse things,
like how Orly will never speak to her again.

   She can see him sitting in one of the offices, but they haven't let
her talk to him. When the Customs officer pulled him out of the
line because he couldn't enter the United States without proof of
citizenship, Orly gave them his father's number. His dad received
the message an hour later on the tarmac at LAX and had to wait
until he could get to the United Airlines lounge before he could
return the officer's call. The second call he made was to Nina.

   "How, Tía, how does a twelve-year-old end up in Matamoros?"

   "He took the bus downtown and from there walked across."

   "No, I mean, how did he even get the idea?"

   "He was reading when I left to run my errands." She didn't
know what he wanted her to say. She was telling him all she knew.
"But he's okay now. He's safe."

   "But you left him alone?"

   "He didn't want to go, and he wasn't alone. My mother and the
woman who cleans the house were here with him."

   "If they were there watching him, then how'd he get out? Tell
me how that happens, if they're watching him."

   "He just left, he walked out the door when they weren't watching. I don't have him locked up. He just wandered off when they
weren't looking. You used to wander off when you were his age."

   "Not to Mexico, not to Matamoros."

   His third call is to Kayla, who has to drive across town to the house, find and scan Orly's birth certificate, and e-mail it to his dad so he can then forward it to the Customs and Border Protection office. All this before they will even talk to Nina.

"Do you have some identification, Mrs. Diaz?" The room has only a desk and three chairs, nothing on the desk, nothing on the walls, no lamp, no plants.

She thinks about correcting her that she's a Miss, not a Mrs., but at this point she just wants to get her godson and leave. "I already showed them my driver's license."

"I mean a passport or passport card."

"For what, if this is my country?"

The officer looks at her without acknowledging her words. Nina wonders if the woman would've asked her that question even a few months ago, if this is how it's going to be from now on.

"Your godson did something dangerous, crossing alone into another country," she says. "People get kidnapped and shot just for being in the wrong place."

"Yes, but not because I let him. He went without permission."

"He was upset?"

"Not that I know." But she wonders if this isn't the reason for the questions and if the boy told them about the pink house. She remembers when she still used to go across and on the way back how they could be with their needling questions, just waiting for you to get mad or say something you never intended that they could then use against you. She feels her heart pounding in her chest the same as when Eduardo called her about Orly. She was just down the street from the bridge but had to sit in her car another twenty minutes to calm herself enough to where she wouldn't break down as soon as she walked inside the Customs office for him. Her hands would be shaking now if she didn't have them tucked under her legs.

"He said he was bored."

"That he was bored does not mean that anything bad happened to him."

"Then you are saying that he just ran away on his own, for no reason?"

"Who said he ran away? Because he went across and came back is not running away. Since when do boys have to have a good reason for doing what they do?"

"You're upset, Mrs. Diaz."

"He's my only godson, I don't have any children of my own. His father brought him to me so I could take care of him, so he could be safe with me at the house. He scared me. You think I don't know what could have happened to him?"

"But you left him alone."

"No, not alone. He stayed with my mother."

"But earlier you said you took care of your mother. So how was she going to watch the boy if somebody needs to be watching her?"

"But not just with her. I would never leave them both alone."

"Who then? Who did you feel comfortable leaving your mother and godson with?"

She is still sitting on her hands but now feels a tremor in her leg as if she might suddenly kick the desk. Here she was worried about Orly revealing something, and now she's the one who almost landed them in trouble. If she says her maid was also at the house, the next question will probably be about whether the maid has permission to be working on this side. And of course she doesn't. Whose maid does? Every morning there's a long line of women on the bridge coming over to work, and then at night they go back across to their families in Matamoros. Right or wrong, legal or illegal, seen or ignored, that's how things work here.

"A family friend, that's who. She comes to visit and stay with my mother when I have errands to run."

The first time she'd called Rumalda a friend, it was to try to explain why she had helped her; this time Nina was calling her a friend because it was the only way to get herself out of this mess. She had done a small favor for the woman, which led her to doing other favors that weren't really favors, which led to another favor for a boy who knocked on her back door late one night, which *was* more like a favor but which she doubts her godson or his father or the officer sitting across from her would ever understand.

Half an hour later she and Orly are in the car, driving home with the rest of the traffic leaving the bridge. They haven't said a word since the last officer brought him to her. Nina waits until she's a few blocks away from the bridge before she turns in at the first gas station she sees and pulls up next to the tire pressure gauge, then shuts off the car and gets into the backseat. The lights are bright enough here to see his face.

"Later on we can talk about what happened, why you left the house, but right now I need to know all the questions they asked you," she says.

"They just wanted to know who I was traveling with and how long I had been in Mexico."

"Orly, mijito, you need to tell me everything. No more playing around."

"I'm telling you truth."

"Por favor." She extends her hand to touch his cheek, but he turns away. "Look at me, Orly."

He looks at her but only long enough to say, "I didn't tell them about the other night, okay, if that's what you want to know."

"Are you sure, not even that you were upset?"

"I wasn't the one who was upset."

"I meant that you surprised me so late at night."

"I didn't say anything about the pink house, okay?"

She wants to ask more—she knows how tricky these officers can be. If they manage to get information from adults, ones who make their living from hiding things and are trying to stay out of prison, how much easier would it be with a twelve-year-old boy? She stops herself from asking only because she worries he might run off again.

She opens the car door and returns to the front seat. They ride the rest of the way in silence. It's dark now and almost time for her mother to be going to sleep. Nina hopes her mother hasn't given Rumalda too much trouble or had an accident because she insisted on getting to the bathroom without her walker. When they get back Nina will need to call a taxi for Rumalda, pay her the extra money and whatever they charge to take her back home to Matamoros.

"I'm sorry," Orly finally says when they're close to the house. He waits, then repeats it when she doesn't respond. He only says it because he knows if he doesn't say it now that later they'll have to talk about it longer.

She lowers the window, and after turning onto her street, she pulls over near the car wash.

"Tell me why," she says, still looking forward as if she were driving down some unfamiliar road with the lights off.

"I'm sorry for running away, even if I meant to come back."

"Not that."

"I'm sorry for going across the bridge and then for everything after I came back. For you having to go get me."

"I mean tell me why you left." She keeps both hands on the wheel.

"Just because."

"Just because why?"

"I was bored."

"There were a lot of other things you could do if you were bored—go to the mall, go to the movies. Not to where you could get hurt."

"I don't want to go to the stupid movies."

She turns toward him but now he's the one looking out his window, staring off in the direction of the car wash.

"Your daddy says he can come to get you."

"I don't want to go home with him."

"He got mad with me on the phone too," she says, hoping this will make him look her way. "Give him time and it will pass."

A small blue truck, low to the ground, eases into the parking lot of the car wash, then the first bay. A minute later the mist from the power washer rises into the light cast from the lamppost.

"I'm tired of everybody lying to me."

She wants to ask who "everybody" is but lets it pass and looks back, waits for him to face her. "I should have told you that night, explained it to you, but the real truth is I didn't want you to know."

"But why, if I had already seen him?"

"Yes, but I didn't want you to know how he got here. I wanted for it to be like you never saw him. I didn't want for you to know about how some mean men had brought him and some other ones for me to hide because it was illegal the way they came here." She pauses to see his reaction, if he'll kick the seat or try to run off, but he only looks at her as he does when he doesn't understand a Spanish word, confused but now also upset, as if she'd told him the meaning of the word but then changed it without telling him. "But not for long, and then they left and it was supposed to be the last time, except for the next day the police caught them after they left the house. I went to bed that night worried that the men who brought the people would say where they had been hiding them and then the police would come to my front door, knocking. But in the morning nothing, no knocks, and the next morning tampoco. But the knock came two nights later, at the back door. It was the boy, Daniel. He had run away when they caught the other ones. At first I wanted to send him away, tell him to leave or I would call the police. But how could I send him away, a young boy just a little older than you, out across the canal to find his way in the night?"

Orly looks at her now, waiting, like there might be more.

"Only until we find his family," she says. "He lost the number to call his father."

It makes him think of how his dad kept asking what the hell was wrong with him—as if he didn't know at least part of the answer to his own question—and how he thought Nina would yell at him too, but when he saw her she hugged him for such a long time he could feel a sob rising in her chest, and then asked him if he was okay, if he'd had anything to eat and if he was hungry.

"At first, I thought I was keeping it a secret to protect you, but now I know it was to protect me."

"Protect you from what?"

"From what you might think of your godmother."

17

Two times is how Nina remembers it. She had heard of girls getting in trouble for doing less with their boyfriends. After the second time she swore to herself no more until she and Jorge were married, which they had talked about in roundabout ways that she accepted only because he was still in the service and who knew where he might be a year or even six months from now. She tried not to panic when she was two weeks late. It was the summer after she had graduated and started working at the Kress store, and each day on her way to work she took a small detour and stopped by the cathedral to say a prayer—to beg, really—that she wasn't pregnant. She remembered hearing talk of a second cousin, a prima on her mother's side of the family, who by then was married more than ten years and every December she and her husband made a pilgrimage from San Luis Potosí to the Basilica in Mexico City, to ask la Virgen for help in bringing them a child that in the end never came. And here she, Nina, was on this side of the river, asking God to do the opposite, to stop any child from coming into her life before it was time, and each day it didn't happen she felt her faith struggling to catch its breath like the flickering candle she made sure to light on every visit. She wondered if her pleas would be met with the same indifference that her prima had received. She had been feeling nauseated in the morning but hadn't thrown up the way her sister-in-law, Bea, had a few months

earlier, just before she learned she and Raúl were expecting. This
was 1970—it wasn't like Nina could walk into a drugstore and buy
a pregnancy test. Maybe Jorge would marry her. Maybe. Her days
and nights had become filled with maybes. Maybe he would deny
it was his or say it was her fault. Maybe he would accept it but still
leave her back home to raise the baby on her own. Maybe Jorge
would accept her and the baby, but her family would still reject
her (that last one seemed like less of a maybe). Maybe she could
just move away to San Antonio or Houston, try to make it on her
own, at least until she had the baby and gave it up for adoption.
Maybe she could give the baby to her prima and at least one of
them would have her prayers answered.

And then later it occurred to her that the baby inside her had
been conceived in Matamoros at Jorge's tío's house and not in
Brownsville, not that this made much of a difference as to what
would happen next but maybe she should be praying closer to
where it happened. Nina knew this was crazy, that there was no
difference between a prayer said in one country and a prayer said
across the border in another. There was no American God and no
Mexican God, there was just God. But by then she was nine weeks
late and crazy didn't seem so crazy anymore.

She went on a Monday, her one day off from work, forcing herself not to think about the cramps that had kept her awake most of
the night and made her want to stay curled up in bed. After crossing the bridge on foot and passing through Mexican customs, she
took a taxi that dropped her off across the street from the church,
ignoring the driver when he offered to wait and take her for a stroll
in the plaza after she was done with her business inside. From
the sidewalk, the pink hue of the Mexican cathedral seemed to
pulsate in the noonday sun. The cramps were worse now and she
fought the urge to go sit on a bench under the shade trees in the

plaza. The church was empty except for some American tourists taking photos of the altar. Unable to lower herself all the way to the cushion without feeling the next spasm, she took a seat in the back and went through her ritual of saying an Ave María:

> *Santa María, Madre de Dios,*
> *ruega por nostros, pecadores,*
> *ahora y en la hora de nuestra muerte.*

By now she had said this last verse dozens of times and not fully seen herself as one of the pecadores, the sinners with a need to beg for forgiveness, now and in the hour of her death. All she wanted was for it not to be real and if it was real to know what to do next. Maybe the problem was more complicated. She promised then that she would never ask for anything ever again, nothing. She would lead her life giving and not taking. If she could have just this one favor.

This time she left without lighting a candle. She needed a bathroom. The cramps had her doubled over in pain. She passed a barbershop and one of the younger barbers rushed out to follow her down the sidewalk, hissing to get her attention. Around the corner, she found a shop where the seamstress had to leave a young bridesmaid atop a wooden box, her arms spread as if in flight, and show her to the modest facilities in the back. Almost as soon as she sat down, she felt her body expel some but not all of the guilt and worry she'd been carrying for the last nine weeks. She stayed seated, listening to the seamstress asking the young woman to stand straighter, like she would when they were taking photos. Then asking her how long she had been friends with the bride, and if she had met the groom, and if she thought they made a good couple, if he came from a nice family. Nina stayed exactly where she was for nearly half an hour, listening to the entire conversation because she couldn't yet bear to stand up and look at the murky remains of the baby she had just lost.

Jorge happened to be back for a visit the following month, but she wasn't ready to talk to him and didn't return his three or four calls. She was better the next time he came to town later that year for the holidays, but now he didn't call, and she waited by the phone, embarrassed for not having returned his calls, each day expecting it to ring, until she realized all the days of his leave had passed and he was gone.

She made herself call the next time she heard he was in town, but he never returned the call. After that, each time she heard he was back she wanted to go over and find a time for them to talk, if only so they could fight and have a proper breakup and not whatever this was, her waiting and him not ever calling. She wrote and rewrote letters, in a few of them even mentioning the baby, but she never mailed them. When she wasn't consumed with what had happened or didn't happen between them, she helped her sister in-law care for her baby boy, Eduardo, only a year old, wondering as she held him and gave him his bottle and changed his diaper if she would've had a boy or a girl, wondering if it really would've been so hard to do it on her own. Even then she knew she would always link this time of caring for her baby nephew with having lost her own baby.

Later, Nina heard from friends that they had seen Jorge dancing with some woman at the Mustang in Matamoros, but she told herself it probably wasn't anything serious. Dancing wasn't anything, lots of people danced and never spoke again. Maybe. Maybe not. It was another six years before she accepted that she was the only one waiting by the phone.

18

A silence fills the house. Not just at night, when he's supposed to stay in his room until morning, but during the day, too, when he's not supposed to ask about or mention the boy. He knows too much as it is.

The silence is the same as it was the morning after his parents told Orly and Alex about the separation, but different from the afternoon when they found out their mom had died. With their parents separating, the silence came from the question of why their mom couldn't stay and everything be like it always was, which was a question that had an answer and at the same time didn't have an answer because as soon as Orly thought he understood, he found out how little he really knew.

Maybe this is part of being an adult, not always having an answer. Knowing certain things but keeping them to yourself, hidden from everyone else. Maybe silence is where you go to figure out questions that don't have answers. Even though Nina explained it to him, he still isn't sure why she keeps the boy in the other house. She said it's because of her mother and Tío Beto, because they won't like it if they find out she's hiding a boy and will call the police to come take him away. But he doesn't understand why she can't just explain it to them, make them understand that if the boy gets sent away it'll solve the problem of his being here but not the other problem of how he finds his family.

One thing he knows to keep to himself is what happened on the street in Matamoros, which in a way was nothing—a bunch of Mexican cops blocking traffic for a couple of minutes, then leaving—but could've easily been something bad. He keeps it to himself especially after getting back and later that night online reading about a shooting a day earlier on the other end of Matamoros. Five people killed, four of them with one of the rival drug gangs and another one who was crossing the street with her little girl when it happened. The photos showed people strewn across the pavement in pools of blood, but without identifying the bad guys. When his father and Nina asked what happened when he crossed, he made his time over there sound as boring as it had been on this side of the bridge. They might have been right about not going across, but it didn't mean he had to prove this to them. Some things are better left unsaid.

The one person he thinks he could tell who might understand and not go crazy is Mr. Domínguez. Orly e-mailed him a few days after he got here, just to say hi and tell him that he had his book with him, but he never heard back and wonders if he uses a different e-mail over the summer, when he isn't always having to respond to his students and their parents.

A couple of mornings after the final parent-teacher conference, Mr. Domínguez was leaving his apartment to go for a run at Memorial Park when four heavily armed officers from Immigration and Customs Enforcement surrounded him before he could get into his car. Did he know where they could find Julián Montenegro? Julian was his partner. My boyfriend, he said when the ICE officer looked at him funny. Ex-boyfriend. They had lived together for a little more than a year but had been fighting for the last few months, more when Julián lost his job at the health club where he worked. Last he'd heard, Julián had decided to return to Mexico. So, he self-deported? The lead officer wasn't buying it, especially not with the boyfriend having a warrant out for his arrest for an unresolved DWI charge. Where in Mexico? But Mr. Domínguez wasn't entirely sure. Julián was from Guanajuato, so perhaps there. He wanted to give him some space before reaching out to him. Space before reaching out? The lead officer—she looked Latina but with blue eyes, so who knows—seemed amused with his choice of words. Then she asked to see some identification, which he provided in the form of a driver's license. The problem was, his work visa had expired ten months earlier, the renewal of which he said was pending, but which in fact had already been renewed once and had reached its limit. It was enough for them to take him. In another two weeks Mr. Domínguez will be deported back to Veracruz, still without knowing where Julian might be.

The silence in his godmother's house ends two nights later. It happens early in the morning when the trash truck that has been lumbering down the street then has to back up the whole way, the beep-beep-beep-beep signal going off, because there's no place to make a U-turn. Orly wakes up to take a sip of water—which he now serves himself in a short glass, then covers the opening with his iPhone—and before he can fall back asleep he feels a heavy thud shake the floor beneath his bed.

At first he thinks something tipped over in the kitchen. A chair? The table? The *refrigerator*? Then the first sound is followed by a wail that rattles him enough to sit up and do away with whatever sleep he had left in him. He wants to crack the door open, but he's afraid Nina might scold him for coming out in the middle of the night even if the middle of the night has already happened. The light seems brighter now at the bottom of the door. He drops to the floor and rushes forward on all fours until he reaches the door, the side of his face on the shag carpet, the tip of his nose edging into the sliver of light.

A minute later Nina's standing at the wall phone just outside the door. First her scaly heels, then she turns and it's the front of her plump toes staring him in the face. He can't see the phone, but he knows it's yellow because the long rubbery yellow cord is dangling in front of him. She uses the wall phone as much as the cordless phone in the living room. The extra-long cord, at first hopelessly tangled in knots, grows taut and then rises and disappears as she walks in the direction of her mother's room. She says to the person on the phone that she needs an ambulance, for her mother, ninety-four years old. There's another moan and Nina asks the dispatcher to hold on. Her voice dissolves to a murmur in the distance. A minute later she's back at the receiver. Yes, ninety-four, she repeats in Spanish. She fell.

Orly wonders if it's okay for him to open the door or if she needs him to keep out of the way, if even now she means for him to stay in his room the whole night. The moans are right around the corner from his room. After she hangs up, she checks on her mother, then dials Beto, tells him what happened, for him to call the rest of the family and later to meet her at the hospital. When she hangs up, he has only a few seconds to scramble back under the covers before she gently opens his door, the hallway light fanning across his bed.

"Orly," she says and touches his cheek, "wake up, mijito."

He squints up from his pillow as if he just woke up.

"My mother had an accident and needs to go to the hospital."

He pushes up on his elbows. "Is she dying?"

"No, mijito, she fell and hurt her leg," she whispers and sits on the edge of the bed. "Most people just go to the hospital to get better."

"And then she's coming back?"

"As soon as the doctors tell her. Right now you need to put on some clothes so you can come with me." She draws back the blanket.

"But I don't want to go."

"Nothing's going to happen. It's just to make her feel better."

"Still, I want to stay here." He pulls the blanket back up to his chest.

"I can't leave you all by yourself."

"Yes, you can, I'll be okay. My dad lets me stay alone sometimes when he goes to play golf."

"But with your brother?"

"Not all the time," he says. "You can ask him."

"It will be longer than a few minutes before I can come back." She tugs again at his arm and this time he pulls back.

"I'll be okay."

There is no siren at this hour of the morning, only the ambulance lights now flashing across the paneling and their faces.

"Orlando, mijito."

"I won't leave," he tells her. "I promise to stay inside the whole time. I won't go anywhere. You can trust me."

She tries to find some proof in his words, in his expression, if he might be trying to fool her again, the way her kids used to try when she first started teaching school. But like it or not she knows she has to trust him—as she already has with so much else.

"Not even to the backyard?"

"No, just inside until you get back."

"And not open the door to anybody?"

"I know, my dad tells me the same thing."

They can hear the ambulance doors opening and closing.

"I'm going to call you as soon as I get there. And if you don't answer me, then I'm going to have to come home to look for you.

You understand me? That I will have to leave my mother there, alone, so I can come find you, make sure you are safe?"

"I'll be here, I promise."

She kisses him on the cheek and leaves when the EMTs knock.

As soon as she closes the door, he goes back to the carpet, this time lying on his back with his head tilted toward the door. The paramedics are trying to figure out how to reach Mamá Meche with the gurney. They wear what look like black army boots but with more traction. They wheel the gurney forward but have to back up into the bathroom in order to turn the tight corner and get to her room. Her cries turn louder when they load her and then reverse their earlier steps. The wheels move forward, the wheels move backward, into the bathroom, out of the bathroom, an inch here, a centimeter there, until they suspend the wheels a couple of inches off the floor and hoist the gurney around the corner. After the second paramedic passes, the last thing Orly spots under the door is Nina's sandals, the nicer ones with the plastic flowers over the straps, for wearing away from the house.

19

She calls as soon as she gets to the hospital and again closer to nine, the time he normally wakes up. He stands at the wall phone listening to her tell him her mother broke her hip when she fell. They just took her in to operate.

"Your tío Beto wants to go by later and check on you, maybe bring you some breakfast."

"He doesn't have to, I'm all right."

"That's what I tell him, pero es bien terco. He doesn't listen to people, only he knows."

"When's he coming?"

"As soon as they bring her out."

He asks her if there's anything he can do around the house, like feed the dog. She takes a moment, tells him she doesn't want him in the backyard, remember? He remembers. The dog can wait, she says and pauses again.

"Listen to me, Orly," she says.

"Yes, ma'am," he answers, because he knows to say sir or ma'am when a grown-up uses that tone and might be about to say something they think is important.

"I need you to be extra careful with your tío when he comes."

"Why, what's going to happen?"

"Nothing, but you know how he likes to ask his questions. He thinks he's a detective. He might want to go looking in the back."

"What if he goes to the other house?"

"Let him, si no he'll think there's something to be hiding. The boy knows not to make sounds or look out the window."

After hanging up, Orly goes to the restroom to pee and splash water on his face. Last night, once the ambulance lights faded and his room turned dark again, it took him close to half an hour to fall back asleep. He was glad Nina hadn't made him go with her to the hospital and wait around with all the other sick people and their families. But now he wonders what it would've been like if Mamá Meche had died, if he was there to see it. It's a weird thing to think about and he feels a little ashamed of himself, guilty as if even thinking about it might make her die and it'll be all his fault. He can't help himself. He thinks being there might have helped him imagine what it was like when they rushed his mother to the hospital that morning, if he hadn't been at camp but was still at home when it happened and she fainted in the garage, just before the movers arrived, surrounded by all the boxes she'd packed to move to her new place. If the EMT let him ride in back, holding her hand, all the way to the hospital. If he was there when she took her final breath. If it was like in the movies when the person's eyelids drop as if they're only falling asleep. Did her eyes stay open in that creepy way where a doctor or nurse has to come around and shut them? Or maybe, if she'd heard his voice, she would've opened her eyes one last time, searching for his.

Beto has barely pulled his work van into the driveway when the dog starts with her barking. He parks halfway under the carport, walks to the middle of the backyard, and gazes at the other house, like maybe if he stays looking long enough he'll be able to see through the walls. See what he suspects his sister is trying to hide from him, make him look dumb for not knowing what's happening right under his nose, in his own mother's backyard. Meanwhile the dog is barking and snarling, tugging against the chain as though she has suddenly rediscovered her purpose in life.

"That animal has what they call behavioral problems," Beto says as Orly unlatches the screen door. "Lots and lots of aggression. My sister, she thinks it's good for protection, but you ask me it's too much. They need to take him to get fixed. You know, chop them off." He makes his thick fingers into a pair of scissors.

"I think it's a girl dog."

"Even worse."

He shakes the boy's hand and sets down a paper bag, the bottom half stained through with grease from his chorizo taco. Orly brings out the paper plates his godmother has started using so he isn't always washing dishes at the kitchen window.

"My sister says she wanted to bring you with her to the hospital, but that you wanted to stay."

Orly nods, but wonders if his tío is trying to trick him into saying something.

"I told her she shouldn't be taking chances, leaving an eleven-year-old all alone in the house. Sometimes she doesn't use her head."

"Actually, I'm twelve. I had a birthday in May."

"Okay then, twelve," his tío says and hands him a taco. "Happy birthday."

"Sometimes my dad leaves me."

"But that's a different neighborhood, where you and your family live."

He takes a sip from his can of Dr Pepper, wonders how much he can trust Eduardo's boy to be straight with him.

"So did she tell you not to be going outside, you know, allá atrás in the backyard?"

He says no, shakes his head, and unwraps the aluminum foil from his taco.

"My sister said you like it with beans."

He nods, but then lifts the edge of the tortilla.

"What?"

"Just checking to see if they put anything extra," he says, the steam billowing from the refried beans. "I prefer it without cheese."

Beto looks at him without saying anything, just stares.

"What?"

"*You* tell *me* what," his tío says and puts down his taco, the sides of it flopping over the edges of the plate. " '*I prefer*'? What the hell way is that to talk? My sister told me you're like your daddy, the both of you like to hang out in libraries, pero híjole. '*I prefer*.' "

"I just don't like it with cheese."

"That's better," Beto says and uses the paper napkin to wipe the orange grease from his fingers. "And anyways, here nobody puts cheese on their beans. That's for other people, allá en Houston and Austin, those places. Here it's puro frijol."

Orly takes a bite of his taco, careful to not let the beans seep out the other end.

"So is Mamá Meche going to be okay?"

"Ojalá que sí," he says and nods. "She's strong, but when they get that old you never know from one morning to the next. Before they took her to operate I reached down and told her in her ear that I loved her. And right then, with her eyes half closed y toda dormida, she says to me she wants to go home. In case something happens, you know, to be here in her house when she dies. In her mind she thinks it's the same house she moved to sixty years ago." He sips his Dr Pepper. "This used to be a different neighborhood back when your daddy was your age, before he moved away. Kids playing in the street, getting into trouble out by the canal. All the families watched out for each other."

"It's quiet most of the time."

"Quiet because most of them moved away. Now people are coming and going, but people who have no business here. That's why there's so many Border Patrols driving around." Beto looks straight at Orly, waiting for a reaction. "You seen any of them?"

"Seen who?"

"The illegal ones."

"Here?"

"Yeah, like around the neighborhood or in the back."

"What do they look like?"

"Like people," he says. "Most are men, but also some women and children. But they're hard to see because they're always hiding."

"If they're hiding, how do you see them?"

"Because they don't want to hide forever, not like las cucarachas. These ones want to go somewhere else."

Orly feels safe nodding to this.

"Sometimes they're on the news," he thinks to say, "if they find a bunch of them working somewhere."

"Now you're talking about up in Houston, that's different. The ones I'm saying just crossed over and want to go someplace like that."

He glances over his shoulder, toward the back door and the other house.

"My sister, she feels sorry for them. She thinks people should help them out, be nice to them. But I tell her, if the law finds out they're not going to like it, her doing favors." He reaches into one of the front pouches of his cargo shorts and takes a business card out of his bulging wallet. With his ballpoint pen he circles the cell phone number at the bottom of the card, Ro-Ru Pest Control. He named the company after the first letters of his boys' names, Roberto and Rudy. Something for them to be proud of later when they're a little older.

"You let your tío know if you see anybody who looks out of place, like they don't belong, eh?"

Before leaving, Beto tells him to lock the door, "just in case." After locking up, Orly walks to the side window and later to the kitchen window, following his tío as he wanders into the carport, peeks inside the trash can for any evidence that his sister or the boy may be lying to him, then drifts into the backyard and toward the far end of the pink house. He squats to glance under the house for a second, then stands and checks the shiny aluminum covering the inside of the windows, searching for a slit or gap along the edges that'll give him a glimpse of anyone inside the house, but all he finds is his shimmery reflection staring back at him in the foil. He does this around every window he can reach and that the barking dog can't.

An hour passes. Then there's another knock at the back door.

20

This is only the second time Orly has seen the boy and the first time outside of the kitchen. The boy raises his hand to wave and then looks around the corner of the house, to the street, and back over his shoulder at the pink house. The overcast sky makes it seem closer to the end of the day but still far from the time of night when the boy would normally cross the yard for dinner. He's wearing the same green shorts from the first night but a different soccer shirt, this one blue and stained with dirt across the chest and a white collar that stands out against his brown skin. The boy lingers in the same spot where Orly's tío Beto was earlier, one foot on the first step, the other in the dirt. But this time Orly leaves the latch on the screen door.

"La señora," the boy says.

Orly looks at him without reacting, not a smile, not a mean or scared face, even if part of him is afraid and wants to tell the boy to go away, the way he imagines Nina or his tío would want him to, though each for different reasons. Orly's Spanish is good enough to explain why his godmother hasn't come back and why both of them are still alone, even if the other boy is already alone most of the time. But if he answers him, how many more questions will the boy have? What happens if he can't explain the rest? What if he doesn't say anything but "Más tarde" and maybe points to his watch or where his watch would be if he wore one, and lets the boy figure it out from there? Nina's the one who told the boy he could stay. She's the one hiding him, he's the one who isn't even supposed to be talking to the boy. Because the truth is, none of this has anything to do with him and in another week it'll have even less. It's the difference between answering the boy's question, letting him know he understands what he's saying, or not answering and making the problem go away, back across the yard to the little pink house and eventually to wherever he came from or might be headed.

"La señora," the boy says, struggling to pull forth the words. "Where she is?"

The way Orly sees it, his options are (a) shrug like he doesn't know; (b) tell the boy what he knows and close the door; or (c) tell him what he knows and then go answer the phone that just started ringing.

Nina says her mother made it through the surgery okay but now needs to rest. She's calling him from Mamá Meche's room. The doctor wants to keep her in the hospital two or three days before transferring her to a rehab center.

Nina asks if he made himself something to eat for lunch. Did he remember to take his medicines and vitamins? There's the chicken salad she made on Sunday and plenty of bread. He can find more bread in the freezer but it's the white kind, not the wheat bread his father says he should eat. He tells her he's still full from the taco he had earlier. She asks if any of the family has called. But no, the phone hasn't rung since the last time she called. She gives Orly the number to the hospital and her mother's room for when they call. She asks how long her brother stayed in the backyard.

All this but without her ever mentioning the other boy. And so neither does he.

"Un poquito más tiempo," Orly tells him and holds his thumb and forefinger less than an inch apart to show him it won't be much longer. They're sitting on opposite sides of the kitchen table now. "Mamá Meche está mejor."

The boy says he came because earlier a man was walking around the other house, trying to look in the windows. It was the same man who wanted to spray the little house and la señora told him no. He's worried the man might be from the authorities. Maybe he should leave, go away before more come. He can leave as soon as it gets dark, go hide somewhere else.

Orly tells him the man might be back but not because he's with the authorities. "Hermano," he says, "de la señora."

But he doesn't know how to explain why the brother of la señora wants to know if somebody is in the little house. Why it matters to him. Why he kept trying to look in the windows. Why a sister would be afraid of her brother reporting her.

"¿Por qué?" Orly asks and points in the general direction of the pink house, which is the closest he can get to saying, "No offense, but why are you still here, hiding, behind my godmother's house three weeks later? What's up with that?"

The boy says he didn't know where else to go, where it was safe. After he ran away from the police, it took two nights to find the house again. Now la señora is trying to help him find his father. She tells him that he should not lose faith. The other night she said he could stay as long as he needs to. Aquí tienes tu casa, she told him.

It's not the boy's words but how fast he speaks that makes it difficult for Orly to understand everything he's saying. This is how he speaks normally, but to Orly it sounds like someone is still chasing him and he's running out of breath and time to say everything.

"¿Pero cómo, la puerta?" Orly manages to ask, by which he means, "But what about the padlock on the door, bro? How do you get out of a house if it's locked from the outside? Explain that one."

Fácil. La señora told him to keep the little house clean, that he could stay and she would feed him but she was not his maid. Especially the bathroom, to keep it clean and always flush the paper. She brought him trash bags, sprays for the kitchen and bathroom, paper towels and a broom. He used to clean the house for his mother after school and here he has nothing else to do. No homework, no soccer to play outside with friends. To make the work last, he cleans every corner of every room, the floors and the walls, the closet and the cabinets, el refri y la tina. Even the foil covering the windows he wipes it clean every morning. He pretends like the house is a hotel that needs to be spotless. One afternoon he was sweeping in the bedroom and saw a piece of plywood lying inside the closet. Already he had been here two weeks and seen it many times but not thought to move it. There was no lightbulb to see what was inside. But when he finally moved the board he found a hole in the floor. The opening was wide enough for a man to drop down under the house and from there get to the canal. He never saw them open it, but it must have been made by the ones who brought him here, the bald one and his partner, the one always laughing for no reason, for the two of them to escape if somebody came trying to knock down the front door. La señora is still mad about the doorknobs they took. He doesn't think she would like knowing they also made a hole in her floor. Or that he used the hole for the first time today.

*   *   *

Twenty minutes have gone by when they hear the driveway gate scrape against the concrete. No need to go to the window or wonder what comes next or tell each other they need to pretend this didn't happen, that they never met without her here, they never talked. The boy is out the door and across the yard, veering wide from the sleeping dog, his bare feet barely touching the grass.

21

From the back gate, Nina heads straight to the little pink house. This is the longest the boy has been locked inside without her seeing him or letting him out to get fresh air, and though he has everything he needs, she hates having to lock him up. She has to keep reminding herself she is trying to help him, keep him safe. She fiddles with her keys before she can get the right one into the padlock.

Nina is turning the knob when he cracks open the door and waves to her. In the other house people hug, here they wave.

"Por fin," she says, her way of acknowledging how long it took her to return. He nods to let her know he understands she was busy.

He only has on a pair of shorts. His soccer shirt, smeared with dirt from his scurrying under the house, is in a tight ball next to the dresser in the other room. He crosses his arms across his bony chest. After weeks inside, the coppery shade of his face and arms has dulled to the color of wet sand.

"I was changing my clothes when I heard the door."

"So late in the day?"

"I took a shower, so I wouldn't have to do it later."

"Without washing your hair?"

"I washed it last night."

She stays looking at him. Something about the way he has a

quick answer for every question makes her think there is more he is not telling her.

He finishes putting on the T-shirt he has in his hand. The crumpled shirt on the floor is one of the three Nina bought him when she got tired of seeing him in the same soiled blue jeans and gray T-shirt. She also bought him a pair of jeans, some underwear, and socks. He had nothing when he arrived, what was she supposed to do? She bought the small television to keep him entertained during those long stretches when he's alone. Other than to feed the crossers she hadn't spent any of the money El Kobc gave her. If she could get rid of it, at least use it for something good, then maybe her first mistake wasn't as big a mistake.

"A man came and was looking in the windows."

"My brother."

"He had an angry face."

"He saw you?"

"No, I got down, on the floor, before he came and began knocking to the window."

"He thinks I am hiding something from him."

"He knows?"

"Only what I tell him, what I think he needs to know."

"And if he comes again?"

"Maybe we find your father before then."

"And if not?" he asks, but gets no response.

She checks the seal on the aluminum foil. The tape along the edge of the front window is curling back on itself where the boy must have been looking outside. Later she'll bring more tape to make sure the foil stays in place.

The fan blows a gust of muggy air in one direction and then the other. He uses the large pedestal fan during the day, dragging it with him room to room. After dark, when there are unlikely to be any visitors next door, he has permission to turn on the air conditioner.

"Your mother, her side is feeling better?" he asks. "She will be coming home?"

"Not until she gets better. The doctor says maybe two or three weeks," Nina tells him. "And how did you know it was her side?"

"Her side?"

"My mother's side, how did you know it was her hip?"

"You told me through the door, before you left to the hospital."

"I told you she had fallen, but not on her side."

"My grandmother, when she fell it was to her right side."

He's never mentioned a grandmother. She stares at him to see if he looks away the same as her godson does when she catches him saying something more false than true. The small television is playing in the other room. Whatever he has on sounds dramatic and maybe violent. She called for them to connect the cable so he wouldn't be so bored. More than a hundred channels to choose from, lots of them in Spanish, and he likes to watch the ones about the dead coming back to life and chasing living people. Things that would keep her up at night.

She opens the refrigerator.

"You didn't eat the rest of the arroz con pollo from yesterday?"

"Not yet."

"Already you need more milk," she says. "The cereal is for the breakfast, not for whenever."

He nods, looks down at the floor.

"Later, after I rest, I will make the dinner and bring you a plate."

She opens the front door and he squints in the sunlight. With his free hand he reaches down to cover a mud stain on his shorts.

"Put the dirty clothes in a bag and when I come back I will take them to wash," she says. "And from now on you need to eat over your plate. That way your clothes don't get so dirty."

* * *

After she's taken a nap and showered she makes tuna patties for dinner, one of Orly's favorites. She serves him three patties, one for herself, and wraps the last three in foil to keep them warm and later take to the other boy. Same meal, the only difference being where they eat and that Orly puts ketchup on his patties and the other boy takes his with mayonnaise.

Orly has been quiet since she came home. He asked about her mother and for how long she would be staying in the hospital and later the rehab center, but after that he had little to say. Nothing about going again to buy raspas like she had said they would last night before bed. He eats with his head down, using his fork to make swirly patterns in the ketchup.

"Do you want more?" she asks when he finishes his three patties before she's halfway through hers.

"I thought you only made enough for one serving?"

"I made extra." She walks to the counter to show him.

"Aren't you saving those?"

She pretends not to hear him and goes about rinsing a frying pan, but afterward says, "For him I can make something else, warm up the picadillo from the other day."

"Daniel," he says.

"Yes, for him," she says. "Daniel," only hers is in Spanish, as she said the night she came to Orly's room to explain to him who the boy was.

"That's okay," he says and takes his plate to the sink. "I'm not that hungry."

"Are you sure? I have to be there for when my mother wakes up, so she isn't confused. It might be late before I get back."

"If I get hungry I can have some cereal."

"For dinner?"

"For a snack."

"If I let you that's all you would eat, snacks."

She runs water over the ketchup he left on his plate, watches the red smear wind its way down the drain. The rest she leaves for later. She has to hurry if she's going to be there when they come around with her mother's tray of food.

"How come he eats alone?"

"Who eats alone, mijito?"

"Daniel," he says, trying to say it the same way she does, the *el* sound humming against the back of his front teeth. "In the other house, he eats alone every night."

She dries her hands and looks at him. "There are worse things than being alone. Nobody dies from being alone."

She grabs a raspberry popsicle from the freezer, removes the wrapper, and sets it on a small plate for him.

"And not every night," she says, walking into the next room. "Today because I have to leave to the hospital. When things are back to normal, then he can eat here again."

"But only late at night, after we've already eaten and I go to bed."

She walks back into the kitchen carrying her purse and with the other hand holding one of her mother's quilts to take to the hospital.

"Ya, I gave to you the reasons. Over there is where he lives, over here is where we live," she says. "So you are not part of it and know nothing of what happens."

"How long does he have to be there?"

"Until we find his father. Every night I try the numbers he gives me to call."

"What if you don't find him?"

"Then maybe he stays. It would still be better, safer, than the place he came from. He could go to school here, make new friends."

She pauses, waiting for him to react in some way. He looks confused and she doesn't know why she had to go open her mouth.

"If you want, we can do a search on my iPad and try to find his dad. It's easy," he says, his face more alive now. "Just give me his last name and the city and I can see if anyone with that name comes up. We could maybe even find him or another relative on Facebook. All you need to do is give me a name." Now she's the one confused, something that happens anytime he wants to show her something on his computer, a world he's built, one of his class projects, or just a funny pet video he found online. She smiles and tells him how nice it all looks or how funny animals can be, but on the inside, a part of her brain dims so she doesn't have to be reminded of the distance between her world and his.

"I told you that I didn't want you to be involved. Nobody needs your help. Your computer cannot control everything in the world, it cannot make time go back so things turn out a different way. He ended up here for a reason. Whatever happens, how long he stays or where he goes, you don't know any of it. You never saw him, remember?"

"But how is it a secret if I already know? How can I know and not know at the same time?"

"Because you don't tell anybody, and you and me stop talking about it and you do what I tell you and stay out of the backyard, asina, that's how it stays a secret." She grabs the plate with the extra tuna patties to take to the other boy.

"Even if we never talk about it again, he's still in there alone most of the day."

"And you, why do you care so much if a stranger is alone, a boy you never met, from somewhere you will never go?" she says.

"That's not for you to worry about. You can feel sorry for him, but his problems are not your problems."

"I thought Tío Beto was going to find a way to get inside. He was looking in all the windows."

"You let me worry about him."

"But it's just weird, someone locked up and eating alone."

She pulls out a chair and sits close enough to touch him.

"Don't be saying weird this and weird that. You saw him one time and only a little bit until he left again. Who is he?"

"What do you mean?"

He knows she wants an answer but he doesn't altogether understand the question.

"What is he to you? Is he your brother? Is he your primo or your tío? What is he to you that you care so much?"

He looks shaken, like she might have slapped him without raising a hand. "Nothing."

She leans back in her chair, tilts her head to make eye contact. She wants him to think about his answer.

"Are you sure?"

He looks up at her and nods.

"Tell me again."

"What?"

"What you just said, say it again. What he is to you."

"He's nothing to me."

"Nothing," she says. "Then you can keep a secret about nothing."

IV

Chivito

22

Later that night, even in bed with the air conditioner turned to the number 4 setting, Daniel can hear when she returns from the hospital, the gate scraping the concrete of the driveway, the hiss and rattle of the motor turning off, the second gate opening and closing, the wooden steps creaking, her tugging on the padlock one last time.

He wishes he had seen the rest of the blue house. She must have a much larger television than the one he uses. Since he arrived, he has been over many times but only with permission to be in the back of the house because her mother is not supposed to see him. At first it didn't make sense why he would have to hide from la señora's mother, but that was before her brother tried to look in the windows.

One night, when she brought him to the other house for his dinner, the old woman woke up and then he had to remain still for several minutes, barely breathing, so she wouldn't hear him. It was almost as bad as when they crossed him to this side and the driver made him get inside the trunk of a car with two men, one a few years younger than his father and the other one much older. There he didn't want to breathe because he could smell some of the smoke from the exhaust, and moving was impossible with the three of them crammed up against the spare tire. He barely saw their faces when they were crossing and then it was so dark inside he could only see them when the brake lights showed the red glow of their faces. They must have been in the car for only five minutes when one of the two men let out a muffled fart, which smelled worse than the car fumes, and less than a minute later he released a second one, but again without saying anything. "No mames, güey," said the younger one, and then he knew it had been the older one.

He also wants to look at the other boy's phone and tablet that are supposed to be like computers. He has seen people with the phones on the streets and on television but never held one himself. La señora told him her godson spends too much time playing games on the tablet, hours and hours, but he knows that sometimes la señora likes to exaggerate. The other night she told him there could be more than a thousand men in Chicago with his father's same name. She says these things so he'll have patience and won't be disappointed every time they sit down to call and don't locate his father. But by now he knows everything takes time and nothing happens from one day to the next.

When his father left Veracruz it was only supposed to be until he could send for him and Gaby, his baby sister, and his mother. But a few months turned into three years and by then his parents were barely speaking and his father only wanted to bring his boy to live with him in Chicago. His mother said no, that she wanted him to stay with her. His father said she was just doing it because she was mad. She said it didn't matter why she was doing it, she wasn't letting a ten-year-old boy travel all the way to Chicago by himself. It didn't matter how many others his age and younger were traveling alone from as far as Honduras and El Salvador. ¡Qué no! she told him. This way, month after month, year after year. ¡Qué no! Until last Christmas his father came down to bring him back himself, but still his mother said no, that thirteen was still a boy and not old enough to be crossing, even with him, and anyway, his home was here with his mother. Because he was sending her money didn't give him the right to take her son. She even sent him and Gaby to stay with her parents, out in the country, so his father wouldn't be tempted to run off with either one of them. Daniel was allowed to see his father the last day before he had to leave again, but only in front of the house with a couple of his tíos nearby, watching them from the wooden gate. It was there that his father gave him the black backpack he had bought him for the journey but that he could now use for the rest of the school year. His father placed his hands on Daniel's shoulders, whispering most of what else he had to say to him so los tíos wouldn't hear. There was something hidden inside the backpack, another Christmas present. He wanted to open it, but his father made him promise to wait until he was home and alone. It was a cell phone, prepaid and already programmed with his father's number on the speed dial. The only thing was, he couldn't let anyone else see the phone, not even his little sister, or his mother might take it from him.

"So I can call you, Chivito, and you can call me whenever you want," *he said, using his nickname for him since he was a little baby. His grandfather used to raise goats and so Chivito was the name he had given to his father when he was little and the one that his father gave to him when he was born, although by then they had stopped raising goats and moved closer to the city. "And then we find a way for you to come live with me."*

For the next few weeks Daniel kept the phone turned off and tucked inside his backpack so he wouldn't be tempted to check his messages. When his sister and mother were away from the house, he would lock himself in the bathroom and check to see if his father had called, which was never the case, and afterward he would plug his phone into the wall outlet next to his bed so it stayed charged for the next time he checked. A month had passed when he finally dared to call his father. It was a Sunday afternoon, a day his father would be home from the hospital where he cleaned; he had told his mother he was going to play soccer in the field near the house with his best friend, Alfonso, who he also hadn't told about the cell phone. Instead he went to the park, where no one he knew would see him pull it out of his backpack. It rang once and then immediately beeped and went to voice mail, but he wasn't sure what to say and hung up. He called again the next Sunday with the same result and wondered if his father had programmed the wrong number on his phone. The next time it rang ten times before someone picked up.

"Chivito?"

"The phone works," he said, because until that moment he wasn't convinced his father would answer. There were voices in the background, people shouting from different directions as if he had caught him in the emergency room of the hospital.

"Something happened, Chivito?" his father said in that same whispery voice he had used in the yard. "Your mami and your little sister are all right?"

"No, nothing, I just wanted to say hi, to ask if it was almost time for me to go," he whispered back.

"Look, right now is not good to talk. They don't like us to use the phone at work."

"You're at the hospital?"

"This is another one, in a kitchen, but only for the ends of the week." He told him to hold on. For a moment the voices sounded far away, but he could hear someone yelling in English and his father straining to find the words to respond.

"Better for me to call you, Chivito," he said after he came back, his voice even lower now. "Soon."

He couldn't tell his father the truth, that he didn't really want to go to Chicago to live with him, not alone anyway. He had said yes only because he thought being there would make his father also want to bring his little sister and his mother, then they would have to talk again and maybe not at first but eventually they would be happy again. That was his plan, one he kept even more hidden than the phone.

When the time finally came to leave and go be with his father it was sudden, without warning, after not talking about it for months. Things had gotten worse in Veracruz. A few weeks earlier the government uncovered another mass grave, this one with seventeen bodies. A cousin of his father had been on a street corner when a black SUV pulled up and three armed men got out and started firing at another vehicle, in the process *killing the cousin and two street vendors. His father said these were the bad guys, the ones moving the drugs. He said there was no more time to wait for his mother to change her mind. He didn't have to tell him this was a secret, but he did anyway, just to make sure Daniel didn't let it slip in front of her or his sister before he left for the bus station. Román, his father's best friend, who he'd crossed with the first time and who had since moved back, would go on the bus with him all the way to Matamoros and arrange for the same people to cross Daniel to the other side. You call me when you make it across, understand? His father said it like getting to that side was all there was to it, like if he could just get across the river his father would be waiting there for him.*

He did call his father, but it was a short conversation because the bald one snatched the phone from him. The price had gone up, he told his father. He needed to send more money and fast, si no, we don't let him go. His father had to pay extra like the others. One woman and her grandfather had to call their family in Florida to get more money. So did the young woman who was traveling with them, but her money never arrived and then the bad ones said she would have to work to pay the extra money. The work came after they got to the motel and she had to go into one room, while the rest of them sat on the floor in the next room, through the wall hearing her cry, then plead, then the sound of the bed hitting against the wall, and then her crying and pleading all over again. Like this for two hours, for three hours, until she ran from the room to the parking lot with just a sheet to cover herself and next thing they knew the police were pounding on the door and when it opened he was running and running in the dark without knowing where to or for how long or even slowing down long enough to care, which was good because it helped him get away from the one chasing after him, but later he realized he'd left the backpack and phone on the floor in the motel room. It took most of the next day to find the railroad tracks they had crossed and another two nights before he could find the car wash and then the house of la señora.

He drifts off, wondering how much longer he'll be here, safe and fed but away from his family, from his mother and little sister, from his father somewhere in Chicago. Maybe it wouldn't have been so bad to have been caught in the motel room, to have stayed on the floor like they were yelling for them all to do. Maybe being sent back home would've been better than being stuck and not arriving at either place.

The cop who'd chased him was also named Daniel, though of course the irony was lost to both of them as the boy bolted through the parking lot, down a caliche road, then over a ditch half filled with last week's rain before slipping under a barbed-wire fence into an empty field. There was also the irony of the thirty-one-year-old Daniel with a two-pack-a-day smoking habit trying to catch thirteen-year-old Daniel who when he played soccer preferred to take the midfield position where he could chase and pivot and accelerate all afternoon in the sun. Then there was the irony of Officer Daniel Aldridge, the son of a Salvadoran immigrant named Eva, chasing another immigrant. His mother had crossed the river on an inner tube thirty-two years ago and within a few days found work as a maid, cleaning houses. A year later she married one of her employers, Charlie Aldridge, a former Texas State Trooper only recently widowed. Not that any of this would've meant squat to the older Daniel, who was losing ground trying to catch his tocayo, as he might have referred to the boy if he had known they shared the same name and if they had met under different circumstances. His mother having once been an illegal wasn't something that he gave much thought to, first because she was naturalized ten years ago, and second because she was just his mom, not Salvadoran, not American, not Salvadoran-American, just his mom. Besides, he had a job to do, even though, in truth, this wasn't actually his job, chasing illegals in the middle of the night. That was for Border Patrol, that was for ICE, not the Brownsville PD. He and another patrolman just happened to show up for what the dispatcher had described as a domestic dispute and now he looked like a dumbass trying to catch some kid who was only getting farther away. Which was something he reminded himself of as the younger Daniel, who to the older Daniel would remain nameless, just one more illegal, seemed to find another gear and blew open the distance between his past and whatever future might be out there waiting for him.

23

Orly spends the next morning inside reading and watching TV. Nina is back at the hospital but says in a couple of days, when they move her mother to the rehab center, he needs to come with her to visit Mamá Meche. She's been asking for him. Before Nina left, she made him promise again not to go into the backyard, and so when he does go outside with his phone he makes sure to stay on the back steps, which technically isn't the yard, though he knows she probably won't see it that way.

He has an e-mail from his father saying Kayla joined him in L.A. yesterday (earlier, on Facebook—where he finds out more about his dad than his dad actually tells him—Orly saw some pics of his dad and Kayla at a sushi bar in Venice Beach), but a few days from now they'll be back in Houston. He heard from Nina what happened to Mamá Meche and that Orly has been good about staying at the house and not wandering off on any more adventures. Assuming everything stays on schedule, which it has been so far, his father should be there for him in five days, Monday at the latest. When he gets there, if Orly wants, maybe they can go to the beach or fishing or both, some guy time. Alex e-mails that he heard about Orly's sick escape to Matamoros, says their dad never thought Orly had it in him to do something like that. Orly getting into trouble at the bridge is the only thing that got their dad off his case about being caught with his phone. This is the first chance he's had to use the campground computer (ten-minute limit!) to check his messages. Anyway, thanks for giving Eduardo something else to be mad about. Alex didn't think he had it in him either. Then Carson texts to say his stepmom figured out how to get them bumped up to first class. She and his dad were in the row ahead of him and this hot Asian stewardess kept serving him champagne—

[Seriously, dude, like she was trying to get me in the mile-high club.]

He sends a selfie of her squatting in the aisle next to him. They landed in Munich a few days ago and spent one afternoon knocking around a Nazi museum. Tomorrow they're taking the bullet train to Paris and having dinner at the Eiffel Tower.

[Au revoir, bitch.]

Other than clicking out his replies and the *swoosh* that follows when he hits Send, there's not much else happening in the backyard. The sun plays hide-and-seek behind billowy clouds. The parrots cross the river, unfurling their sovereign green flag east to west before dipping beyond the roof of the pink house. La Bronca stands up long enough to shake the dirt from her coat, turn her enormous head this way, and flop down in the cool dirt on her other side. The dust is still settling around her when the most mulish of the clouds begins to part and the sun opens up to the valley below.

Orly peels off the silicone case and rubs the back of his phone on his shorts until the silver gleams. It takes a while to figure out just the right angle, but soon enough he has the sunlight bouncing off his phone and across the backyard, toward the front door. The glare shines off the Apple logo and if he squints long enough, he can almost see the light sparkling off the padlock. He has to move to the left edge of the steps, dropping one leg into the grass to steady himself, so he can aim the tiny ray of light at the window that faces the blue house. Here it reflects across the aluminum foil, flickering off each tiny crevice of the silver surface. Then he waves his other hand in front of the phone and the beam sputters across the foil. A minute later, the clouds drift back and the beam is lost. And now he's just some kid sitting on the back steps twirling his phone for no particular reason. The early afternoon is humid in that way that makes him want to go lie down. He stands up to go back inside, but right then the clouds shift again and there's nothing but sunshine bearing down. Not only that, but across the yard the surface of the aluminum begins rippling until a few seconds later a rectangular window, about half the size of his iPhone, swings open. The opening is turned sideways and when he flashes the light in that direction the little porthole shuts. Then when he kills the light, the window opens. The problem is, he can't see anything more than a nose or maybe an eyeball. If it's an eyeball it makes sense why Daniel would close the tiny door anytime Orly flashes the beam of light in that direction. Seeing his nose in the opening, pressed up against the glass, would be way funnier, though. Orly holds on to the back doorframe and angles himself off the top step, but now he sees even less of the opening. He promised Nina not to step into the yard, but he's pretty sure what she meant was for him not to go to the other house, which he isn't planning to—he just wants to step a few feet into the yard to get a better angle and then he'll come right back to where he was. Three or four steps, five at the very most. Just to see Daniel's nose or eyeball, whatever it is he keeps putting in the tiny aluminum window. How's that going to hurt anything? But he barely takes his first step onto the grass when the dog comes back to life and starts barking her head off, and a second later he hears Nina's car pulling into the driveway.

* * *

Maybe because she feels a little guilty for being away the last two days, maybe it was all she had available, or maybe it was just time, but tonight Nina makes fideo. Orly helps by setting the table and serving their drinks, water from the dispenser for him, a Fresca in the can for her. She takes the fideo from Simmer to Off.

"But with one more plate, mijito," she says.

"For Tío Beto?"

"For Daniel. I was thinking about what you said, about him eating allá solito. For the time my mother is away from the house it won't matter if he comes to eat with us."

"Are you sure?"

"For now, yes." And before he can ask more questions, she's on the other side of the screen door, headed across the backyard.

A few minutes later she returns with Daniel, a new checkered button-down tucked into his shorts, his hair damp and combed to one side, but still barefoot.

She serves Orly first, then their guest, then herself, and sits closest to the stove in case she needs to get up. She asks Daniel if he would like to say the prayer and they bow their heads. He gives thanks for this food they have before them, for her kindness and a safe place to stay, and for the new friends he has made.

"Daniel had never eaten fideo before he came here," she says. "Like you."

"My mom tried to make it once from a cookbook," says Orly, "but it didn't turn out right and my dad had to bring food home from Carrabba's."

"And what is Carrabba's?" she says.

"It's a restaurant close to my dad's office." Then he turns to Daniel and says, "Restaurante italiano."

"Daniel wants to learn how to speak in English."

Daniel nods to this.

"Carrabba's is like when we go to Pizza Hut?" she says.

"Sort of, but fancier."

"Carrabba's," Daniel says. "Italian foods."

Orly gives him a thumbs-up.

Nina asks Daniel if he has ever tried pizza and he smiles, looks at her like she asked if he's ever tried something called water.

"Muchísimas veces." He raises his hand and flicks it back like too many times to even count. "El pepperoni, el chorizo, el queso."

Maybe she will bring it for them one of these nights for dinner, which gets a thumbs-up from both boys. So does saying they can play on Orly's computer while she cleans the kitchen. Later she will sit with Daniel to make the phone calls.

Orly brings his iPad to the kitchen table and scoots his chair next to Daniel's. Orly shows him the hedge maze he started designing this afternoon on *Minecraft*. Most of it is built, but he needs to add more 3-D blocks to his straight lines and right angles and dead ends, enough to make the hedges so high that no one would ever find their way out of the dizzying labyrinth. He asks Daniel if he wants to add the next layer.

"It's easy," he tells him. "Fácil."

Orly shows him how and then hands the iPad to him. Daniel uses his index finger to guide the crosshairs to the exact place on the screen where he needs to tap so he can set the next block of leaves, then find the next spot and tap again, one block of leaves after another, following the pattern that Orly already laid out.

After they finish the hedge maze, Orly asks Daniel what else he wants to do, but Daniel doesn't know what to say because he isn't sure what else you can do with an iPad and Orly isn't altogether sure how to explain it to him. So instead of explaining, he types into the search bar and a few seconds later clicks on the Google images that show them the port of Veracruz, the beach, the harbor, and the plaza in front of the cathedral. On the last day of class, Mr. Domínguez used the projector to share these and other images of waterfalls and mountains and said Veracruz was historically significant because it was where Cortés and his men first landed before conquering the Aztecs, which eventually led to Spain colonizing Mexico. He said he'd have a lot more to tell them next year when he had them again in seventh grade. If he could, Orly would repeat everything Mr. Domínguez had said to the class that morning, but instead he says the only thing there really is to say: "Veracruz."

Daniel nods slowly, not agreeing exactly and not disagreeing, but only asks, "¿Me permite?" And then in the search bar he taps out "Coatzacoalcos," a word Orly's never seen and at first doesn't think is even a word and is pretty sure he wouldn't be able to pronounce if he had to. But here are the images of another city. Here no one is on the beach, there are no resort hotels along the shore, the river that leads to the sea is dark brown and as still as glass, the suspension bridge reflected off its muddy surface, and the streets are narrower and clogged with red-and-white taxis and people on motorcycles and delivery trucks passing through a commercial district with people selling fruit and vegetables and newspapers and brooms and plastic shoes along the median of a long street. Orly shows Daniel how to get the street view and move forward. Here some of the homes are yellow, others orange, others lime green, some blue, a few pink, medium-sized and bigger, driveways, no driveways, all with security gates, and then later many more homes with no color to them, the tiny yards fenced in with upright sheets of corrugated metal. Then Daniel gets them back out of street view and clicks on other images of the city. Here they also find photos of two men who have been shot in the street and of workers in white hazmat suits carrying a body from a mass grave. The federales wear the same gear they wore in Matamoros, but here there are also photos of men in regular clothes wearing balaclavas and holding AK-47s who are not part of the federal police or military.

"Esto también es Veracruz," Daniel says. "Coatzacoalcos, Veracruz."

And then Orly understands that Veracruz is the name of both a city and a state, and there's probably a lot more that Mr. Domínguez hasn't told them yet.

"Coatzacoalcos, Veracruz."

Orly wants to repeat the name of Daniel's city back to him—try anyway—but he's afraid of mangling the word and sounding dumb, so instead he just nods. For a second Orly wonders if he should show him Houston, but he feels awkward, maybe even a little embarrassed, though he knows it's not his fault that the streets are usually clean and they have so many malls and museums, and when the cops show up it's usually only to direct traffic after the Thanksgiving parade or in Montrose or because it's rodeo season. He was just born there. It wasn't anything he chose.

But now Nina's done with the dishes and it's time for them to make some phone calls. Daniel goes to the kitchen cart where she keeps the microwave and from the top drawer pulls out the spiral notebook with the log of numbers they've already called. He has a new number he wants her to try tonight, just to see.

Orly sits next to his godmother, but she tells him she needs more room and waits until he scoots over to the end of the table before she starts. She and Daniel sit across from each other as he reads the first number to her and she dials. Daniel looks at her and she gazes at the ceiling, waiting for it to ring.

"Ocupado," she says and shakes her head.

"Beezy."

"Busy."

"Beezy."

"Busy."

"Beezy."

She raises her hand for him to stop. "Busy."

She writes the word out phonetically, then scratches this out and writes it again, this time in Spanish, and points with the pen to the second syllable.

"Busy."

"Busy," he repeats. "Busy phone."

"Eso."

He jots down "busy" next to the number and gives her another to dial. She barely raises the phone when she hears it ring once and gently hangs up but still with the receiver to her ear.

"No contestan," she says after about a minute

"Not home," Daniel says.

"Nobody home," she says back to him, worried that Orly might have seen her click the receiver too soon.

"Mijito, isn't it time for your bath?"

"I took a shower this morning."

"Bueno, entonces go brush your teeth."

"Already?"

"Look at the hour."

When Orly leaves, she asks Daniel for the next number, and it goes on like this for another twenty minutes. Busy, no answer, or no one by the name of Daniel Mendoza here. Toward the end they do reach someone with a similar name, but this one goes by Daniel Alberto Mendoza and he's only six years old and his mother wants to know why this woman is asking so many questions about him.

Then he remembers his father used to work part-time in a Chinese restaurant, washing dishes, but he never told him the name of the place and Daniel doesn't know if he still works there. Maybe they could call all of the Chinese restaurants around Chicago and ask for him. But she raises her hands and acts as though he's trying to hand her a stack of phone books with numbers to call. He obviously doesn't know how many chinos there are in the big cities and by extension how many restaurants for the people who like to eat their food.

"Muchísimos."

"Too many peoples."

She nods to this and he gives her the next number on the list. She smiles at him because smiling is better than letting him know that with every day that passes they seem further away from finding his father and a little closer to someone finding out she's hiding a young boy inside the little house.

24

The next day, Orly waits until she's down the street and past the car wash before setting the timer on his iPad for ten minutes, which he figures should be enough time to make sure she didn't forget something and decide to suddenly come back. Nina was planning to leave earlier for the hospital, but she couldn't find one of her mother's knit caps and before she knew it, it was close to noontime. She made him an early lunch and left the house while he was still eating his quesadillas.

He answers a few e-mails but keeps his replies vague about what he does during the day at Nina's house and instead talks more about what he wants to do when he's back in Houston. Nothing about Daniel hiding in the house behind him, locked inside all day with the windows covered in aluminum foil, or all the other people who used to be in there with him or how he slipped away from the motel and the cops, and nothing about how he found a way to get out of the house, which is the detail he most wants to tell his brother about but he can't really talk about it without saying the rest. A hole in the floor, which he likes to think of as more of a trapdoor, is the sort of thing you only see in movies. None of his friends' houses have trapdoors, not that he knows of, anyway. It's not one of those details people like to point out when showing off their houses. *Here's the media room, here's the library, here's the wine cellar, and oh, by the way, should you need*

it, here's the trapdoor. Our smugglers are away this weekend, so feel free
to come and go as you like.

Using the trapdoor is all he wants to do today. He thought he
had done something different and exciting when he crossed the
bridge, especially when he couldn't cross back, but when Daniel
told him how he got here, Orly's life felt boring all over again. He's
still a little freaked out about what might be lurking underneath
the pink house—and "lurking" really is the only way to describe
it. The crawl space is less than two feet high and looks murkier
around each foundation block. Cobwebs hanging from the crossbeams, rags that look like they were left behind by the last person
who crawled under there and was never seen again, a den where
a tlacuache could be waiting for him. It's almost enough to make
him stay inside and avoid it altogether.

He walks out the front door and then to the left side of the blue
house, far enough so La Bronca won't care that he's in the backyard, and then follows the chain-link fence until he reaches the
back side of the pink house. The place with the most clearance
to get under the house is the same spot where he pulled out the
boards that he smashed and tossed into the canal. He taps on his
flashlight app and holds the face of the iPhone flat at the opening
and the beam of light shines under the house practically through
to the other end, where between the various blocks, he can make
out the edge of the dog's rump.

The problem is there's no way for Orly to crawl on all fours,
hold the phone upright to guide him, and at the same time avoid
whatever might be down there, around this or that block, until he
finds the trapdoor. What he needs is a headlamp, which, unless he
tapes the iPhone to his forehead, there is no app for.

Daniel said the opening in the floor was on this side of the house, and so Orly drops onto his back and scoots forward until the top half of his body is under the house and he can shine the light on the underside, but he sees nothing that looks like an opening, just boards that make up the floor and other boards that hold up the floor and connect to the foundation blocks. For a second he imagines what would happen if he bumped one of the blocks and this made the house squash him flat and how it'd take them forever to raise the house again and find what was left of him. Then he feels a spider or a caterpillar, something hairy, crawling on his neck and he swats it away and scrambles in the opposite direction as fast as he can, which on his back is actually much harder and slower to do than going the other way.

Once he's inside the other house, he checks in the bathroom mirror to see if whatever it was crawling on him left a mark, but his skin is clear except for some dirt on his neck. Maybe he imagined it. Maybe he just needs to wait until Daniel comes out and can show him how to get to the trapdoor.

Orly opens his iPad, but he doesn't have any new messages, so he rereads some older ones, especially Alex's and the part where he says he and his dad didn't think Orly had it in him to go to Matamoros. It does seem kind of crazy now, crossing the bridge to another country. But it's the part about Orly not having it in him that stays with him. He knows this is the reason his father sent him down here, because he doesn't think Orly's tough enough to be the kind of boy he needs to be to someday grow into a man. But he is, he is, he is. His dad just doesn't know it.

Flat on his belly and pulling himself forward on his elbows and knees, Orly holds the iPhone in his mouth, folding his lips over his teeth so he isn't biting the screen or leaving spit on it. The house is low enough that he has to crawl on his stomach, keeping his head low so he isn't bumping it on the crossbeams. The light jiggles across the boards, never settling on any one spot, but he stops every foot or so to take the phone out of his mouth and shine it directly overhead, runs his hands over the boards, knocks to feel if there is a difference. On the opposite side from where he entered, La Bronca growls at the beam of light flitting about her domain. The chain keeps her from getting around the foundation block and doing anything more than poke her snout into the dark belly of the house. Once Orly is in a ways, the underside doesn't seem as dark as it did when he was thinking about all the reasons this was a bad idea. He knocks on the next board and suddenly the floor above his head creaks. He knocks again, harder, and this time hears a knock come from above the floor. He crawls another foot and knocks again, and then a second later a shallow light filters down, followed by Daniel's face hanging upside down through the trapdoor.

Orly isn't sure what he was expecting once he made it inside—he only had the trapdoor on his mind. But the space is both larger and smaller than he imagined. Larger because there's no furniture in the bedroom except a mattress on the floor and a small sofa in the living room. And smaller—tiny—when he imagines it crammed with people.

Daniel shows him the TV and tells him it has one hundred and thirty channels, he counted them, even shows him a few to prove it. He offers him some cold water from the pitcher in the refrigerator, but Orly tells him no, gracias. He pulls out his iPhone, but his inbox is empty and his battery has less than ten percent. He isn't interested in his e-mails; he just doesn't know what else to do. If they're not watching TV or drinking water from the pitcher there's not much to say, not much to ask about, not much of anything to do but stand around a dim room with someone he barely knows. Awkward moment, Orly thinks, which Daniel is probably also thinking, only in Spanish. But then a minute later Daniel says they should go outside, and he leads the way.

Once they get into the yard, they don't have a clue what to do now, either. All they know is they have two or three hours to themselves, without any grown-ups watching over them.

Orly grabs the soccer ball off the back steps, but Daniel spends the first few minutes watching the clouds, feeling the pulse of the sun on his face. He promises Orly they can do whatever he wants, but for now he just wants to be outside after being shut in all night and most of the morning. Except for the other day, when he came to the back door, this is the first time he has been out during the day.

"No hay felicidad completa," Daniel says, which is something la señora is always saying. That there is no complete happiness, that with each bit of happiness comes some sorrow. Last night she said it after mentioning how it was nice they could all eat together, but it was happening only because her mother had hurt herself and gone to the hospital. After he ran from the motel, he slept one night in the back of an old truck, lying flat under a tarp so no one would see him, and the second night in a ditch, where he worried that a snake or other animal might get him. All he wanted was to be inside somewhere, quiet and safe, and now that's all he has, being inside, quiet and safe, all day and all night, nothing more.

"Vivo en una jaula rosada," he says. He lives in a pink cage.

Orly's not sure what he's supposed to say to this, if there's even anything to say, but then a few seconds later Daniel smiles his toothy grin and pops the soccer ball out of Orly's hands and once it's on the ground he dribbles it, barefoot, with a series of fleet kicks to the middle of the yard, blocking his defender from taking it back. They take turns trying to score on each other, a pair of trash cans standing in as goalposts, the broad side of the blue house as the backstop.

The score is only 4–2 in Daniel's favor, but each time he scores he looks up to the sky and drops to his knees, his arms spread wide like he just made the winning goal in the World Cup. Then he stands up and bows to the imaginary crowd in each direction. So annoying.

Orly says he needs water, so they go inside the blue house. He serves them each a cup from the dispenser. He downs his in two gulps and serves himself another. Daniel takes a sip and stops to look at the water, which tastes nothing like what comes from the tap in the other house.

"Qué padre," he says and sniffs the water before taking another sip.

"La agua es fresca," Orly tells him.

Daniel nods. It's actually supposed to be "el agua," even with the feminine noun, but he lets it slide. He gets what Orly was trying to say.

After they finish off the leftover fideo, Orly says he wants to show Daniel something. Then he pulls out the family album and they sit on the sofa as he turns the pages. Instead of giving Daniel a long, involved story for each image, Orly keeps it simple, telling him who's a tía, who's an abuela, who's a prima, and so on, even if some he doesn't remember exactly how they're related. When Orly turns to his parents' wedding, Daniel points to the photo.

"Tu mamá," he says, and now it's clear that Nina showed him the album.

Orly nods.

"Qué triste," Daniel says.

It *is* sad, Orly thinks, more than sad and more than he has words to explain, and even if he did have the words he probably wouldn't be able to say them all without losing it, crying like some baby right in front of him. So he leaves it at "triste."

Just then his phone dings and it's a text and an attached pic of Carson at the Eiffel Tower.

[Guess where I'm@?]

"¿Un mensaje?" Daniel asks, but Orly says it's nada and swipes the screen to clear it.

He's putting the album back in the closet when he spots the corner of an oversized envelope sticking out from under two large quilts. It's supposed to be stowed away, hidden far back where no one will find it, or if they do, not care what's inside. But that plan didn't take into account two young boys with nothing but time on their hands. The envelope is manila, with the address lines left blank and the inside bubble-wrapped to protect the images.

These are all from long before he was born and she became his Nina. Younger than she is in the few photos of her in the other album, a lot younger even than his mom or any of her bridesmaids. Her hair is dark, long, and straight, past the middle of her back, and in one of the photos she's smiling like he's never seen her smile. So much so that he finds himself smiling at the photo, the same way he can't help but yawn when he sees someone else yawn. Daniel is smiling too. "Bonita," he says. "Muy bonita," Orly agrees. Here she's at homecoming, a sash across her chest, her date in his football uniform, one hand holding his helmet, the other wrapped around her waist.

"¿El novio?"

Orly shrugs. It's hard to imagine his godmother calling anyone her boyfriend. Over here she's sitting at the edge of the pool wearing a black one-piece bathing suit, laughing and gesturing at whoever's holding the camera to take the picture already. There she is riding on a float with her hair in a bun and wearing an embroidered dress, waving to the little boys and girls along the parade route. Here she's with two teenage girls washing a car in someone's driveway, jeans rolled up over meaty calves, shirttails knotted at the midriff, one of the girls spraying the others with a bouquet of water. On the opposite page she's in a graduation gown with three of her friends. And in another one she's in front of a water fountain next to the same boy from the homecoming photo, only now a little older and in a sailor's uniform. And then it ends. Not at the end of the album but a full six pages early, it just drops off. Thirty or forty photos in all, most in black and white, with only the last few images in color before the pages go blank. Like they ran out of film or she was called away before there was time for the rest of her life to happen.

They still have most of the afternoon left. Orly says they should go somewhere.

"Vamos." He motions toward the driveway.

"¿Adónde?" Daniel says, but without moving.

"Para la raspas!" He has enough money for both of them. The little trailer is around the corner, just a little ways from the car wash. They can walk there in no time. "Cinco minutos." He points in the general direction, makes his middle and forefinger into little walking legs to show him how easy.

"¿Tu madrina?"

"A las cinco," Orly says and checks his phone. They have at least an hour until she comes home. He moves toward the gate.

"¿Y la pinche migra?" The other boy takes half a step back, shaking his head.

"No migra, muy rápido." He moves his two fingers even faster like they're on a moving sidewalk.

But Daniel's not buying it. Stuck inside for almost four weeks and then to be caught because they went walking down the street in the middle of the afternoon, to buy raspas. Nomás no. He shakes his head again.

Orly could go for the raspas himself, but it's hot enough that the ice will start melting and the syrup will run down his arm before he makes it back. It feels like it got hotter just mentioning the raspas, and now any bit of relief depends on their going to the trailer.

They sit on the back steps. A flock of parrots glides off in the distance, rising higher and higher before veering beyond their view. Two boys should be able to leave the house to get snow cones on a blazing summer afternoon. Even if his godmother found out and got crazy mad, especially at him for coming up with the whole idea, for leaving a second time, for promising her not to but doing it anyway, even then they should be able to go. She just wants to control his life because she's doing something she's not supposed to and because of that he can't do anything. Like it's his fault, like he started any of it. Isn't summertime when you're supposed to do all the things you can't really do the rest of the year? His dad still traveling with his girlfriend, Alex barely off probation, Carson in Paris, probably drinking more champagne, and he can't even walk down the street in the middle of the afternoon for a raspa.

Another group of parrots swoops across the length of the yard before reversing course and veering south, their squawking seeming louder the farther they get. One bird peels off from the rest and dips somewhere beyond the pink house and the back gate. He waits for it to come back into view and when it doesn't he says, almost in a whisper, "The canal."

"¿El canal?"

"El canal."

And now Daniel nods.

"El pinche canal," Orly says and smiles, even lets out a little laugh, because all along there it was right in front of them.

Orly has on his sneakers, but at the last second he flips them off and goes barefoot too. The distance to the raspa trailer turns out to be shorter if you follow the canal, but the trail itself is cut off in places with backyard fences that force the boys to drop down and walk along the edge of the water or wade across so they can follow the trail on the other side. Because it hasn't rained as much as usual this summer, the water reaches only to their knees. Still, it's slimy and feels like they're wading through oil, the goopy mud squishing between their toes, until they climb the bank on the other side. The dirt path is steep and hard to get up, but then they figure out the path is for going down to the water and the concrete embankment for reaching the overpass.

From the guardrail, it's another sixty feet to the yellow trailer. The lot is empty except for a truck parked outside the dollar store. Still, Daniel isn't sure it's worth the risk and asks Orly to just bring the raspas so they can eat them down here, where no one will see him walking around. But after coming this far, Orly shakes his head.

"¿Estás seguro?" Daniel asks, still inside the guardrail.

Orly turns in every direction, even steps onto the bridge, to make sure it's safe. Then he waves him over and they both make a run for it.

With the afternoon sun bearing down on the asphalt it feels like they're scurrying across the comal where Nina makes the tortillas. They rush all the way to the trailer and the narrow strip of shade created by the overhang, near the window where they order.

Daniel asks for the tamarindo flavor and Orly gets the leche his great-grandmother had last time. They take a taste of each other's and decide they made the right choices. Daniel's tongue is a brownish yellow, Orly's rose-colored, a few shades off from the house behind his godmother's house.

They've eaten only the top part of their raspas when a white Suburban with a green stripe pulls up to the curb and idles there in the bright sun.

Daniel notices the agent first and takes a deep breath and holds it. He and Orly look each other in the eyes for a moment, neither uttering a sound, each letting his gaze drift over the other's shoulder, ready to drop their raspas and take off en chinga when it's time. They could run in the same direction or split up, so at least one of them has a chance to get away. If Daniel gets caught, it's over, end of the summer, end of their big afternoon adventure, end of trying to contact his father. If Orly gets caught, they call his Nina for the second time in a week. If he gets caught, they ask why he ran, they ask who the other boy was who ran in the other direction, they ask how he knows him, they ask where he lives.

But instead of either of them running, Orly half turns and waves hi, same as his dad when they first got to town. This agent isn't reacting, though, and only keeps staring in this direction. Then Orly nudges Daniel and when he waves the agent finally eases off, which is when the two boys get back to breathing.

The traffic is heavier on the overpass when they head down to the canal. Daniel leads the way this time, crisscrossing the water more than they had earlier. Orly doesn't know what he'll tell his godmother when she asks how he spent his afternoon, how much he'll have to lie or if he can get away with saying he just hung out, reading and playing on his iPad, and let her think he was doing what she hoped he was doing. If not telling her he went for raspas with the boy is the same or worse than her lying about hiding him.

When they're close to the house, Daniel reaches out his sticky hand to help Orly up the slope. Orly is lowering the clasp on the back gate when his tío's van pulls into the driveway and both boys hit the ground and steal across the grass and then under the edge of the house. They've barely crossed into the dark before Daniel gets to the faint shaft of light from above.

"Aquí está," he says, and up they go.

Beto pulls in as far as he can and then grabs the bag of pan dulce sitting next to him on the passenger seat. The sweet bread is still a little warm and he cradles the bag in his forearm as if he were carrying a newborn.

The boys take turns peeking through the tiny porthole in the foil. On the way back, Orly felt like he had to pee and didn't know if he could make it all the way to the house. He even considered doing it in the canal, but now he feels like he couldn't do it if he had to.

Beto walks around to the back and knocks on the screen door. The dog is barking at him, lurching against the chain, choking on its rage. When he sees the security door is unlocked, he knocks one more time, calls out "Hello," and lets himself in.

"La puerta," Daniel says, as though Orly needs reminding that he should've locked it before they left the house. A few minutes pass before his tío walks down the back steps.

"¿Qué está haciendo?"

"Nada," Orly says, because his tío is just gazing in this direction as if he suddenly notices something different about the little house.

Beto sets the bag on the back steps and walks to his van. One of these days he needs to organize his equipment so the pumps go where the pumps are supposed to go and the toolbox shuts all the way. It's been over a year since he cleaned up back here, and even then it was only to make sure the pumps and bait stations weren't anywhere that his boys' little hands could reach if they happened to open the panel doors. It worries him that they might be messing around with the chemicals inside there and get hurt, and so he hides the van keys when he gets home, sometimes so good that even he can't find them. He pulls out the spare tire and the jack, and places them on the driveway. Finally, beneath all this, he finds his crowbar and stuffs everything back where it was.

After he picks up the white bag, the boys can't see him anymore from the side window and have to move to the front door. Sitting on the floor, their backs against the door, they feel the house shake each time the dog rises up and the chain jolts against the foundation block.

"Ya está bueno, bow-wow," Beto says to the dog. "Why you have to always be so mad? Mira, I brought you a little present." He drops the crowbar in the grass and holds the paper bag open just out of reach of the dog but close enough to make it bark louder when it catches a whiff of the pan dulce.

"Ya ves, I'm your friend, bringing you a little snack. What do you like more, las empanadas o las donas? You look like an empanada doggie to me." He takes the glazed donut for himself, clutching it between his teeth, and flings the empanada into the grass. The dog half sniffs it before scarfing it down.

"No que no, doggie. Now you and me, we're talking the same language."

He finishes the last of his donut and La Bronca is whining for more, wagging the knot of matted fur that makes up her tail.

"How about a concha?" he says, looking into the bag. "Let's see, I got a chocolate one and another with the yellow flavor." La Bronca is sitting on her haunches, waiting while he digs into the bag and lifts one piece of the shell-shaped bread and then the other. "Better make it the yellow one. Everybody knows doggies aren't supposed to be eating chocolate conchas."

This one he tosses just behind the animal so she has to turn to get to it and all the yellow flakes that fall into the grass. Then he picks up the steel bar and high-steps it to the door.

He places the bag of pan dulce to one side but holds on to the crowbar, in case he needs some protection. First he pounds on the door with the plump side of his fist, hard enough that Orly can feel it against the back of his head and through the rest of his body. Daniel inches away, first scooting, then turning around and crab-walking as he keeps his eye on the front door. His arms are shaking so much that he has trouble not tipping over to one side.

A few seconds pass before Beto pounds on the door several more times and leans in to listen for any movement inside the house. Then again. Still nothing.

His first whack with the crowbar misses the padlock and leaves a dimple on the doorframe. His second one connects with the base of the lock but only makes it rattle in place. His next try hits the shackle, sending the lock jangling side to side. And then again and again and again and again and again and again, the whole house shuddering now, till he feels the steel bar pulsing through his hands and arms and finally has to sit on the steps to catch his breath.

The dog starts barking again, and so Beto tosses it a square piece of pink cake, the colored sprinkles popping off the frosting as soon as it tumbles into the dirt. The dog is still sniffing out the crumbs in the grass when Beto slips the forked end of the crowbar into the shackle of the padlock and leans on it with his entire weight until the whole lock busts apart and a second later the hasp splinters from the doorframe, leaving only the dead bolt in place. The noise is so jarring that he doesn't hear his name. It doesn't help that the dog has given up on the crumbs and is back to barking.

"Tío Beto?"

He turns to find Orly standing at the bottom of the steps, waving to him. His shirt is smeared with dirt; he's holding a soccer ball under his right arm.

Beto begins to wave back but stops to switch the crowbar to his other hand.

"I came to bring you pan dulce." He motions to the bag with his chin. "I knocked a bunch of times on the other door y nada, couldn't find you nowhere."

"I was in the back."

"This is the back, we're in the backyard now."

"Behind the backyard," he says. "I kicked my ball too hard and it fell into the canal."

"In the water?"

"It started floating away, so I had to run after it. I dried it off, there in the grass."

"You weren't inside because you were chasing a ball, barefoot, that's what you're telling me?"

"Yeah, behind the pink house. I took off my shoes before I got in the water."

Beto glances back at the house as if he needs to verify the color, and then turns back to the boy. "Yes, sir."

Orly nods. "Yes, sir."

Beto shakes his head, wondering who the kid thinks he's fooling. He's ready to get it out of him, make him explain himself, but right then the gate opens.

His sister stands just inside the yard, tilting her head to one side, unsure that she's seeing what she thinks she's seeing. It takes her a moment to make her way across the yard. Orly steps aside and the dog's barking drops down to a menacing growl.

"And you," she says to Beto, "what gives you the right?"

"Ya, it was time."

Without taking her eyes off her brother or the busted lock, she sends Orly to wait for her inside the other house. She stays at the base of the steps, staring at her brother, the leather strap of her purse tight around her fist.

"Time for what, Beto?"

He looks for someplace to set down the crowbar and instead hooks it on his belt, where it sways against his right leg. "Don't be playing all pendeja like you don't know. Mom told me, she said she was hearing the voices again. She even told me the boy had tried to run away."

"¿Y le créiste, una viejita ninety-four years old que they have on so many medicines? The one who wakes up in the middle of the night and says she needs to go milk the cows? The first night they had to tie her hands to the bed rails because she kept pulling the wires and tubes from her arms and chest, that one you believed and not your sister?"

"That's our mother you're talking about."

"You think I don't know who she is? I live with her, for the last eight years, or you forgot? I'm the one who feeds her and changes her when she has accidents in the bed. Me, not you, I'm the one that's been at the hospital almost all day, every day, and even sometimes at night when you leave after you said you were going to stay. I know who she is."

"And because of that you think you can hide a bunch of mojados behind her house. Did you think I wasn't going to keep coming around until I got in?"

"Ya con tus mojados, I told you no more, that what you saw was the last time I let them stay."

He glances back at the locked door. The dog has retreated to her usual spot under the house.

"If you're not keeping twenty or thirty of them in there, then unlock the door. Let me in if you really got nothing to hide."

"And if I do open it, then what? You'll leave me alone, let me figure out my problems on my own?"

"You want me to promise that I'll let you keep twenty or thirty mojados in here and with my mother in the other house?"

"If I have what you think I have, then you can do whatever you want, call the police, take Mom to the nursing home. But if not, you leave me alone."

"Open it."

"Promise me, Beto."

"Open it or I'll just call right now and it'll be over." He pulls the phone from the leather pouch on his hip and taps on the screen to show her how fast he can make it happen.

She doesn't know what she was thinking, that it wouldn't end like this or worse. She wants to tell Beto about the young boy and why she's been trying to help him find his father. If he wasn't lost and alone and hungry she wouldn't have let him stay. What's so hard to understand about that? She wants to believe that ignoring Beto will make him give up, but she realizes, as she should have the first time, that her brother isn't going anywhere. She can make up a lie, some story to buy herself some time, but in another day or two they'll be standing in this same spot, and with the boy crouched and terrified on the other side of the door. Maybe it is better if they take him, return him to Mexico, to the mother who from one day to the next lost her child.

Nina reaches around him and unlocks the dead bolt. "Then see for yourself," she tells him. "If you're so worried about what I've been hiding."

Beto uses the hook end of the crowbar to nudge the door open the rest of the way. The sunlight pouring in the front door is the only light in the room. He stumbles around looking for a lamp and finally yanks on the pull chain near the kitchen window. In the sink, a couple of bloated Froot Loops drift in a bowl of watery milk. The rest of the dishes are stacked neatly in the dish rack.

"Looks like somebody was here," he says.

"Maybe they were" is all she offers him in response.

"Are you saying the maid was staying in here, because it smells like someone was cleaning."

He opens the refrigerator and finds the leftovers she brought over the other night. The quart of milk is almost empty, the expiration date still a week away.

"She doesn't eat very much, does she?"

But Nina is distracted, glancing around the house to where the boy could be hiding—in the shower, under the kitchen sink, in the bedroom closet—and wondering how long it'll take her brother to discover him. She wonders if Beto will run him off or call the police or immigration to come take him.

"And the doors?" he asks when he notices the knobs are missing.

"I'm replacing them," she answers. "That, and now the door-frame."

"Only because you forced me to, that's the only reason. If you could, you would blame everything on me. Make it my fault you had to come back to take care of Mom, my fault you had to sell your little house. Everything my fault, like the family was keeping you from having your own life, like you never had your chance."

She lets him go on mumbling to himself; she's heard it all before. He glances into the bathroom and makes his way to the bedroom, where he finds an old mattress flopped over on itself. The light is brighter here than it was in the living room. Nina follows him into the room only as far as the closet, the one place he hasn't looked yet. It seems ridiculous to her now, allowing him in the house so he can prove he was right. She almost wants to do it herself, say, Here, right here's what you're looking for, and get it over with. But her brother walks past the closet and goes straight for the pile of clothes folded neatly on the floor by the far window.

Using the fork of the crowbar, Beto flicks aside the shirt and shorts, even the baseball cap, and finds a pair of tennies worn down along the heels and the outer edges. Then he steps closer and puts his work boot next to one of the tennies, close enough to see that it's much smaller than his own and closer in size to what his boys wear. And for the briefest moment he imagines Rudy and Roberto Jr. wearing these shoes, and not the two or three pairs they own because their mother keeps buying them more than they need. And once he lets himself imagine Rudy and Roberto Jr. wearing the tennies it isn't so difficult for him to imagine how crazed with worry he would be if his little boys were hiding in some place like this.

But a few seconds later he's angry at his sister for causing all of this, for making him feel things he doesn't understand or want to understand.

"What kind of trouble did you bring to my mother's house?"

"Let me explain, Beto."

"Move," he says when she stands in front of the closet door.

"You don't have to do this."

"Move." And this time he nudges her aside. He yanks open the closet door and sees exactly what he's supposed to see—nothing but dark space, a void with no past, present, or future. He lets go and the door swings closed.

"I don't want to hear it, Tencha," he says, using her real name because he wants her to snap out of it, whatever dream she's been having. "No more with your excuses. However you do it, all I know is that this, what you have going on here, it needs to be gone by the time Mom comes back home next week. I didn't cause problems before only because you said it was over and then after that I didn't have the proof. But now I do."

"It's not that easy."

"Easy or hard, it's not our problem," he says. "Fix it for good or

I will." He stares at her a few seconds, so she knows he's serious this time, and goes out the front door, stopping only to grab his half-empty bag of pan dulce.

After her brother pulls out of the driveway, Nina goes back to the other house to find Orly. He tells her everything but leaves out the part about going to get raspas without her permission. He explains about the trapdoor and how Daniel found it when he was sweeping inside the closet, that he didn't make the hole, only used it a couple of times, but was afraid to tell her because she might be upset. She unlocks the door and makes him show her where.

"Here," he says, pulling out the plywood cover from the closet floor. She can barely make out the edges of the hole where the laminate was cut into with something jagged and the floor was stomped on until it gave way and fell into the moist dirt beneath them. It's not really her house, but the damage to it angers her more than anything else El Kobe and Rigo did while they were here, more than her brother breaking the lock on the door. It feels like each of them has taken something from her that can't be replaced or made to look and feel right again, like it was before. Even in the dark corner of a bedroom where no one can see it.

"He wanted to feel the sun again."

"He could have asked me."

"He thought you would say no."

She grows quiet, wondering if it's worth arguing about.

"And what else?"

"That's all."

"Are you sure?"

"He called it his cage, he said that now he lived in a pink cage."

Orly looks toward the front and then down at the hole in the floor, anywhere but his godmother's face. She wonders how many more ways there may be to remind her that she did something wrong.

"But to where, mijito? To where was he going after you saw him leave the yard? You need to tell me. Something bad could happen to him."

She holds his chin so he'll look her in the eye and know how serious this is.

"I tried to ask him, but he just ran away without telling me where he was going. I was afraid Tío Beto was going to hear me calling him to come back."

She notices the blush of his tongue and knows that he and the boy must have gone for raspas. At first she wants to get mad that he was trying to fool her, this after the bridge. But when he lowers his head she lets him stay this way and walks back to the other house. She needs to go lie down, rest from dealing with her brother, from hiding so many parts of her life, from what to do next.

25

It's all true, what Orly told her. How could it not be? Close to five weeks of living inside the little house with no hopes of where it might lead to or if it would lead to anywhere other than someone coming to break down the door and drag him away. All this was true. She knew it before she heard it. She had her own cage. Stuck inside and not able to leave for days at a time unless it was to take her mother to one specialist or another, to stop by the Walgreens for more medicines, more bandages for her scrapes, more bottles of Ensure, more overnight protectors for the bed. But at least in her case she wouldn't have minded if years ago someone had broken down the door and dragged her away from this.

She lies on her bed and closes her eyes, meaning to sleep if she can, but there's a tap on her door.

"¿Qué fue?"

Orly cracks open the door. "Are you okay?"

"Just resting."

He's never seen his godmother curled up in bed, especially not during the middle of the day, and he doesn't know what to do now, wishes he hadn't knocked.

"Come here, mijito." She moves over to make room for him, but he stays put.

At home, he wasn't supposed to go near the bed when his mom

was resting. Sometimes he couldn't help it and went to her any-way, but it always felt like she was on her bed floating so high above him, beyond the roof and trees, up in the clouds, and there he was on the ground connected to her with only a frayed rope he had to cling to so she wouldn't slip away.

"Please." Nina holds out her hand to him.

He sits on the edge of the bed and she takes his hand in hers. They watch the fan oscillating from one corner of the room to the other, as if the next gust of air will bring some change to their situation.

"Sometimes grown-ups, people who should know better, they make mistakes. More than we like to say. We think we are doing good, but it turns out bad in the end."

"It's because Tío Beto had to come ruin everything."

"He should not have broken the lock, but I was already doing wrong."

"You were just trying to help Daniel so he could find his father."

For a second she looks as sad as his mother did sometimes, but Nina does it without turning away from him and instead looks him clearly in the eyes. She wants him to see her, all there is she can show him, all there ever was, the tears in her eyes, the quiver in her lower lip, the sorrow and regret on her face, and know that she needs him to stay and hold on to her hand.

"At first I hated that he was here, that he came back and made me have to decide what to do with him. I would open the door in the morning and wish that I had been dreaming the day before and the day before that, wish that I hadn't let him hide here. Who would do such a thing? Open the door to let trouble into their house? It was different than before, because now nobody had said he would leave on such and such date. Each night we were hav-ing no luck calling. I began to lose hope, more than even he was, and when people get that way, desperate like there is no other way, they begin to tell themselves stories just to get to the next day. And the ones who are really desperate begin to believe these stories. I was afraid of who might be out there that I was sending him to, if it turned out not to be his daddy. I told myself that if we couldn't find him then it was better that Daniel stayed with me, that he would be happy and safe here, if I was his family. Here, he would have food and a school to go to and I would never leave him behind. I would buy him clothes for school and the room where you sleep could be his."

She looks up at Orly's face for some proof that she is making sense.

"If he stayed, he would see it was better. I told myself I had to find a way of making him stay. So I began to not call the numbers he told me. I pretended to call when really I was not pushing all the numbers and then I would say it was not ringing. That the number was no good. I would tell him there was no sound and he would go to the next number. One or two numbers I would dial all the way and then the next two I would only pretend to call."

"But you still wanted to help him."

"That was the first story, but there was another story I knew but didn't want to believe, because it was more true. That I was not doing it for him, but for me. Because I wanted him here with me and didn't want him to leave and for me to be alone again."

Now he's the one who looks at her for some proof she means what she's saying, searching for her face in the fleeting shadows.

"Being older doesn't mean you stop making mistakes, it only means your mistakes can hurt more people."

26

There under the bridge for two hours, maybe three, maybe longer—enough for the voices of people waiting in line at the raspa stand to grow faint. Daniel knows it is late because the sun has gone down and earlier there was more traffic passing above him, the rhythmic thumping of tires rolling over one crack and then another before reaching the smooth pavement, city buses going to and from town, fathers and mothers heading home for dinner. He imagines one of those sets of tires must belong to la migra they saw earlier when they were buying the raspas. Daniel still can't believe he and Orly waved. ¡Qué locura! He imagines the agent driving back and forth, trying to spot the boy from earlier who looked like he didn't belong. If he hadn't been with la señora's godson, who looked like he could belong anywhere, it might have ended there and not here, however it'll turn out in the end. If he concentrates and listens to nothing else, he believes he can tell if it's a car or a truck or a green-and-white Suburban passing overhead, if the vehicle is moving closer to the raspa stand or away from it.

The trunk they had stuffed him into was darker, but the trunk also felt safer. He could have died in the trunk if the ride had lasted much longer and they kept inhaling the fumes, but at least then he knew how it would happen and after a while he wouldn't feel anything and just go to sleep. Under the bridge the list of bad things seems endless. Maybe it's worse for there to be some light and be able to see around, imagine all the ways it might happen. Earlier he found a syringe in the grass, near where the embankment connects to the underside of the bridge. At the very top, crammed into a crevice above one of the cement blocks buttressing the bridge, there's a T-shirt stiff as a ruler from dried spray paint. He hasn't crossed to the opposite side because he saw something zigzagging in the waist-high grass and thought it might be a stray dog or a snake.

He sits in the middle, equal distance from either side of the bridge, so he has a chance to run one way or the other depending on which direction they come after him. He doesn't know what he'll do if they come from both sides at the same time. His hands are filthy from scrambling through the dirt when they were still sticky from the raspa and he wishes he had stopped to wash them in the bathroom, that having clean hands would somehow make a difference in his getting away. Dipping them in the canal only made them feel grimier. He wants to go back and, if la señora's brother has left, sneak inside the house to wash his hands and face, to change out of the clothes she bought him and put on the ones he came here with. Then he would leave again and know things would turn out okay.

He doesn't know why he didn't just stay in the motel. He wonders what story he would be telling now. Yesterday on ¡Despierta América!, during the news portion of the program, they showed a house where la migra had found forty people being hidden in a garage with no water, no toilet, nothing but forty bodies sitting or squatting across the floor. This morning he kept turning between Univision and Telemundo to see what happened next, if they were locked up or sent back to their home countries, but there was no mention of it, as if it didn't happen or it happens so often that it isn't worth mentioning more than once and then moving on to the next story.

If he had stayed in the motel, by now he would've been back in Veracruz and his father would have found a better way to bring him or he would have stayed with his mother and little sister. Here he can't go back and he can't go be with his father. If he had known the choice was between being sent back home and waiting, for what he doesn't feel like he knows anymore, he might not have run. He was stupid to come again

to la señora's house, to stay locked in her little house, night after night
calling numbers for nothing.

He'll wait along the canal and just before it gets dark crawl back
inside the pink house and take whatever food and water he can carry
with him. He wants his family to be together, but maybe together is no
longer possible and he has to choose between one and the other, between
what he can and can't reach the easiest. He doesn't know which way he'll
go, if north or south. All he knows is that here is not there.

Nina finds him just as he opens the back gate and is about to slip
under the little house. She hadn't been sure if she would see him
again. There's no shortage of things they can talk about, but she
tells him only that after dinner they will call to see if they can
locate his father.

"Ya no," Daniel says, shaking off the idea. "I need to go."

"But leave to where, mijito?" she says, surprised that she called
him something she reserved for her godson. He shrugs, but looks
up when he hears the tenderness in her voice.

"Listen to me," she says and kneels before him to keep his attention. "You can't lose your faith. You can be tired, you can be afraid,
you can miss your family, but if you keep hold of your faith, then
everything is going to be okay."

"I had faith, like you told me," he says to her face, "and nothing
happened."

It takes her a moment to realize he's crying. And she does
something then she hasn't done before—she touches him. For
the last month there hasn't been as much as a handshake or a pat
on the back or a tousle of his shaggy hair. At first she means to
only rub his shoulder, let him know it's going to be okay. But her
touch, instead of soothing him, only brings more tears that turn
to sobs and now she's hugging him not just to calm him but also

to keep him from falling there in the dirt. Minutes pass this way, with nothing but his crying softly in her arms as she rubs his back in big circles and later tiny and tinier circles until he's better and can look at her.

"Mijito, our faith does not run out because things don't turn out the way we want, when we want. You think your mama or your daddy has given up that they will see you again? No, every night they go to sleep thinking of you, every morning they wake up thinking of you. It doesn't matter the distance or how difficult it becomes, whatever stands in our way our faith only gets deeper. In there," she says and taps him on the chest. "Remember, in there no one can take it from you."

27

She buys pizza because this is one of their last nights all together. She doesn't need to tell them things will be changing soon. Orly's father will be here in four days, and today wasn't the last time her brother will come around.

She serves herself one slice of the pepperoni and another of the sausage and leaves the rest for the boys, both of them eating like she hasn't fed them in a week.

"Bien rica la pizza," Daniel says. "Delicious."

"Muy rica," Orly agrees.

She's glad she bought a kind they both like, but reminds them to not be talking with their mouths full.

After dinner Orly takes the pizza box out to the trash can and washes the dishes. Daniel brings out his notebook with all the numbers they've called these last five weeks. The numbers are marked with an X for a wrong number, a question mark for no answer, and a line crossing it out if it was a non-working number. Tonight she wants to try the ones where no one answered, some of which they've called more than once. Maybe they were on the other line and couldn't answer. Maybe they were working and now their hours have changed.

"¿En serio?" Daniel says and looks at her as if she just told him they should throw away the notebook and start all over again.

It's worth a try, she tells him. She tells Orly he has better eyes than she does and maybe he should sit closer to make sure she's dialing the right number. He smiles and pulls his chair up next to her, then nods when he's ready.

She dials the area code and then asks for the prefix and finally the last four digits. It takes longer because she mumbles each number back to herself like she's playing bingo.

Just as he thought, the first five numbers are still not working and the next four keep ringing and ringing. She ignores Daniel rolling his eyes, a bad habit he must have picked up from Orly, and goes on to the next number. If the number is working, she lets it ring at least fifteen times before she hangs up. Daniel's job is to keep his index finger on the number until it's time for him to lower his finger to the next one. When someone does happen to answer, he holds the pen ready to mark another X across the listing.

"Bueno, ¿puedo hablar con el señor Daniel Mendoza?"

From there she asks her usual questions of where he is from and if he has a young son traveling to meet him. Even when he's not named Daniel Mendoza these calls always go on longer than necessary, with her asking the person if he knows anyone else who goes by that name, a father who might be missing a son, who was traveling to be with him but never showed up and hasn't contacted him to say what happened. Then she spends another minute apologizing for the bother of her phone call, explaining she's just trying to help the young boy and his father.

If she let him make the calls, Daniel knows he would be done with the first or second question, maybe even hang up right then without the disculpe or gracias. First of all, he would recognize his father's voice and his father would recognize his and call him Chivito, as he has since he was a little baby. He told her this the first night they dialed the numbers, but she made it sound like it could be dangerous if he were the one calling and a stranger answered, like no strangers were to be trusted in this country because any one of them could report a boy calling from this number, from this house, and then who would be the one in trouble. It was her phone after all, not his. His phone he left back in the motel and now can't remember any more than the first four or five digits of his father's number. And then what more was there to say? He didn't leave it on purpose.

He listens to her talking to the latest Daniel Mendoza, her voice rising with each pointless question. Until they started calling, he never realized how common a name he and his father shared. He scans his notebook to find the next number, but when he looks back, she's staring at him, not saying anything, the phone pressed up against her chest, her expression changed like something bad has happened. For a moment, he imagines the call is being traced back to this number and it will be only a matter of time before someone comes pounding on the door to drag both of them away.

"Busy number?" he says.

She shakes her head and her eyes begin to water. A single tear runs the length of her face but without her wiping it away. She looks at him as though it's the first time he has been in her kitchen and she's trying to memorize his face.

"Tu daddy." She holds the phone out to him, her hand quivering before him. "Ándale, habla con él."

He looks at her, then at Orly, who smiles and then motions for him to put the phone to his ear.

"¿Estás segura?" he asks.

As sure as she can be, she tells him. His full name is Daniel Mendoza Gutiérrez, like he said his father went by. De Veracruz and now in Chicago. She pauses like maybe it was a mistake, another wrong number or she misheard the person who answered, and they should move on to the next one. But then she says the man has been waiting almost a month for this call. That no one answers the cell number he has been calling. Ándale, she says again to the boy. He takes the phone and looks down at the receiver in the palm of his hand.

"¿Chivito," he hears a voice call out to him, "eres tú?"

28

There are still details to arrange. Los arreglos. After they hang up, his father calls a man who knows a man who puts him in contact with a woman down here taking a load in the next three or four days, maybe sooner. It depends. She specializes in arranging transport for children, the boy will be taken care of. Money will need to be wired. Once it arrives, they will receive a call notifying them of when the boy will be picked up. The father can expect him two or three days later.

But all that is for tomorrow and the days to follow. Tonight, since her brother busted the padlock, Nina says there's no point in Daniel sleeping in the other house. Even with the dead bolt that still works, it feels less safe to her. At first, she makes a bed for him on the sofa, but then Orly asks if they can sleep on the floor, the way he and Alex do when they come with their father. Like a sleepover. Daniel has never been to a sleepover, but he likes the idea of not being alone in the other house.

She spreads a pair of quilts on the floor and brings out more sheets, blankets, another pillow, and two glasses of water. Then she dims the lights and gets down on the floor to bless her godson. She thanks God for keeping these two boys safe today and for allowing them all another night together. She ends, as always, by making the sign of the cross, en el nombre del Padre, y del Hijo, y del Espíritu Santo, Amén and giving him a kiss on his cheek.

"¿Y mi bendición?" the other boy says and clears the hair from his forehead.

She moves around to the other side of the quilts. This is the second time this evening she will touch him. Until a couple of weeks ago, she still thought of him as the mojadito out back, one who showed up like the stray cats she feeds on the back steps and who one day would disappear just as easily. The first time she asked him how he had slept last night it felt as if she crossed some line far beyond what she had when she started doing favors for her maid. She was risking her own freedom and her mother's well-being if she wasn't around to take care of her. What did she care how he slept? She was giving him a place to hide, food to eat. Looking back, she can't say when this changed, when it became about more than just hiding him, when he became more than her mojadito out back.

"¿Seguro?" she asks, to make certain she heard him correctly.

He nods and closes his eyes for her to begin. She thanks Diosito for the miracle of finding his father and asks that He please bless this boy on the rest of his journey, keep him safe and in good health as he travels to Chicago, help him study and do well in school. En el nombre del Padre, y del Hijo, y del Espíritu Santo, Amén and with the same kiss on his cheek.

The sleepover is less like when Orly and Alex camp out on the floor or when he stays over at Carson's, because Daniel falls asleep almost as soon as Nina leaves the room. Maybe it's Orly's fault for not explaining to him how sleepovers work. That you're supposed to stay up late eating all kinds of food and playing games or watching movies, and basically trying to see how long everyone can stay awake.

There are questions Orly wanted to ask him as soon as Nina

brought him back inside the house. Questions he kept to himself because his godmother might have said it was none of his business, but not now since they spoke to Daniel's father and he'll be leaving in a couple of days. He wants to know what it's like to be illegal not because you're doing something you're not supposed to, but only because you want to be with your family and because they want to keep you safe. What it feels like to always be hiding and feeling like you can be caught at any minute, even if after the crossing part you haven't done anything else illegal. What it feels like to know that someone is thinking day and night about how they might get you back. But as soon as Nina said good night to them, the boy lay on his back and a couple of minutes later was taking deep nasally breaths that could almost be called snores. Orly might as well have been in the other room, counting the number of spaces between the panels.

Maybe it's better they didn't watch any movies. Daniel likes zombies and Orly hasn't seen anything scary since sneaking into the movie his brother was watching, before seeing his mom in the other theater. He remembers having a bad dream that night after they came back from the movies. The dream had little to do with anything he'd seen in those few minutes while squatting in the dark. Instead he was inside his house in bed and outside were four men wearing fencing uniforms, all in white, including the mask, but carrying long white rifles, which seemed weird since he'd thought they'd be carrying long pointy swords. Anyway, for some reason his bedroom was now downstairs, closest to the sunroom and the back door, and the men were looking in his windows and he had to lie perfectly still under the covers, not even breathing, so they wouldn't see him. Then suddenly he escaped out the back door and dove into the pool, but he couldn't come back up to the surface for air or he'd be shot by the fencing guys, who were now scanning the water for any movement.

From underwater he could see their cloudy images circling the pool. But then he realized he wasn't at home but in the pool at the townhouse, which his mom had never taken him to but he somehow knew this was it, knew how the lounge chairs were arranged, where the Coke machine was in the cabana, where they hung the orange-and-white life preserver on the black iron fence, all this from beneath the water. He woke up gasping, and only then realized he was sweating and somehow had gotten tangled up in his flannel blanket and comforter.

He was trembling and wanted to yell for his mom to come up, but he knew Alex would hear him across the hall. He walked downstairs to his parents' bedroom. Normally he would've just opened the door, but that was before the family meeting and the news his mom was moving out. Now he wasn't sure if he should knock gently or call out until she got up to open the door. He didn't want to startle her. He tried tapping on the door and calling her, and when there was no answer, for a second he wondered if he was still dreaming, a dream within a dream, and he had come downstairs but had landed in a different house. Then, on the end table down the hall, he spotted the framed photo of the four of them sitting in a patch of bluebonnets. It was the same photo they'd used on their Christmas card four years ago. The photographer had selected the location for their annual family photo and now they were all smiling for the camera, doing their best to ignore the hovering bees and the fact that instead of sitting in some idyllic meadow they were alongside the frontage road as an endless stream of cars and trucks zoomed toward the coast for the weekend, any one of which seemed like it could veer off the highway and put a sudden end to their family outing.

The door creaked when he opened it, but it still wasn't as loud as the sound machine on her nightstand. He was about to come around to her side of the bed when he saw she was turned the other way and was holding his dad from behind. It was the same way she held Orly when she rushed upstairs to his bedroom because he'd had a bad dream and she would wrap her arms around him until he stopped sobbing and fell asleep. He was surprised to see his dad in the bed. Most of the coverlet and bedsheet had bunched up near his ankles. For a moment Orly wanted to believe they were back together and she wasn't leaving after all, but then he remembered what he'd seen earlier that day in the movie theater and was pretty sure that wasn't happening. His dad must have arrived home late from his trip, sometime after Orly and Alex had gone to bed. At first, after his mom announced she would be moving out, Alex had seen their dad sleeping on the living room couch, his feet propped on the armrest because he didn't completely fit on the cushions. Then a few nights later their dad went back to sleeping in the bedroom with their mom, but they wouldn't go to bed at the same time at night and he always came out before she did.

Orly stayed looking at his parents for a few minutes, the way his mom fit so perfectly around his dad, his arm cradling hers over his chest, her knee gently spooning the back of his, their feet snuggled somewhere beneath the coverlet, and it seemed like the most natural place in the world for the two of them to be. He thought it was something he should remember, an image he wasn't ever going to see again.

Over on the next quilt, Daniel is mumbling in his sleep. It sounds like it could be English, it sounds like it could be Spanish, it sounds like it could be something in between, a secret language he's inventing in his sleep and will forget before he wakes up.

Orly wonders if he's dreaming of seeing his father in Chicago or his mother in Veracruz. Where Daniel would choose for them to live if it was his decision and not theirs. If later he'll dream of his time here, hiding in the pink house or hanging out in the backyard and going to get raspas.

Then Orly realizes how he still knows so little about the boy next to him. Like opening an album or looking at a framed photo, these images make us want to believe we know everything there is to know about a person, a stranger or even someone in our family, our mother or father, but of course we never do.

29

The phone rings late the following day, just before dinner. The woman calling says the boy's father gave her this number to call with the arrangements. She says the boy needs to be ready to leave tomorrow early in the evening.

The next day, to prepare him for the trip, Nina washes his clothes and uses the money from El Kobe to buy things Daniel might need on his trip. The Cricket cell phone is only temporary, and when he gets to Chicago if his father wants he can give him money to buy another one. She also hands him half a dozen snack bars to carry in case he gets hungry and a small amount of money to put in his sock, sealed in a plastic baggie, in case he should need it for something unexpected. From his left shoe, she removes the insole and to the bottom of it tapes a strip of laminated paper with two phone numbers, hers and his father's, and then sticks the insole back in the shoe. Anything bad happens, he needs to call one of them, and if nothing happens, he still needs to call her to let her know he located his father. And make the call as soon as he arrives, don't keep her waiting to hear from him.

Orly gives him his backpack, since he always gets a new one for the school year anyway. He also gives Daniel his e-mail address and says they should stay in touch, partly because he wants to stay in touch and partly because he knows that's what people say when there's more than a good chance they'll never see each other again.

Suddenly a car is pulling into the driveway. Another young one driving, same as the first time, this one wearing a track suit like she just came from exercising. Nina opens the gate and the young woman begins to walk toward the back before Nina tells her to come to the front door. No one lives behind the house anymore.

Inside, the driver squats down and asks the first boy she sees if he's Daniel and if he's wanting to go to Chicago and if he's ready. Then she looks over at Orly, but he just smiles at her. This one's mine, Nina tells her.

Now it's time for the good-byes. Orly reaches out to give him a fist bump, like he did the last time he saw Carson or when Alex left for camp. But Daniel shakes his head and leans in to hug him. It isn't a pretend hug, either, the kind most of his friends gave him at his mom's funeral because they felt sorry for him but also didn't want to get too close. At first Orly isn't sure what to do with his arms and hands. When Nina or some other grown-up hugs him, he usually only leans in and holds still, like he's getting measured or they're taking his temperature, but here Daniel isn't moving away and is waiting for him to hug back, like this means something he understands and Orly will understand too if he stops thinking about what was, what might have been, what could be, and instead sees what is. Orly remembers when Daniel first knocked on the back door and the way he wanted to close the door on him, pretend he couldn't understand what he was saying, and thinks how different his summer would've been if he hadn't cracked open the screen door. His dad will be here in three days to take him home to Houston, and he feels like a lot has happened since he got here—finding another boy in his godmother's kitchen, running away to Matamoros for an afternoon, crawling under a pink house, sneaking through a trapdoor, crisscrossing through the canal to get raspas—and yet most of it he can't tell anyone and needs to keep between them. And so he hugs Daniel back just as tightly and in ways maybe tighter, because he has more he's holding on to.

Nina wonders why they didn't take care of this part before Daniel's ride came. If she embraces him she might not be able to let go, not without losing control of herself. She wanted to cry as soon as she saw the car in the driveway and now has no choice but to wipe away her tears as he comes to give her a hug. Daniel holds her hand and tells her Thank you, which he's done many times since the phone call to his father. She wants to say it was nothing but doesn't, because right now it feels like something more than nothing.

Of all the mistakes she's made in her life, she thinks this might be the biggest. Sending him with a complete stranger, to hide in another house, in a truck or van or trailer, air-conditioned or not, however they take them, passing them on like merchandise ordered from a distant location. Without knowing if these are people she can trust, if they will feed him when he is hungry, hold him when he gets scared, protect him from anyone who might try to hurt him or take advantage of him. She hasn't turned on the news since the arrangements were made—she can't stand to watch any more stories about the Border Patrol uncovering another house with thirty or forty people hiding like scared and beaten animals, another story about even more people dying in the back of a trailer with no air-conditioning. Never in a thousand years could she imagine doing anything like this, sending this young boy off to all the dangers awaiting him in this merciless world. Never, never, never, never, not if God willed it. But then there is so much she can't imagine. Having to leave her child because there isn't enough to feed him, promising to bring him soon and knowing that soon won't be soon enough, and then learning he is in danger if she sends for him but in more danger if she doesn't. A lose-lose situation, no matter what she chooses for her child.

Now they're walking out to the car and the boys start laughing between themselves in the driveway, some joke held over from their adventure to buy raspas.

"Bueno, ándale," the young woman says and holds open the back door. "I have more to pick up."

"How many?" Nina asks.

"Tonight, only two more, a little brother and sister, eight and nine."

"So young."

"But only with other children, that way they're safer. The parents have to pay more up front, but this way they send them less worried."

From the glove box, she pulls out a small notepad and scribbles down a name and number, then tears the sheet off and hands it to Nina.

"If later you need more help," she says.

"He was the last one."

The young woman looks at her a moment and nods.

"Maybe later it's different. People have different reasons for changing their minds."

Once they're inside the car, the woman tells Daniel how to lower the passenger window. Then one last time he waves to Orly and Nina, who stands in the driveway making the sign of the cross as the car pulls away.

Nina goes inside to grab her purse and car keys. She had promised her mother she would bring Orly by the rehab center to visit tonight. She does this now because earlier she was busy getting things ready for Daniel to leave and couldn't get to the rehab center, and because she needs something to get her mind off his leaving. She tells Orly he can bring his computer to keep him company in case he gets bored watching the TV with them.

Like most things in Brownsville, the rehab center is only a ten-minute drive from the house. It isn't as busy as a hospital in the way Orly had imagined it when Nina first told him about coming to visit his great-grandmother. From her other visits, Nina knows the security guard and two of the nurses at their station. Mamá Meche's room is down the hall from the visiting area and looks out onto a courtyard.

"I brought you a guest this time," Nina says. "You remember Orly?"

"Bah, now she thinks I broke my head and not my hip when I fell." Her mother straightens herself up in the bed. "Tell me how I'm not going to remember my great-grandson, el hijo de Eduardo?"

"I was just checking."

"Check yourself," she says and calls Orly over so she can give him a hug and a kiss on the cheek. "Tonight, you are going to sit right next to me."

She tells him to set the extra chair alongside the bed and takes his hand in hers, which is nice and all but means he can't use his screen. He follows most of her new novela and how the tequila baron doesn't want his daughter falling for the lowly jimador and how he's already picked someone else for her to marry but the other guy only wants her money. They watch the first half of the novela before Mamá Meche dozes off during a commercial break, which Nina says has never happened during one of her programs. She tries to gently rouse her mother but stops when she hears her snoring. Nina goes to ask the nurse if they changed her mother's medication or if she missed her afternoon nap.

Orly still has his hand in hers and slowly slips his fingers out of her palm, which she keeps tightening as if she might be dreaming. Her other hand is bruised and partly bandaged from the IV she had in the hospital. On the hand closer to Orly the veins that cover the back of her hand bulge like the exposed roots of an ancient tree. One of the larger veins starts near her wrist and runs up to the dip between the knuckles of her forefinger and middle finger. She even has veins on her fingers, though they're not as thick. Following them with the tip of his finger reminds Orly of all those nights he fell asleep in his dark bedroom feeling the different grooves on the paneled wall. He closes his eyes and follows this vein to that vein that dips between another pair of knuckles and crosses another and another and another vein, the pattern even more random and mysterious than the gaps in the wall. His father, his brother, his Nina, his tío Beto, all his other tíos alive and dead, they all came from these hands. Her skin feels thin enough that Orly imagines he could peel it back to her wrist, then her elbow and shoulder, neck, head, and then do it over and over, layer by delicate layer until he uncovered the little girl with the giant bow in the photo album. Nina wanted to show him where they came from, but where they came from is nothing more than that—where they came from. It isn't where his story ends, only where it begins.

Back at the house, it's late when Nina says the prayer with Orly and gives him a kiss on the cheek.

"Where do you think Daniel is now?" he asks her before she can leave the room.

"I don't know, mijito. It's only been two hours since he left. It might take a few days before he sees his father again."

"But we were kind of like his family. You were like his mother or a grandmother and I was like his brother or a cousin maybe."

"For a little while, yes."

"Do you think we could keep being his family, even if he lives somewhere else? Not all our family lives in one place."

"That's true."

"Maybe we'll see him again someday."

"Maybe, but it would be difficult. He's going to have a different life now."

"But family is family."

"It is, mijito, but sometimes being in a different place, even if the place isn't that far away, makes it hard to get back."

Nina gives him another kiss and tells him they can talk more in the morning. For now he needs to rest. So does she. She's exhausted after her long day and feels like curling up on the sofa and going to sleep in her clothes. It's all she can do to put away the dishes Orly used for one last bowl of cereal and then get herself ready for bed.

She's about to get into bed when she hears a sound at the back door, not exactly a knock, more like a thump. She tells herself no, to stay where she is, to not be fooling herself imagining someone at the back door. At this hour Daniel may already be somewhere north of the final border checkpoint. Her mind is playing tricks on her. That's what happens when you haven't been sleeping, worried about your mother, worried about two young boys you need to take care of. But there it is again, the thump. And a second later La Bronca starts barking.

She feels her way to the kitchen without turning on any lights in the house or outside. She knows it won't help her see whoever it is moving in the shadows who doesn't want to be seen.

"¿Quién es?" she says. "¿Quién es?" But then a moment later without thinking what she's saying, it changes to "¿Quién eres?"

Who are you? She realizes she's saying it no louder than a whisper because she's only saying the words to herself. She realizes this is the first time she's ever asked herself this question. "¿Quién eres?"

Someday, not too long from now, as much as she hates to think about it, she's bound to lose her mother. It could happen from one day to the next, faster than Nina or Beto wants to believe. She doesn't know if she'll hold on to the house, if she would even want it, knowing Beto is likely to fight her on it. But either way it doesn't mean she can't have her own life now. It doesn't mean she won't be here or somewhere else for when her Orly wants to visit her. It doesn't mean that later things won't be different and she'll have reasons for changing her mind about some of her choices.

This time the thump against the screen door is followed by a woeful meow and the fury of La Bronca, especially when it leads to Nina setting out a bowl of milk for the stray cat.

After the cat has had its fill, Nina goes back inside and searches her purse for the scrap of paper the driver gave her before leaving with Daniel. From the hallway closet, she pulls down the second photo album and flips through the first half of it until she finds a blank page. With the plastic peeled back, she unfolds the paper with the phone number, lays it flat, and seals it up, where she can find it later. She still has plenty of pages to fill.

Acknowledgments

So many people helped me in large and small ways to tell this story. I want to thank Hipólito Acosta for his books *Deep in the Shadows: Undercover in the Ruthless World of Human Smuggling* and *The Shadow Catcher: A U.S. Agent Infiltrates Mexico's Deadly Crime Cartels*. His advice and insight helped clarify several sections of this novel. My gratitude goes out to Antonio Almazán, a San Antonio–based attorney, who educated me on the particulars of immigration law. Dr. Barbara Bergin, Dr. Felix Hull, Dr. Mary McCarthy, and Dr. Tony Zavaleta each gave their time and expertise toward helping me better understand my characters. Oscar Saldaña, a Border Patrol agent in the Rio Grande Valley Sector, opened my eyes to the current trends in human trafficking and directed me to the sites of former safe houses along the border. The International Boundary and Water Commission added detailed information about the width of the Rio Grande River in South Texas. Jody Agius Vallejo, with her book *Barrios to Burbs: The Making of the Mexican-American Middle Class*, documented a vital story that helped inform the world of some of my characters. At the University of Texas at Austin, Liz Cullingford (Department of English), Domino Perez (Center for Mexican American Studies), and Richard Flores (College of Liberal Arts) secured the time I needed to research and write this book.

My agent, the tenacious Richard Abate, never stopped believing. Thank you to Tim O'Connell, my editor, for seeing what more this book could be and then knowing just what to say to get me there. Thank you to Anna Kaufman for guiding me handily in all those moments when I needed it most. Thank you to Michelle Tomassi and everyone else at Knopf for all you've done to bring this book into the world.

My prima, Loida, gave voice to my voice. My tío Nico's words inspired my words. Laura Furman and Antonio Ruiz-Camacho brought clarity and promise to the first draft of this novel. My brother and sister-in-law, Idoluis and Toni, and my longtime friends Letty and Bitty served as my memory when I couldn't get back home to Brownsville. Alfonso Saldaña (and his family and friends) became my eyes and ears in Matamoros. My son, Adrian, guided me through his virtual world of *Minecraft*. My sister, Sylvia, and my cuñado, and my close friends and confidants Scotty, Manuel, Joel, Mr. John and Ms. Pat, Heide, JHC, TJ, Bill K, and Josie and Murray encouraged and sustained me through the long haul it took to see, understand, and finish this book. And thank you to my dear family, Becky, Adrian, Elena, and Luna, for the love and the joy and the wags, and for making time for me to walk out our front door and take those eighteen steps to my office door.